MAID OF MURDER

AN INDIA HAYES MYSTERY

MAID OF MURDER

AMANDA FLOWER

FIVE STAR
A part of Gale, Cengage Learning

GALE
CENGAGE Learning

Detroit • New York • San Francisco • New Haven, Conn • Waterville, Maine • London

GALE
CENGAGE Learning™

Set in 11 pt. Plantin.

LIBRARY OF CONGRESS CATALOGING-IN-PUBLICATION DATA

Flower, Amanda.
    Maid of murder : an India Hayes mystery / Amanda Flower. — 1st ed.
        p. cm.
    ISBN-13: 978-1-59414-864-4 (alk. paper)
    ISBN-10: 1-59414-864-3 (alk. paper)
    1. Women librarians—Fiction. 2. Murder—Investigation—Fiction. I. Title.
PS3606.L683M35 2010
813'.6—dc22   2010007269

Published in 2010 in conjunction with Tekno Books and Ed Gorman.

Printed in Mexico
2 3 4 5 6 7 14 13 12 11 10

For my parents
Rev. Pamela Flower and Thomas Flower
and
in memory of
Calvin

ACKNOWLEDGMENTS

Special thanks to Rosalind Greenberg for plucking my manuscript out of the thousands, and to my editor Jerri Corgiat for helping it shine.

Thanks to my Sisters in Crime, Maria Hudgins and Sarah Parrott, for their critiques and support, and to my dear friends, Melody Steiner, Jen Pula, and Melissa Williamson, who read and commented on the manuscript.

Hugs to Mariellyn Dunlap for her edits, friendship, and willingness to always accompany me on a road trip, be it near or far.

Love and gratitude to my mother, Rev. Pamela Flower, who read every word ten times over and was there every step of the way.

Finally, to my Father in Heaven, thank you.

CHAPTER ONE

As a child, I dreaded the Fourth of July despite the fireworks, the barbecue, and the general flag flapping. The holiday signaled that summer was half over. And though my mother chided me about my attitude, called me her pint-sized pessimist, and told me to see the "glass half full," I moped through the holiday. I knew—come the next day—the discount store and supercenters would have fresh back-to-school displays of yellow number two pencils and college-ruled notebook paper. I was a fair student and mid-list popular, but I never wanted to go back to school. As an adult, when I actually had to work every day, my attitude toward Independence Day changed. To me, any day that starts as a paid holiday is a good one.

But that Independence Day morning, my brother called.

When the telephone jangled near my sleeping head, I sat bolt upright and sent my cat Templeton flying across the room in a hissing cloud of black fur.

Who died? was my first thought, followed closely by, who's about to die? for waking me.

I groped for my glasses, shoved them on my face, and looked at the clock. It read four minutes after six in electric blue numerals. The phone rang again. I snatched it up.

"India?" My brother's voice, hyped up on caffeinated pop and mathematical theorems, zipped out over the line. "Could you look up Yang-Mills Theory for me at the library today? I think I'm really onto something. I'd do it myself, you know, but

I'm hitting a wall here with work. And the library's slow, right, because it's summer—"

"Mark," I interrupted.

"Huh?"

"The library's closed today." I swatted a hank of long, dark hair out of my face and tucked it behind my ear.

"It's closed? But why?" He sounded shocked.

"It's the Fourth of July. You know, Happy Independence Day and all that." I glared at the clock. "It's also six-oh-five in the morning on a day I don't have to work," I added in case he was having trouble grasping the point, which Mark often did.

"It is?"

"Where are you?" I asked while rubbing my gray eyes, which were gritty from sleep.

"In my office?"

"You don't sound very sure of that."

There was a pause. "Definitely my office. I'm working on this really great theorem. I think I have it now, India. My dissertation—"

"I understand," I stepped in before he could enter another long-winded explanation about The Dissertation. He'd worked on it for half a decade. It'd become a bit of a swear word in my parents' house.

"Well, Mark, I better let you get back to it. Call me at the library tomorrow, and I'll see if I have time to look up that Yohoo-Miller thing for you."

"Yang-Mills. It's a partial differential equation that—"

"Whatever." I moved to hang up, but his lingering silence was palpable. I sighed. "Was that all?"

Mark swallowed hard. "I know she's getting married."

Geez. I knew he'd eventually find out one way or another, but I wished it had been after the ceremony.

"Mark, I—"

"Don't lie to me; I saw it in the paper. She's getting married next weekend. You knew. I can't believe you didn't know."

"Uh." What could I say? I did know. Mark would be devastated when he found out how well I knew. I tucked that thought away to deal with later.

"Why didn't you tell me? It's not like I'd care or anything."

Sure, I thought, and my watercolors would make me millions of dollars someday. I took a deep breath. "I didn't know how to tell you, and Olivia didn't want to hurt you, either."

"Thanks, anyway," he whispered and hung up.

I stared at the receiver, then knocked it against my forehead a few times before dropping it back in its cradle.

After fifteen minutes, I threw off the sheet and stomped to the bathroom. "Next time he has a day off, I'm calling at three in the morning. That little . . ."

After a shower and breakfast, I no longer felt so hateful toward Mark. I knew I should have told him that Olivia was getting married. I should have told him months ago when I learned about it, but there never seemed to be a good time. And the way marriages go these days, I thought, it would be much easier to announce that Olivia was getting a divorce in a couple of years.

I clicked on the TV.

"It's going to be a beautiful Independence Day, folks," the weather girl from the Cleveland station said. "We might break some records. Temperatures in the upper nineties and ninety percent humidity, Remember, don't mow your lawn until after sundown. There's an Ozone alert—"

I clicked off the screen.

By nine that morning, I was sprawled across a sheet I used to cover my poorly chosen couch in order to avoid touching the hot, itchy fabric. It was beautifully upholstered in royal purple velvet. I had found it at an estate sale in Chicago. It had cost a mint to have it shipped to Stripling, and, not until it was safely stowed in my apartment did I learn that it was uncomfortable in the summertime and a magnet for black cat hair. My long legs hung over its end, and Templeton lay in the same position next to me on the floor. I periodically spritzed him, then myself, with ice water from a spray bottle that I normally used to wet down my unruly hair. Templeton shook his head like a dog every time he was hit with a spray of water but didn't move out of its reach. Even an aquaphobic feline welcomed the cool mist in my air conditioning–deprived apartment. While Templeton shook his head for a fourth time, I tried to build up the courage to call my brother back and tell him the truth—that I did know that Olivia was to be married this weekend in Stripling and that I, India Hayes, who had sworn after the last wedding that I would never be in a bridal party again, am to be one of Olivia's doting bridesmaids.

The phone rang.

I told Templeton, "I'll get it, but tomorrow I'm teaching you to answer the phone."

He didn't respond.

"India?" It was a voice easily as perky as the weathergirl's.

I swallowed hard. I knew that voice. "Hi, Olivia. You aren't in town, are you?"

Templeton gave me a look that to me said, "Spritz me, baby." I obliged.

"Just arrived. We're at my mother's now. Stripling is just how I remember it. It's so cute. The perfect place for a wedding, don't you think?"

"Really darling."

She missed the sarcasm. "As you know, it's a holiday."

"I heard something about that." I spritzed myself in the face.

"Very funny. Anyway, my mother is having a little Independence Day gathering at two in honor of my return, and I am inviting you to come."

"Well, I was planning—"

"Please, India? I haven't seen you in forever, and I want you to meet Kirk. You can bring a date if you want."

I snorted, but after ten more minutes of listening to Olivia's pleas, I finally agreed. As bridesmaid-in-waiting, I had an obligation.

After she hung up, I pulled the sheet over my head with a moan and asked Templeton to put me out of my misery. I peeked out from the sheet when he didn't respond. He looked like an overbroiled chicken splayed on the hardwood floor. "If you are not going to help me out, I'll just have to call Bobby, won't I?"

Templeton blinked at me. I picked up the phone and hit speed dial. When Bobby McNally answered, I said, "I need a favor."

"It'll cost you," a churlish and groggy Bobby answered.

"How much?"

"How do you like children?"

I groaned.

CHAPTER TWO

Bobby opened his front door with a flourish. "So, I won't have to answer even one question for the horrid Library Quest?"

Bobby and I were the two full-time reference librarians at the Ryan Memorial Library at Martin College. Every year, the admissions office planned Martin's Campers Week in late July, a week where Martin alumni can send their precious darlings, known to Martin as future tuition-payers, to terrorize college employees. Library Quest was the bane of our existence because the admissions staff, usually recent Martin grads who had majored in recreation, released about fifty kids into the library at a time for a game of Fun Facts. One of the asinine rules of the quest forbade kids from using the Internet to find the answers to the list of questions they clutch in their hot little hands. Let's just say that the up-and-coming generation doesn't know how to use a print index. Shoot, *I* could barely use one.

"Not a one," I said.

I stepped into his Spanish-style bungalow, a half block from campus. The homes circling the perimeter of Martin were an eclectic bunch, constructed by turn-of-the-century Martin faculty. Bobby told everyone his home had been designed by a Spanish professor in 1910. He had yet to produce the documentation required to support his claim. He bought the house last year and coddled it like an infant.

Bobby perched on the sofa to tie his shoes. Tall, well built with black Irish coloring, he was a handsome lad of the Emerald

Isle with a colorless Midwestern accent. He was also annoyingly persistent when he was scheming his way out of work. "Not even a science one? You always give me the science ones. If I knew anything about science, I wouldn't be working at that miserable excuse for academia."

"Wow," I commented. "You should work for the admissions office." I headed for a chair, caught my flip-flop under a sixty-four by forty-eight, stunningly beautiful, and perpetually wrinkled Navajo rug Bobby had found at a Columbus bazaar, and my knees hit the floor. Fickle inertia. "Ow."

"Pick up your feet when you walk," Bobby advised.

I rolled to my seat on the offensive rug and examined the strawberry on my knee. The lute-playing characters on the rug mocked me. "This is a hazard."

Bobby picked up the black-and-white photograph of his father in his police sergeant dress uniform that I had knocked off an end table and shook his head. "Not if you know how to walk. If I got a dime every time you hit the skids, I'd be a rich man living in the Virgin Islands with a model on one side and a waitress on the other."

"Bobby," I growled.

He gave me a hand up. "Hey sweetheart, I'm doing you a favor. Let's go."

We climbed into my ancient made-in-America sedan. The car was a hodge-podge of parts of several automobile manufacturers. The late great-uncle who'd willed it to me had loved to tinker. Unfortunately, his favorite tinker toy was his car. Most of the car's body is powder blue, but a smattering of rust red and olive green decorated the front and rear fenders.

"You really need to get a new car," Bobby said. "This thing's an embarrassment."

"If you hate it so much, you could've driven."

"Yeah, but I don't know where these people live." Before I

could tell him offering up the address wouldn't have pressed me much, he said, "Okay, tell me again why I am being subjected to this barbeque."

"I doubt the Blockens will have barbeque. Too messy."

Bobby shot me a look.

"I told you about the wedding."

"Oh please, I know how many weddings you've been in, and this is the first time I've had to babysit you."

"This one's different."

"Why?"

I ground my teeth. "Because of Mark."

"Really?" Bobby said, sounding intrigued. "How's that?"

Uh-oh, I thought, I know where this is going. "Mark had a thing for the bride, but it was a long time ago. And I haven't seen any of the bride's family since then, so it may be awkward. You're the distraction."

"Tell me about this thing your brother had for the bride."

I thought about the telephone conversation I'd had with Mark earlier that morning with a wince. *Had* may be the wrong tense when describing how Mark felt about Olivia.

I eyed him. "You really want to know?"

"Of course I do. I should know what I'm getting myself into. I left my body armor at home, so no cat fights, please."

"Olivia lived on the same street two doors down from us. Her parents still live there. Mine moved after Dad's accident."

I thought back to the day Olivia and her parents arrived with that huge moving truck. It was amazing how well I remembered even though I was barely four at the time. It's funny the memories that the mind retains with crystal clarity.

I was wearing a tie-dyed T-shirt that my mother had made. It was too big for me, but she had said there was no point making it smaller because I was growing like a weed on steroids. I was already the tallest girl in my preschool class.

From my yard, I watched the couple and their daughter with glossy brown hair, cut to the shoulder, go in and out of the house. The girl skipped around the yard, twirling. Her mother yelled at her several times about grass stains. The girl waited until her mother's back was turned and twirled again.

The moving van had been in front of the house for two hours before I worked up the courage to walk over. I inched up the street, stopping every few feet to inspect the ground as if the cracks in the sidewalk were oh-so-interesting. Eventually, I found myself in front of the house. It was a huge Victorian at least a hundred years old that sat on two lots. The rest of the houses in the neighborhood, including mine, were made from the same faux colonial cookie cutter used in the 1950s to satisfy the baby boom generation and sat on postage stamp-sized properties.

The mom and daughter looked at me. The girl smiled, but her mother pursed her lips. "What is she wearing? It looks like a neon pillowcase."

I looked down at my shirt, which I had been so proud of up until that moment, and felt ashamed. The pair in front of me wore clothes bought at the mall. I knew because it was the kind of clothes my older sister, Carmen, complained we never bought because Mom and Dad said shopping at the mall fed consumerism. I started to back away. I desperately wanted to go home and change my shirt.

The girl looked at her mother with her chin jutting out. "I like her shirt, and she's going to be my friend." She walked to my side and took hold of my hand. Together we sat on the grass cross-legged and watched the big men unload the truck.

Bobby's voice shook me out of the memory. "I'd appreciate it if you not daydream while driving. I do have a will to live."

I shot him a look. "Do you want to hear this, or not?"

He made a gesture as if he was zipping his lips shut.

I knew it would take much more than an imaginary zipper to keep Bobby quiet. Nevertheless, I continued. "I think Mark fell in love with Olivia when we were still in grade school. Even at age six she was beautiful, and she knew it too."

Bobby made hissing cat sounds.

I laughed. "Maybe I was a little jealous. She also knew how much Mark liked her, but she never showed any interest until high school when she and Mark dated briefly. I think she only did it because she was between boyfriends at the time and Mark was a senior when we were only sophomores. Even dating a senior nerd like Mark was more impressive than dating someone in our own class. It was never serious on Olivia's part. She dated a lot of different guys from skateboarders to jocks. I guess she counted Mark as her geek quota. When they broke up, he didn't take it well. He called her, hung around her house, waited for her after school. It was awful. Even when she was with someone else, she was all he talked about. Well, besides the Pythagorean Theorem, that is. After Mark graduated, he went to Martin in order to stay close to Olivia, despite the fact that he could have gone just about anywhere with his test scores."

"I bet your parents loved that he gave up the Ivy League for a girl."

"When it was her turn to choose a college, Olivia went to a school in Virginia. That's when it got really bad."

"Bad how?

I bit my lip. "Look, we're almost there."

Bobby crossed his arms across his chest. "Fine. I'll make up my own ending."

"Don't even think about it." I took my eyes off the road to give him my best dirty scowl, a look I perfected at the library's reference desk.

"What?" he asked innocent as a baby lamb. I knew better.

"You're wondering if you can use that story in one of your

ridiculous plots."

Bobby had a penchant for writing short fiction for romance magazines. He'd sold several to publications like *Minx* and *Velvet Rose*. I had proofread far too many of them to want my brother to be the inspiration for the next confounded hero.

"I wasn't thinking that."

"Yes, you were."

"Okay, I was, but my readers would love it. It's got all the elements: scorned heart, love lost—"

"We're talking about Mark here. Please. I might have to pull over and throw up. It's wrong to use his heartbreak that way, especially for a measly two hundred bucks."

"Hey, *Minx* paid me six hundred last time for *Secret Kiss,* a three-part series," he said proudly.

I shook my head and turned the car onto Kilbourne Street. I pointed at a two-story colonial. "That's where I grew up." Someone had painted it a dark khaki. I grimaced.

"Very suburban," he remarked.

Two houses down, I parked in the driveway of a large Victorian, complete with wraparound porch and suspended swing, outshining all the other abodes on the block. When I lived on Kilbourne Street, the Blocken house had been painted a simple white with navy trim; now it was a supposedly Victorian pink with darker pink trim. I'm sure the decorator called the colors "damask" and "mauve."

I wasn't halfway out of my car when I heard a high-pitched yelp, resembling a frightened puppy at the groomer's.

"Incoming," Bobby said as he slipped expertly out of the passenger-side door.

"India!" Olivia ran toward me with her arms outstretched and welcoming as if I was a returning war hero. Thankfully, I cleared the car door before she hit. She grabbed me in a crushing hug. Because she's so thin, this would have surprised me if I had not known about her lifelong obsession with fitness. There was a kickboxing-hardened body hidden under her elegant sundress. After an excruciatingly long minute, she released me. All the while, Bobby smirked at me over her head. He was enjoying himself a little too much, in my opinion.

Olivia looked much the same as she had in high school—same build, same endearing smile and flawless complexion. However, her hair was red, and so expertly done that I wouldn't have suspected anything if I hadn't known her for twenty-some years as a brunette.

"I'm so glad to see you." She repeated the sentence at least three times until she finally noticed Bobby standing beside my car with that infuriating grin on his face. "And who's this?" she asked with the tone of an eighth-grade girl spotting a tenth-grade hottie.

Bobby looked especially fetching standing in the afternoon sun, dressed in pressed chino shorts and blue knit shirt I knew he'd picked to match his eyes. One of the arguments I had used to persuade him to accompany me was that he might meet a new lady friend. Bobby was always on the prowl for a new heart to break. Fortunately, I knew this from observation, not experience. When I started working at Martin's library, Bobby's looks had intimidated me, but sometime during the last three years, he'd grown familiar. I was only reminded how handsome he was when women reacted to him like Olivia just had. Or when female undergraduates strutted up to the reference desk to ask me when the "hot book guy" would return. I've never told Bobby about the "hot book guy" thing; his ego is far too large already.

"Oh, I'm sorry, Olivia," I said, as if I should have introduced him while she was crushing my bones into powder. "This is Robert McNally. He works with me at Martin."

"Really?" Olivia on her strappy high-heeled sandals sashayed over to Bobby and took his outstretched hand. "Hello, Robert. I don't remember librarians being as hot as you when I was in college."

I stopped myself just short of asking her if she's ever stepped inside her college library.

"Call me Bobby," he replied, his eyes looking her up and down.

"Call me Olivia," she cooed.

Call me disgusted, I thought. "Olivia, I'm dying to meet Kirk. You know . . . your fiancé?"

Her head snapped up. She removed her hand from Bobby's light grasp. "You're going to love him." Olivia led us up the front walk.

Hanging back, I squeezed Bobby's arm. "She's engaged, for Pete's sake."

He smiled back, pretending not to hear.

The front door opened into the living room or, as Mrs. Blocken liked to call it, the parlor. The inside of the house had changed as well. Mrs. Blocken had obviously maxed out her creative resources and her husband's credit cards. The interior was faux-finished within an inch of its life.

Olivia's parents stood by the door, ready to greet their guests. I met Mrs. Blocken's gaze and the temperature dropped several degrees. Then again, some things never change.

CHAPTER THREE

I hadn't spoken to Olivia's parents since the unfortunate incident at Olivia's high school graduation party. Sure, sometimes I would spot them in the local market but would dive down the next available aisle before they could recognize me.

"Look who's here," Olivia told her parents.

Mrs. Blocken extended a narrow hand with polished nails. She barely brushed my hand with hers. "Thank you for coming."

Mrs. Blocken had abandoned the helmet bob that had bolstered her through the decades. In its place, she'd fashioned her hair in a short cut. Her hair was only a deeper shade of red than her daughter's. The coif framed her face and elongated her tight neck. Plastic surgery? I thought so. She wore a sundress so frighteningly similar to Olivia's that I blinked. Bobby noticed the twin routine too, judging by the amused expression on his face.

I introduced Bobby, and Mrs. Blocken held out her hand to Bobby in the same manner that she had to me. However, when he took it, she held on longer than necessary. Bobby's physical appearance enthralled all generations of women. "And will you be India's guest for the wedding?"

A look of panic flashed across Bobby's face.

I took mercy on him. "No, unfortunately Bobby is working next Saturday. He's a fellow librarian at Martin."

Mrs. Blocken eyed me. "Then who are you bringing?"

"No one," I said, the fake smile on my face already starting to hurt. "I didn't think it would be fair to bring a date since I will be so busy as a bridesmaid."

Bobby snorted, and I covertly stomped on his sandaled foot.

Mrs. Blocken's attention returned to Bobby. "Are you all right?"

He gave her one of his charming smiles. "Whatever you're cooking smells heavenly."

She beamed. "Why, thank you."

I mentally rolled my eyes and turned to Dr. Blocken, who stood quiet beside his wife. Even though he tipped the scale at three hundred pounds and resembled a bear, Dr. Blocken was an utterly forgettable man in the shadow of his wife's personality. He practiced dentistry in one of the oldest dental offices in Stripling. I recently heard from my mother, who had an ear for town gossip, that Mrs. Blocken wanted her husband to retire that year so that they could jet set through the Keys and the Continent. My mother told me that Dr. Blocken was resisting her. He would eventually fold, I suspected, but I liked him better for trying to stand up to Regina Blocken.

Dr. Blocken pushed his glasses up the bridge of his nose. His nails were bitten to the quick. "I thought I saw you shopping for groceries the other day, but whoever I saw disappeared, and I couldn't be sure."

I laughed hollowly.

Bobby disentangled his hand from Mrs. Blocken, and she paraded us to the backyard.

Even though the sponged and dry-brushed walls of the Blocken home grated on my nerves, I preferred the cool relief of the Blocken's central air to the sweltering backyard. Bobby didn't appear too thrilled, either.

The lawn was expertly maintained. The grass, if measured,

would prove to be exactly one inch high, and the flowers and plants were the attractive, if unimaginative, sort found outside of banks and office buildings. Every exposed patch of dirt was buried in a mound of pungent black mulch.

Two umbrella tables sat on the generous patio. A gorgeous woman and a burly, thirty-something man sat at one of the tables. A sullen-looking teenager slouched alone at the other, slumped on a patio chair with her arms folded in a defiant, piss-off pose. She wore baggy boys shorts and a T-shirt that read, YOU'RE NOT THE BRIGHTEST CRAYON IN THE BOX, ARE YOU? She had her improbably yellow hair cropped close to her head.

With a start, I realized the teen was Olivia's fifteen-year-old sister, Olga. I only recognized her because, despite the hair and the shirt, she was the identical version of Olivia's teenaged self. I looked at her and at Olivia and back again. They had the same smooth forehead, straight nose, and wide mouth. For some reason, I found seeing Olga sitting at that table looking like she was ready to bolt more jarring to me than seeing Olivia earlier in the driveway. The last time I saw Olga she was eight or nine. That is how much time had passed between then and now, between seeing Olivia and her family every day to not at all.

Olivia introduced the stunning woman, model-thin with a thick mane of curly black hair, as Bree Butler, Olivia's former college roommate and maid of honor. I guessed she was of Mediterranean descent, maybe Greek, although her last name suggested nothing of the kind.

Bree stood and hugged me. "Olivia always talked about your misadventures together. Did you really get lost in the sewer for two days when you were eleven?"

I glanced at Bobby for help, but he was lost to me, floored by Bree's beauty. "More like two hours."

"Bree's a special education teacher at a public elementary school in Virginia," Olivia told Bree. "India's a librarian at Martin College. You probably have so much in common."

Right, I thought.

Bobby added, "I'm a librarian, too. India and I are coworkers."

Thank you, Bobby.

Bree giggled for no good reason. "I'd love to see Martin while I'm here." She seemed to recollect me. "Can I get you anything? Something to drink?"

I glanced at the picnic table three feet away lined with soft drinks, iced tea, and lemonade. "Nothing thanks."

"Bobby, can I get *you* anything?" Bree asked.

He shook his head mutely. It would be a long time before he recovered his voice.

"Olivia?" Bree asked.

Olivia waved her hand at the burly man. Using my world-renowned powers of deduction, I concluded that the man was Kirk, Olivia's fiancé, and that he could bench-press my weight. Without looking at Bree, she said, "Bottled water, make sure it's spring water, in a glass with a handful of ice."

"Right away." Bree scurried off.

I glanced at Bobby to see if he'd noticed Olivia's dismissive tone. If he had, he didn't indicate it. His eyes had followed Bree.

Kirk rose from the table and lumbered toward us. He was an inch shorter than Olivia, who stood approximately five feet five. His hair was too blond and his skin too tanned. Husky and thick-chested, he reminded me of a lumberjack except he wore prep, not flannel, in a tight black T-shirt and tailored jean shorts. The effect was very S.W.A.T. meets weekend-wear. His biceps were so pronounced, his arms couldn't rest easily at his sides. I towered over him in my flip-flops. Bemused, I wondered how Mrs. Blocken was going to trick him into wearing lifts during the ceremony. He kissed Olivia on the cheek.

After Olivia made introductions, Kirk extended his hand first to Bobby then to me. The men shook harder than necessary in a testosterone Alamo.

I wondered if he could crack a walnut with his calves.

Kirk turned to me. "I've heard so much about you. Did you really set your parents' garage on fire?"

Olivia had evidently presented me as quite a hellion. "I was experimenting with a wood burner and a hot glue gun."

Bree returned with Olivia's water. Bobby preened, running his fingers through his impeccable mane then shaking it out.

"Kirk, do you want something to drink?" He nodded at her glass, and she half-turned to Bree. "Bree?"

Bree scurried off. Bobby watched her go, then looked at Olivia. "How did you and Kirk meet?"

Olivia laughed. "We work together."

So much for the great love-lost plot Bobby desired. She raised Kirk's hand to her mouth and kissed it. Kirk beamed. If they started making out, I'd make a break for it.

"Kirk owns a small chain of gyms in Virginia called Kirk's Fitness Center."

Catchy, I thought. That explained the muscleman bod.

Olivia rubbed Kirk's arm like she was polishing a trophy into a special shine. "In college, I majored in physical therapy. After graduation, the first place I applied was at Kirk's Fitness Center, because it came with a free membership."

Kirk looked lovingly at his bride-to-be. "I hired her because she was so hot."

Well, that certainly was a resounding affirmative action endorsement.

"KFC is the most sought-after gym in northern Virginia," Olivia said.

"KFC?" I swallowed a joke about fried chicken.

"Kirk's Fitness Center is more than a gym; it's a destination with spa treatments and juice bar."

I wondered if Olivia had recently written a brochure. I'd probably go for the juice bar but that was about it.

"It must be difficult to own your own business in today's economy," Bobby said.

"Fitness is big business, really booming. No matter what the market is doing, there are always fat people trying to get thin. We opened our fifth center last week."

I stared at Kirk, thinking that he was the polar opposite from Mark, making me even more sure that Mark had never had a real shot with Olivia. I wished Mark could realize that and move on.

I turned my body away from the group so they couldn't see my expression. I watched Dr. Blocken place a plate of hot dogs and hamburgers from the grill next to the platter of fried chicken. Thank goodness for the veggie tray, I thought.

"Please, everyone. The food's ready," Mrs. Blocken called from the patio. We trooped to the picnic table. I filled my plate with carrots, celery, and a heaping helping of potato salad. Bobby and I sat with Bree and sulky Olga. During the meal, Bobby lobbied for Bree's attention. They discussed their respective jobs and families, trading all vital statistics. I began to wonder how long politeness required me to stay at the Blockens. One hour? Two? Certainly not three.

"I wish my mother could have come to the wedding. She's so fond of Olivia," Bree told Bobby. She dabbed a napkin to her eye.

"Why couldn't she?" Bobby asked.

"She hasn't been feeling well." Bree looked mournful.

"I'm sorry to hear that. Are you close?" He all but batted his eyelashes at her.

Bree nodded. "She was a single mom, and I'm her only child."

"Family is definitely the most important thing in my life."

I swallowed a snicker. Bobby only visited his family on Christmas and every third Thanksgiving.

Bree beamed at him over her cheeseburger.

Feeling frumpy and churlish in comparison, I turned to Olga. "Nice T-shirt, Olga."

She snorted some type of response that, even though I don't speak teen angst fluently anymore, I interpreted as, Leave me alone; I'm busy being unhappy.

Taking another tack, I said, "I like your hair color," I paused. "It's vibrant."

She touched her hair, but didn't respond. Not even a snort. But just when I was about to give up on her, she mumbled, "Oh em."

"Excuse me?" I asked, leaning closer.

She looked me in the eye for the first time. "O.M. My name's O.M. Never call me Olga. Ever."

"No problem."

Olga—sorry O.M.—must have used up her daily word limit. She was silent for the remainder of the meal. I shrugged and enjoyed the food, watching Bobby salivate over Bree and counting the ways I could tease him about it later. At the next table, Olivia, gathered with her parents and Kirk, organized wedding logistics.

I overheard Mrs. Blocken say, "The doves will arrive early in the morning on the wedding day."

"Mother, I told you that I don't want doves. What if they get loose? It's too much of a bother."

"What if the birds poop on the guests?" Kirk asked.

Mrs. Blocken gaped at Kirk. I choked on a bite of potato salad.

Olivia gasped. "Ohmigawd. They'll ruin everything. Mother, cancel the doves,"

"If the bird handler wants the good money that your father

and I are paying him, he'll keep those doves in line," Mrs. Blocken said.

Considering her tone, if I were one of those doves, I would certainly control myself.

"But Mother . . ." Olivia said.

"Honey, it'll be charming. I'll handle it. You don't have to worry about a thing."

"How can the handler stop the birds from pooping?" Kirk asked. Obviously he hadn't spent much time with Mrs. Blocken. It was probably a very good thing that he and Olivia lived in Virginia, hundreds of miles from Stripling.

Mrs. Blocken gritted her teeth.

"Olivia should have everything that she wants." Dr. Blocken bit his thumbnail. "If she doesn't want the doves . . ." he trailed off. His thumbnail started to bleed.

Mrs. Blocken slapped his hand. "Stop that."

A cell phone played the "Star-Spangled Banner." Everyone began patting themselves down.

"It's me," Olivia announced with a satisfied look.

After several "Uh-huh," "That's rights," and "Okays," Olivia snapped her cell shut. She turned to her party. "Great news. Topaz is coming."

Everyone except Bobby and me, who had no idea what this meant, and O.M. too, because it would hurt her image no doubt, cheered happily at this report. I took this as a bad sign.

Chapter Four

I leaned across the table and asked Bree, "Who's Topaz?"

Bree looked unhappy to have her conversation with Bobby interrupted. She studied me with appraising eyes. "Topaz is the dress designer for Olivia's wedding. She's bringing the bridesmaids' dresses for us to try on." I had the feeling she wanted to add *silly* at the end of that sentence.

My stomach tightened in dread. I knew the dress would have come up eventually. I was a bridesmaid after all. But not now, not here, not with an audience.

Bobby pried his baby blues from Bree to grin at me. The jerk.

Fifteen minutes later, the Blocken doorbell rang. Olivia and Mrs. Blocken rose as one. Topaz had arrived. She came too quickly for me to come down with the flu or the *E. coli* virus, which I planned to contract in the next ten minutes. I slumped in the patio chair, defeated. Bree said Topaz would need help bringing in the dresses and hurried after them. Bree's absence freed Bobby to torture me.

"That was really good planning on Olivia's part, wasn't it, India? I mean, what better time to have the dresses fitted than when all the bridesmaids are together at her mother's house?"

I gave Bobby my best withering glare. O.M. watched our exchange with mild interest. Or, was she watching Bobby with mild interest? I'd have to remember to keep him away from her.

Moments later Olivia, her mother, and Bree returned to the

patio with a tall and graceful black woman, presumably Topaz, the dress designer who made house calls on national holidays. Her hair was cropped close to her head, revealing its perfect form and reminding me of an Egyptian bust of Nefertiti. Olivia and her entourage made a quick circuit around the patio with breathy introductions. "This is India Hayes, Topaz. She's a childhood friend of mine. She's bridesmaid number three."

I smiled politely at Topaz, flabbergasted that Olivia had the audacity to number her bridesmaids, and that I was number three out of three.

Topaz gave a pleasant but noncommittal smile.

"I hope it wasn't too much trouble to come out here on a holiday," I said.

"No trouble at all," she replied, but her eyes flickered. I was willing to bet that she was collecting time-and-a-half.

Mrs. Blocken broke in. "We should begin the fitting. Who would you like to see first? India?"

Why am I not surprised? I thought. Without a word or a glance in Bobby's direction, I followed Topaz and Olivia into the house.

Inside, Topaz handed me a garment bag.

Olivia said, "You can change in my old bedroom." She was practically jumping up and down in prenuptial ecstasy.

I trudged upstairs. Although I hadn't been in the Blocken house for several years, the layout was as familiar to me as my childhood home. Olivia's room was on the second floor, the second doorway on the left, and looked the same as it had when we had graduated high school. I was relieved to discover that at least one memory of Kilbourne Street had not changed.

I walked across the lush carpet and threw the dress bag on Olivia's old double bed in disgust. I stalled for time by snooping. Olivia's personality had defected when she'd fled to college by way of Dixie. Left behind was the image of Olivia Mrs.

Blocken had tried to create throughout Olivia's childhood. The room was painted lavender and the furniture was a matched set of white provincial, consisting of two dressers, a writing desk, and headboard. On the dresser, Olivia had abandoned her silver-plated brush and mirror, as well as various childish knickknacks. A white shelf nailed high on the wall above the desk held a complete set of ceramic girls in frilly Victorian-inspired gowns with numbers in front of them, one dainty lady for every birthday through eighteen. At sixteen, Olivia confessed that she hated those figurines, and she didn't know what in the world she was going to do with them. I smiled at the memory.

I sat on the bed beside the garment bag. I had to ask myself why I was even sitting in Olivia's childhood room with that garment bag. I was absolutely positive that a woman could be a bridesmaid too many times. Olivia's wedding would be my sixth tour down the aisle in a hideous monster of a dress. Somehow I can never say "no" to a betrothed's teary-eyed request, be it my sister, a friend from art school, or a third cousin twice removed.

I had to admit even to myself that wasn't explanation enough for me to be in this particular wedding. Olivia had broken my brother's heart. It was seven years ago now, and although Mark had been in other relationships since, they'd never match his memory of Olivia. His depression that had followed Olivia's graduation party had put a wedge between her and me that the geographic distance between us could not mend. When she had called to ask me to be in her wedding, I was shocked and maybe even a little flattered. Okay, a lot flattered.

"Please, India," she'd said, "I've always wanted you to be in my wedding. I can't imagine getting married without you there."

I tried to say something, but she didn't give me a chance. "Don't you remember how we said we would plan each other's weddings? How you promised to wear gloves at my wedding, and I promised to wear a black dress at yours even though I thought it was morbid?"

"I—"

"What about the time I agreed to that save-the-mourning-doves rally with your family just so I could keep that creepy Brad Coldecker away from you."

I'd forgotten Brad Coldecker. He'd been a college student and a member of one of the environmental groups that my parents ran. I didn't remember which group it had been. There'd been so many. Brad Coldecker was convinced that by flirting with me, he would get closer with my parents. Apparently, the fact that I was thirteen at the time made little difference.

"You don't have to do a thing. All you need to do is show up and be there. I need you there."

Then, I'd heard myself say "yes," and, before I knew it, I'd been giving her my dress measurements and my address for the invitation.

It wasn't until later that my chest tightened and the reality of what I'd just agreed to sunk in. That's when I forgot Brad Coldecker again and remembered Mark.

I told myself that it would be fine, and that I was there in Olivia's old bedroom for the finality of it, because I wanted to witness the end of my brother's obsession. Surely, even Mark would have to let her go when she was married. Or maybe I was just there because I couldn't say *no* to Olivia when it was her turn to ask, especially after saying *yes* to the third cousin twice removed. As this was the sixth wedding I would endure, it has been established that I wasn't particularly good at saying no.

I reluctantly thought of Mark. Last time, he'd comforted himself with the black-and-white world of mathematics and dedicated the same obsessive energy he had in pursuing Olivia to solving story problems I had no way of deciphering. I hoped that he would be able to do that again. I also knew when my parents found out, there would be heck to pay because they couldn't forget that Olivia was the catalyst that had caused Mark to fall apart.

I shook the melancholy thoughts from my head. If I didn't want Olivia to bop upstairs and offer to help me dress, I'd better get moving.

I gave a long and heartfelt sigh. "I can burn it after the wedding."

That cheered me a tad. I had had a nice bonfire after the third cousin twice removed's wedding and could look forward to another one.

I unzipped the garment bag in a dramatic flourish and suffered paralyzing blindness. I wasn't blinded by a chemical discharge or random laser or anything that friendly, but by the dress itself—a bright squint-worthy gold. Rumplestiltskin gold. I yanked the dress from the bag in hopes that the brilliant gold was a layer of psychedelic tissue paper. No such luck. I pushed the empty garment bag onto the floor and spread the dress out on the bed for a better look at my fate. The design of the dress was relatively simple. It had a floor-length full skirt with a sleeveless off-the-shoulder top. I could not overcome the color. The shimmering gold fabric attracted light like a bike reflector. I hoped that the wedding invitations recommended guests bring sunglasses and SPF forty-five. I doubted they'd ever need them more. By that time, I had been in Olivia's room a full fifteen minutes without a peep. I knew that at any second, she'd be tapping on the door asking if I needed any help, or, worse, her mother would.

I stripped and tugged on the dress. It zipped up, but it was remarkably tight, highlighting every imperfection my figure had to offer. I stood in front of the mirror in Olivia's childhood bedroom and felt the sudden and uncontrollable urge to burst into tears. The dress was hideous in every conceivable way: cut, color, and style. I giggled, somewhat manically, I'm afraid. I doubled over, and something popped in the back of the gown. Apparently, my stock bridesmaid dress measurements had changed since the third cousin twice removed's ceremony.

A friendly tap-tap rapped at the door. "India, do you need any help?" Topaz asked.

I calmed down enough to say, "I think the dress is broken."

"Let me in, honey, I'll fix it."

I cracked open the door, hiding behind it for cover, and allowed Topaz to slip in the room. I slammed it shut before anyone else could eel in.

"Shoot, girl, you almost took off my foot."

"Sorry."

"That's all right—" Topaz stopped when she saw me in the dress. I'm sure I was not what she'd envisioned when she'd created the gown. "Girl."

That was about all I could get out of her for the next twenty minutes as she circled around me, pulling, pinning, and ripping seams.

Every few minutes, Olivia called, "Is everything okay in there? Is there anything I can do? Can I come in?"

Each time, in unison, Topaz and I yelled, "No."

"Well, honey, the dress will fit, but I don't know—there's nothing I can do about the color," Topaz finally said.

I shrugged in defeat.

"You're definitely a winter, honey. Winters should never wear gold."

She left me to change back into my capris and tank top. When Topaz and I walked downstairs, the whole party greeted us with a collective groan.

"Where's the dress?" Olivia asked.

"There was something wrong with the zipper. Bree, would you like to try your dress on next?" she asked before Olivia or

Mrs. Blocken could make further comment.

I mouthed *thank you* to her.

Ten short minutes later, Bree floated down the stairs in an exact replica, be it a smaller one, of the bridesmaid dress of my nightmares. On Bree the gown was stunning. Her tanned skin and the shimmering fabric fit together perfectly. Appreciative murmurs swept the room. Bobby's expression was comically enraptured.

Mrs. Blocken glided over to Bree's side and circled her several times. "Perfect, perfect." Olivia joined her. "I told you this color would be perfect, Olivia. The ladies will be like golden stars adorning you," Mrs. Blocken said.

From my seat on the floral printed sofa, I gagged. O.M. straddled the threshold of the open French doors that led into the backyard. Her face encompassed all the horror I felt. It gave me small comfort.

"Olga," her mother called. "Try on your gown."

O.M. backed outside onto the patio.

Mrs. Blocken looked up in disgust. "Olga, *now.*"

O.M. shook her head.

Mrs. Blocken marched over to her daughter. "Young lady, you will do as you're told." The doorbell rang, playing *Für Elise.* Happy for an excuse to exit the room, I offered to answer it. To my dismay, I opened the door to my brother's eager face. His blond hair was sticking up in all directions, his beard was unruly and in desperate need of combing, and his T-shirt hung crookedly on his thin shoulders—sure signs that he'd been up at ungodly hours with mathematical equations, theorems, and other things I hoped never to understand. Mark looked just as startled to see me as I was to see him.

"India?" He adjusted his wire-rimmed glasses on the bridge of his nose. "What are you doing here?"

"Mark, this isn't a good time. I'll talk to you later." I started to close the door.

He began nodding, then, "Hey, I didn't come here to see you. I have to speak to Olivia. It's urgent."

"Not now. I'll tell her you'd like to talk her. Now, please leave."

The conversation from the living room moved closer.

"India, who's at the door?" Olivia called.

Hearing her voice, he barreled past me, ramming the brass doorknob into my hip. I swore under my breath.

"Olivia, I have to talk to you."

She froze. Her sunny party expression vanished.

"Olivia, dear, you shouldn't abandon your guests," Mrs. Blocken's voice preceded her into the entry. "We weren't—" She stopped suddenly seeing Mark, whose gaze never left her daughter's face. "What's he doing here?" Mrs. Blocken's demand was laced with disgust. "Is this your idea of a joke, India?"

"I—"

The remaining party members materialized behind Mrs. Blocken.

"Olivia." Mark said her name like a prayer. "I have to speak with you. Please."

"Get him out of here this instant, India," Mrs. Blocken ordered. "I'm holding you responsible for this. I didn't want your family to have anything to do with the wedding, but Olivia insisted that you take part. I see now that my earlier judgment was correct."

My face burned. I grabbed my brother's arm more roughly than necessary and shoved him toward the door.

Bobby mumbled a hasty good-bye to Bree. As I was pushing my brother out the door, he grabbed the frame. "Mark," I hissed.

He clung tight. "I really need to talk to you. I'll be in my office at Martin all day tomorrow. Meet me, please!" He called over his shoulder.

I pried Mark's right hand from the jamb, and Bobby worked on his left. When Mark let go, I pushed him outside, Bobby on my heels. The door slammed behind us, and we heard the bolt slide home.

On the front lawn, Mark shook out of my grasp. "Let go."

Hoping the Blockens wouldn't overhear, I demanded, "What are you doing here?"

"I had to speak to her. She's making a mistake," he said, obviously unconcerned with eavesdropping.

His face was the color of the inside of a watermelon, and his thin chest heaved up and down so rapidly I thought he would hyperventilate.

A neighbor across the street glanced up from her faded azaleas. Bobby stood beside my car, suggesting we leave before the Blockens called the cops.

I ignored him. "She's getting married in a week. Leave it alone."

Mark rushed to his car and threw open the door. "I wouldn't expect you to understand. It's obvious where your loyalties lie."

"Wait," I called, running after him. He peeled away from the curb and down the normally quiet Kilbourne. I watched him drive away and silently prayed that he wouldn't die in a horrific accident.

Bobby walked up behind me. "Thanks for inviting me. This was fun."

CHAPTER FIVE

A gauze bandage was more likely to fix the ozone layer than a Martin student was to enter the Ryan Memorial Library on Saturday of the Fourth of July weekend. Regardless of this basic logic, I held my post behind the reference desk bright and early the next morning. I disliked the location of the reference desk. "Island" would be a more apt description of the area, which was a glorified high counter floating in the middle of the main floor. In it, I felt exposed and cut off from the safety of walls and back exits. After reading library management journals, the previous library director relocated the reference area directly in front of the library's main entrance, hoping that after a patron ran into it, he'd ask a question. Although the undergrads had more bruises than before, the arrangement was not exactly working as planned—and wouldn't, as long as Internet search engines dominated the average student's research methods.

By ten o'clock, our only patron was an elderly journalism professor who sat in the back of the main floor cursing at the microfiche machine. Occasionally, a loud bang drifted from the professor's general direction, but the library staff turned a deaf ear. The professor had a reputation for biting off heads. I was flipping through a new botany text to distract myself. Mark's emotional drop-in visit to the Blockens' yesterday reminded me of Olivia's ill-fated high school graduation party. His two appearances were so similar that the thought of one always reminded me of the other, and I wished that I could forget them both.

The party had been half graduation party, half bon voyage. She had received a summer internship in Virginia, so she was heading south in mid-June as opposed to August. I'd snuck out of my house to go to the party. I didn't want my brother to know where I was going. He was having a hard time accepting Olivia's decision to move to Virginia. He had been constantly calling her and dropping in on the Blockens all spring hoping that he could change her mind with sheer persistence. The family became increasingly annoyed with Mark's pursuit. Mrs. Blocken thought I was egging him as some kind of practical joke. "This isn't funny, India," she told me on numerous occasions.

The party was the highlight of the graduation season and held in the Blocken backyard. All of Mrs. Blocken's friends were there, including the mayor and his wife and the president of Martin College and her husband.

Just when the party was at its height, Mark stumbled through the Blockens' opened gate. Olivia sat on her boyfriend-of-the-moment's lap, a baseball player from a rival high school. I stood with some classmates, only half listening to their chatter about summer jobs. Because I wasn't paying attention to the group, I was the first one to notice my brother. I started to make my way to him, but there were too many partygoers between us for me to reach him before he called out.

"Olivia!"

Olivia, who was whispering something to her jock boyfriend, either didn't hear him or pretended not to, but Mrs. Blocken certainly did. She had her gaze trained on Mark with a glare that could have melted iron. She started toward him. Mark saw her coming and backed up into the buffet table. Somehow he managed to kick out one of the legs from under it and the table fell. Cucumber sandwiches, olives, and cake toppled to the ground. The well-groomed guests gawked at Mark, who had potato salad in his hair and punch down the front of his shirt. He struggled to get up and hurried toward Olivia. His tumble had gained her full attention. She'd left her jock and stood a few feet from him.

"Olivia, I love you." He smiled at her as if he believed that she would return his affection. "Please stay, or if you really want to go to Virginia, I'll transfer down there."

Olivia looked at him for a long minute as if she realized for the first time that he wasn't joking. Up to that point, she always accepted Mark's attentions as if it were a game that they played. I had to admit to myself that I thought the same way, but seeing Mark there covered in punch in front of all those guests, there was no question that he was earnest.

"I don't love you," she said. "I'm going to Virginia alone."

Mark sucked in a breath as if he couldn't get enough air. I was frozen with embarrassment. If the earth would have opened up at that moment, I would have willingly dove in.

Snickers and giggles coursed through the group.

"Your brother is such a freak," one of my classmates whispered into my ear.

Mrs. Blocken shook with rage. "Get out, and stay away from my daughter."

Mark kept his gaze fixed on Olivia.

"Leave," Mrs. Blocken said.

A group of varsity jocks were quickly closing in on my brother. They would like nothing better than to throw a nerd like Mark over the Blockens' fence.

Luckily, they didn't get that chance because Olivia spoke first. "I don't want you at my party, Mark. Go home."

Tears welled up in his eyes, and he staggered away, back through the open gate.

Later, I found him curled in a ball in his apartment. I called my sister, and she took over with her usual efficiency, and, in the fall, I ran away to art school.

The phone at the check-out desk rang.

A moment later, Lasha Lint, the director of the library, bellowed, "Botswana, phone."

Startled, I jumped. Lasha shook the receiver at me. Black, solid, relatively young, and loud, Lasha is nothing like the withering-violet type that many think of when they conjure up the image of a librarian. With a brutal penchant for nicknames, she hadn't called me India since my first day at Martin.

"Botswana," I said as I hopped off my chair, sending it skidding on its polished wheels into the reference counter. "That's a new one."

"I've been studying the atlas, honey."

I chuckled and took the phone from her.

"India, do you know where Mark is?" my mother asked in the tense, low voice she used to console divorcées.

I prickled. "No, I'm not his babysitter."

"I'm not asking you where he is, I'm asking if you know where he is. I know where he is," she rambled.

"Then, why are you calling me if you already know where he is?"

Lasha shamelessly eavesdropped. I leaned against the checkout counter and rolled my eyes.

"Your brother called from campus. He was babbling."

A hereditary trait, I noted.

"He said something about Olivia and a fountain. He was—he sounded strange. I'm worried about him. If you could walk over to his office and check—"

"I can't just leave the library—" I started to say, but was interrupted by shrill sirens that shook the book stacks.

Lasha rushed to the window. "A police car and two ambulances. They're heading to Dexler."

"What's going on?" my mother asked. "Are those sirens? India!"

"I'll have to call you back." I hung up and turned to Lasha. She had her nose pressed up against the glass.

"Go on, Iran."

I staggered out the loading doors into the stifling heat and sunlight. Gathering my bearings, I jogged across campus to Dexler. As I closed in on the building, I saw three police cars, a fire truck, and two ambulances gathered around an iron fountain. The fountain, entitled *Empowerment,* was a twenty-foot metal embarrassment to modern art that a donor with more cash than class unloaded on the college. Never one to upset benefactors with impending tasty bequests, Martin accepted the sculpture, but tucked it behind the Dexler Math and Science building, the least visible location on campus.

I forced myself to slow to a walk and tricked myself into believing that the sirens had nothing whatsoever to do with my loony brother. A handful of summer faculty and students had clustered about thirty feet from the fountain. A uniformed campus security guard blocked their view to whatever they were trying so desperately to see.

"It can't be Mark. He wouldn't—" I refused to allow my brain to complete that thought. When I reached the assemblage of Martinites, I asked a dour chemistry professor, "What's going on?"

"Nobody knows. Something about Mark Hayes," the professor said with a glint of excitement in his eyes.

I forced my way past the security guard who looked just old enough to star in a zit cream commercial. He stood on his tiptoes to peek at the action and didn't notice me until I was already well beyond his reach.

"Wait! You can't go back there," the boy-officer cried,

astonished that anyone would cross his imaginary line. Obviously, he hadn't been at Martin long.

I hurried around the left side of the fountain's base. A cluster of public servants in different official uniforms stood over something on the ground. An EMT wheeled a stretcher over to the group. They swallowed the EMT and the stretcher into their ring. I stopped, afraid to proceed, afraid for Mark. An image of a somber orderly pulling a sheet back and asking me to identify the body entered my mind. Suddenly lightheaded, I doubled over, gulping deep breaths. I had to stop watching crime shows.

"Miss, you shouldn't be back here. Are you all right?"

I stared at a pair of black walking shoes. After two more deep breaths, I straightened to stare into the concerned face of a middle-aged EMT. White remnants of sun block glistened on his bald head. The dizziness passed.

"Is that," I stopped and began again. "I'm looking for my brother, Mark Hayes."

The EMT nodded. "Don't worry, Miss, he's fine. He's a little shaken up, but fine. I'll take you to him."

Mercifully, the EMT led me away from the cluster of emergency workers to an ambulance. Mark was perched on the end of the ambulance's bay. Despite the heat, a heavy wool blanket enveloped his frame. A dark-haired man in khakis and a green polo shirt asked him serious-sounding questions. Mark stared at the ground, his thin shoulders shaking.

"Mark!" I rushed past the khaki-clad man. "What happened?"

I hopped up beside him on the edge of the ambulance. He sniffled. Fat tears rolled down his face and stalled at his beard. I patted his arm, wishing that my sister Carmen was there. She was better equipped to handle emotions.

The khaki-clad man uttered a frustrated sigh. "Who are you? We're in the middle of an interview here."

I recognized the man's face, but couldn't put a name to it, a fairly common occurrence for a community of Stripling's size. "I'm his sister. India Hayes. Can you telling me what's going on?"

"Well, Miss Hayes," the man said. His voice had the lilt of recognition. "A woman tumbled into the fountain and was badly hurt. Your brother's a witness."

"Who's the woman?" I asked, but already I knew.

The man consulted his minuscule memo pad. "Olivia Blocken."

CHAPTER SIX

"Olivia," I whispered.

The man peered at me. "Do you know her?"

"She's a friend. Is she okay?"

Breathe. In and out, in and out, I reminded myself.

Mark snuffled. I patted his arm again. I really wished Carmen was there.

"She's alive, but unconscious. She received a nasty gash and bump falling into the fountain, or whatever the hell you people call that thing."

I let out a breath. "And she'll be okay? She'll recover?"

"Hopefully we got to her in time." He flipped through his notebook.

Mark stopped weeping and sat staring in the direction of uniforms by the fountain. His face looked carved from stone.

"Does her family know? Have you called them?"

"They've been notified and will meet Olivia at the hospital in Akron."

"What does Mark have to do with this?"

"If you would give us a minute, that's what I am trying to find out," khaki man said.

The light dawned. "You're a police officer."

He held out his hand. "Detective Rick Mains."

I stopped short of shaking his hand. "Rick Mains? Ricky Mains?" And I remembered where I had seen Mains before. He was one of a long line of high school boyfriends that Carmen had dated before she'd settled down in college. Mains was one of the long-termers. Four months.

Mains grinned. "You remember me?"

"I'm sure Carmen does too," I said.

Mains guffawed the same intrusive and uproarious laugh that had caused Carmen to dismiss him for the happy hunting grounds of higher education.

I frowned. The current situation was not conducive to any levity, and what I'd said wasn't funny, anyway.

Regaining control, Mains smiled. "I'm sure she does. Now, if you don't mind, I only need a few more minutes with Mark."

I scowled, but stepped away from the ambulance. At the fountain, the small cluster of people divided again, and a female EMT rolled a stretcher toward the other ambulance. Although I couldn't see her, I knew that Olivia lay on the stretcher. Two EMTs lifted Olivia into the ambulance. Sirens blared, and the ambulance raced off campus. The emergency workers cleared the scene, uselessly wiping their sweaty faces in the humid air. The half dozen police officers circled the fountain, like August yellow jackets around an especially fragrant garbage can.

Mid-morning and the humidity had already plastered my hair to my neck and face. I heard snippets of Mains and Mark's conversation. Mark was harder to hear. I found myself in one of those rare moments when I longed for my cell phone, if only to call my mother and tell her that Mark was okay. She would be climbing the church's narthex by now. My cell was uselessly sitting in my office back at the library.

Turning my thoughts from my mother, and from Olivia and the stretcher, I mentally replayed the scene at Blockens' yesterday afternoon and Mark's strange appearance. Why had he asked to see her? Did he honestly think that she'd leave Kirk for him? Did she actually come? I wondered. There was no other reason for her to be on Martin's campus than to see Mark.

Why would she come? To appease Mark? To finally settle things between them?

I held my knit blouse away from my body, hoping a non-existent breeze would cool me.

"Miss Hayes," Mains said, breaking into my thoughts.

"Call me India," I said, startled.

"Okay, India." He smiled. "Your brother's free to go."

Mark removed the blanket from his shoulders. I gasped. He was soaked to the skin, and his clothes were covered with watery traces of blood. Olivia's blood. I swallowed hard.

Mark was completely composed. He folded the blanket and handed it to an EMT as if he were computing simple trigonometry. From personal experience, I knew this was a bad sign.

"Do you need a ride home?" I asked. "I could take you to Mom's, if you want," I added, although I couldn't think how that would be helpful. "Or Carmen's? Wherever you want to go."

In my peripheral vision, I could see Mains still watching us.

"I don't need a ride," Mark snapped.

I jerked back, stung.

"I have work to do in my office. You can leave."

"Hey," I snapped back. "Don't get pissed at me because—"

"I'm not pissed at you." Mark, who usually hated that kind of vulgarity, said.

"Then don't be such a—jerk. I'm here to help you. Mom called, and I—"

"Great, just what I need, my mommy and baby sissy to watch over me. Call Mom and tell her everything's fine. Okay?"

"Why are you acting this way? Everything is not fine." I stepped closer to him and lowered my voice so that Mains wouldn't overhear. "What happened to Olivia? Did she meet you here?" I couldn't hide the disbelief from my voice.

"Is it so hard to believe that Olivia would want to speak to me?" My brother's voice cracked.

"No. Not at all." I hastened to reassure him. I could deal much better with an angry Mark rather than a weepy Mark. "What happened?"

He dropped his head. The white-hot sunlight reflecting off his blond crown nearly blinded me. "I don't know. She called my office last night and said that she'd meet me by the fountain in the morning. By the time I got here, she was already in the water. I pulled her out and called 911. She was bleeding. From her head I guess, but there was blood everywhere. I couldn't remember CPR. I couldn't do anything."

"You called 911." I tried to console him.

"Like that's enough. If she dies—"

"She won't die. Now, what time were you supposed to meet her?"

"Nine-thirty. I found her at nine-forty-five; I looked at my watch." Tears banked on his lower eyelids.

The last remaining EMTs piled into the lone ambulance and exited Martin at a sedate speed. Mains had disappeared. I looked around and finally spotted him standing by *Empowerment* with a handful of cops.

"Are you sure you want to go back to work?"

His shoulders sagged. "I'd like to go to the hospital to see Olivia."

A Blocken lynching played out in my mind. "I don't think that's a great idea."

A silver luxury car pulled up to the fountain. The driver, a solid man with silver hair leaped out of the car before it was fully settled into park. The man was Sam Lepcheck, college provost and spin-doctor *extraordinaire,* and his presence was never a good sign.

Lepcheck approached Mains and conversed for a few minutes, then nodded and scratched his chin. I could hear the bad press headlines careening through his mind. "Stripling native tumbles into Martin's hideous fountain," and the like. Lepcheck sucked in a big gust of air—Mains must have told him that the victim was Regina Blocken's daughter. So much for the amicable town and gown relationship that Lepcheck tried so desperately to foster. Mark's name floated across the pavement to us.

I grabbed my brother's arm. "It's time to go."

I dragged Mark across campus toward the library and my car before Lepcheck decided to make my brother the fall guy. Mark already ranked on Lepcheck's hit list because he hadn't completed his Ph.D. Martin prided itself on having roughly ninety percent of its teaching faculty toting doctorates, and although Mark planned to reach this accolade sometime before his seventieth birthday, his pace was a bit slow for Lepcheck. Fortunately for Mark, and, I supposed, unfortunately for Lepcheck, Martin had a notoriously poor math department, and staffing was always a challenge. So the college had hired Mark on the basis of his master's degree and his alumnus pledge that he would complete the higher doctorate.

Halfway to the library, Mark froze. "Theodore! I left him in my car."

"You left your cat locked in your car? It's over ninety degrees."

Theodore was Mark's twenty-five-pound Maine Coon cat, and a permanent fixture around campus. Mark found him as a kitten abandoned outside Dexler three years ago and had no idea how much cat he was getting. Maine Coons are known for their impressive statures, but Theodore was at least ten pounds overweight. Mark taught Theodore to walk on a leash, and it wasn't uncommon to see the two of them strolling across campus together. Many students carried cat treats or goodies from the cafeteria in their knapsacks for Theodore, resulting in his present obesity.

"I left the windows down," he defended himself.

Mark and I raced back across campus to the small faculty lot behind Dexler. The fastest way to reach the lot was to dash by the fountain. I saw Lepcheck's gaze follow us as we flew by. We were the spitting image of respectable faculty.

Mark's hybrid car was one of three cars in the lot, and like he promised, the windows were down. I reached the car first. Theodore lay on the backseat of the small car, on his back, his front paws suspended listlessly in the air. I threw open the door and touched him. He chirped pathetically. Mark reached my side and cried, "Is he okay? Theo! Theo!"

"He's overheated. You don't leave him in the car like this a lot, do you?"

"No, just this once. Theo, I'm sorry." he sniffled and patted the cat's upturned belly.

"Let's get him out of the car and cooled off," I leaned into the car to pick up Theodore. When I placed my hand on his round tummy, he attacked. His claws dug into my bare arm and he bit down hard on my fingers. "Ow! Get him off me."

Mark grabbed Theodore's paws and pried them from my skin. I knocked Theo on the head, and he relinquished my fingers. I inspected my arm. Tiny puncture marks and purple bruises dotted my forearm and hand. Blood welled up from deep scratches. I jumped away from the car and cradled my arm.

Mark pulled Theo out of the car. "Poor baby." Theodore lay in his servant's arms, purring happily.

There was no time to tend to my wounds. With Lepcheck lurking about I needed to get Mark off campus. I ushered man and cat toward the library.

CHAPTER SEVEN

Taking a less direct way to the library, we avoided Lepcheck and the fountain. I made Mark put on my lavender cardigan. It wasn't much of a fashion statement, but at least it covered the bloodstains on his white dress shirt. Luckily, he was wearing dark jeans, so I didn't have to sacrifice my skirt. Just inside the service door, Mark slumped in a padded folding chair with growling Theodore stretched across his lap.

"Stay there," I ordered both of them.

I hurried through the workroom and collided headlong into Jefferson Island, the cataloger. The collision was more painful for me, since Jefferson is six-four and three hundred plus pounds. A transplanted Georgian who detested the north with every fiber of his being, Jefferson had dressed conservatively in a white button-down shirt and gray polyester pants. He also wore a red leather bolo tie with a pewter Dachshund charm in honor of a childhood pet.

Now he regarded me through narrowed eyes. "Miz Hayes, please watch where you're goin'. You nearly bowled me over."

I rubbed my aching nose. "Sorry, Jefferson."

"Rush, rush. All you Yankees rush. It gives me a headache. Even with all that rushin', nothing gets done. Who gets the books on the shelf around here? Me, that's who. Who—"

His bulk thoroughly blocked my path. Frustrated, I interrupted his pity party. "Move."

Shocked, Jefferson stepped aside. "Pardon you, young lady."

Lasha stood behind the checkout desk reprimanding a student worker. "If you put the books in the wrong place, you might as well as burn 'em, because we sure as hell are never going to find them."

The student, a thin junior, ducked his head to hide a defiant smirk.

"I don't care if it takes you all day. Take that cart up, and do it right."

The student scurried away. Lasha scrutinized him with beady disgust. "I thought they taught them numbers and letters at Martin; it appears I was sadly mistaken." She looked at me. "Romania."

"Lasha, can I speak to you in private?"

"Sure thing," she said. Jefferson stood two feet behind me, watching our exchange. "Georgia, watch the desk."

"That's not in my job description," the cataloger blustered. "It's not my responsibility to watch the desk."

"It's only for a few minutes, and if you get into any trouble, ask one of the student workers." She slid past him. "Are you coming, Latvia?"

Lasha shut her office door behind us. The office was the size of closet and half of the limited space was taken up by a metal desk. She sat behind the desk in an office chair she'd bought with her own money. "What's up?"

I sat in one of the two arm chairs in the room. My knees butted up against the front of her desk as I told her about Olivia, and Mark's involvement with the accident. She expressed sympathy, and I thanked her. "Of course, I am worried about Olivia, but I'm also concerned about Mark. I was wondering if I could take the rest of the day off."

Lasha waved away my request. "I think this constitutes an emergency situation. Just go ahead and leave. Looker will have to come in earlier." Looker was Lasha's nickname for Bobby.

He reveled in it. "We're understaffed today, as it is. Dixie and a half-handful of students aren't going to cut it."

"He'll love that."

"That's why you can call him." Before I could protest, she rose and slipped out of the office, throwing over her shoulder, "Use my phone."

I called Bobby's home, but no one answered. I tried his cell. "Bobby—"

"No to whatever you are about to ask me. No. The answer's no."

"Bobby, I wouldn't call if it wasn't urgent."

"Like yesterday was urgent?"

"It's Mark," I blurted.

"What happened?"

I ran through the same story I'd spilled to Lasha, a tad more dramatically—Bobby's tougher to sell.

After I finished, Bobby asked, "Is Olivia okay?"

"I . . . I don't know. Last I heard, she was unconscious."

I heard hushed conversation on Bobby's side of the line. "Who are you talking to?"

More muffled voices, one of which sounded suspiciously female. "Bree," he finally answered.

"Olivia's Bree?"

"I'm showing her around Stripling."

"Uh-huh. You work fast, *mi hermano,* I'll give you that."

"Listen, Bree just called the Blockens on her cell. She's heading to the hospital to meet them." Dramatic pause. "I'll come in."

"Thanks, Bobby, you're the best. I swear to God, you're an angel. If I had any musical talent, I'd write a ballad about your greatness."

"Charming. There's a *but.*"

"A *but?*" Suspicion arose.

"Oh, yeah. Library orientation. *All* freshman English classes."

In the third week of August, the freshmen would arrive on campus. The new students have a few carefree days before the upperclassmen arrive lurking for prey, and the administration slams them into classrooms with overburdened faculty. By the second week, early post-adolescent synapses zap and the freshmen realize that college wasn't ultimate recess, but *school*. During this time of painful discovery, the English professors farm out their freshman classes to the reference staff (i.e., Bobby and me) to teach the students how to use the library.

"Bobby, no."

He said, "Take it, or leave it."

"Arrgh. Okay, I'll take it."

"Great. Tell Lasha I'll be there in twenty minutes. Oh, and India, you might want to get on the Internet and look up the latest trends for teenyboppers. I think you can really grab them early if you pepper some of their lingo into your presentation."

I hung up the phone.

After telling Lasha that Bobby was on his way, I returned to the workroom to retrieve Mark. He'd propped himself against the loading doors. Theodore purred in his arms. A small cluster of female students, a few of them library workers, surrounded them.

Erin, a willowy redhead, cooed. "He's adorable."

I hoped she referred to the cat, but she watched Mark from under her eyelashes.

I mumbled a greeting, then took Mark's arm. "Ready to go?"

Mark bit his lip and nodded. I told the students that I had a family emergency and Bobby would be coming in early.

"Bobby, huh?" Erin said with orchestrated disinterest. Everything about her screamed seasoned. I'd seen Bobby check her out when he thought no one was looking and vice versa. I'd have to keep an eye on them this year. I don't know if I could stand this job if Bobby got sacked for behavior unbecoming a librarian.

Once we were in my car, I called Mom and told her I was bringing Mark to her house.

"Why? What happened? Is Mark okay?"

"He's fine. We'll be there in a few minutes. Gotta go." I snapped the phone shut.

During the short ride to our parents' house, Mark sat silent, Theodore cradled in his lap. At each stop sign, I glanced at him, wondering if the day's event would be enough to send him back over the edge.

CHAPTER EIGHT

I turned the car into my parents' driveway. They lived in a brick, L-shaped ranch with dark purple shutters and bright red front door that they bought after my dad's accident. While trimming a sycamore tree on the property of Stripling Presbyterian Church where my mother was pastor, my father fell from his self-made rigging and broke his back. He was paralyzed from the waist down.

Roses and black-eyed Mexican sunflowers bloomed in full glory along the wooden ramp that led to the front door. Wearing a pair of overall jean shorts and a pink tie-dyed T-shirt, my mother waited impatiently on the ramp. She'd separated her long hair into thick gray pigtails.

"India, I don't appreciate you hanging up on me. I was worried sick about Mark, and then I had to worry about you on top of that," she said as I wrestled the car door open. Mark exited easily.

"And Mark, where have you been? Why the cryptic phone call? Honestly, both of you. Carmen would have at least called to tell me what was going on. I was waiting and worrying, afraid to leave for the church because you might—" She stopped abruptly. "Is that blood on your shirt? And you're wet."

Mark wrenched away and set Theo down on the driveway.

"What happened?" Mom demanded. She directed this to me.

I slammed the car door shut. "I'd tell you if you'd give me a chance."

"Don't take that tone with me, young lady. Is that your blood Mark? Are you hurt?"

She started toward my brother again, but he scooped up Theodore and sprinted into the house, a good move on his part.

"Just tell me if he's hurt," Mom said. This time I heard real fear in her voice.

"He's not hurt, but Olivia is." That shut her up and gave me a chance to tell her what had happened. "I'm going to head over to the hospital to see how she is."

She waited, looking nervous, until Mark disappeared through the front door. "Are you sure you don't want me to go to the hospital with you?"

"Yes," I said a little too quickly. "I think it would be better if I go alone."

"I'll take care of Mark." She was halfway to the front door by the time she'd completed her sentence.

The hospital in Akron's proper is a city unto itself, and each year more of its outbuildings swallow parts of Akron's downtown. The large state university in Akron was doing the same thing coming from the opposite directions. I wondered when the two finally met who would overtake whom.

I left my car in the parking deck closest to the Emergency Room entrance. I knew the layout fairly well because my father spent three weeks in the hospital after his fall.

As I stepped through the mechanical doors, the faint scent of antiseptic hit me, reminding me of my father's accident. I had been in Chicago, finishing my freshman year of art school. Mom had called from the emergency room and told me to come home immediately. I told her I had one more exam to take the next morning and I'd drive home after the exam.

"I shouldn't be surprised that you'd treat this family crisis the same way you've acted about your brother's problems." Before I could respond, or even think of a response, she hung up.

The next day with my car waiting outside the visual arts building, packed to the gills with clothes and dorm room trappings, I took the final, confusing the impressionists with the expressionists. I drove the six hours home, straight and alone. Choosing the wrong bank of elevators when I arrived at the hospital, I lost myself in its endless corridors and passages. A friendly, large-toothed nurse helped me find my father's room, on the opposite side of the hospital, where he was attached to metal rods and plastic tubes.

Mom and Carmen hovered over my father with anxious chatter and didn't even notice when I walked into the room. I didn't call attention to myself. Instead, I focused on Mark who had huddled in a corner, his long arms wrapped around his body like a straightjacket. He was even thinner than he had been over Christmas, the last time I'd been home. I walked over to him, took his hand, and led him out of the room.

The rest of the summer, as Mom had shopped for a new wheelchair-accessible house and had dealt with hospital bills and dad's rehab, I had taken care of my brother. I had driven him to appointments and to Martin where he was taking independent study courses in higher math. I had made sure he took his medicine everyday, and had even contemplated transferring to Martin for the next school year so that I could watch out for him, but Carmen had talked me out of it. And I had never thanked her for that.

Now, on the day after the Fourth of July, the emergency room was crowded with firecracker mishaps and holiday binges. The injured and families of the injured in varying degrees of pain and distress filled the main waiting room. No Blockens. A pair of old men watched a baseball game playing on a TV tethered high in the corner, and children squabbled over toys in the corner while their parents flipped through dog-eared magazines. A dishwater blond woman shot them dagger looks and bent over her dog-eared copy of *The Bell Jar.*

Glancing from face to face, I felt my first twinge of apprehension. It was instinct that had made me head to the hospital as soon as I could. I hadn't wanted it to be like that last time when I had put something trivial by comparison first. But this was different. This wasn't *my* family in crisis. I shouldn't have come. I've never been a Blocken favorite, except to Olivia, and my family wasn't too high on their charts either. In some way, I knew Mrs. Blocken would blame Mark for the accident.

Before I could flee, though, Bree appeared carrying a paper cup of coffee. "India?"

"How is she?" I asked.

"She's in surgery now to release fluid from her brain."

"Oh," I replied. If I said anything else, I would've thrown up on her sandals. Even paper cuts make me queasy. After a beat, I asked, "And the rest of her family?"

"A private waiting room down the hall." She glared at the men who cheered the game on the television set.

"Did you see her?"

Bree shook her head. "They took her straight from emergency to surgery."

I absentmindedly rubbed my left shoulder. My shoulders always ached when I was nervous or tense due to years of being hunched over a painter's easel.

"I can take you to the waiting room. Olivia's family will be happy to see you."

"No, I don't think that—"

"This way," she said. She turned around and headed down the corridor. Just as she was about to disappear around a corner, I jogged after her.

"Down the hall" was almost the other side of Mars. I followed Bree's brisk pace through the hospital corridors, weaving in and out of wards and around hospital staff in ugly white sneakers. I stared resolutely at the back of Bree's trim ankles as she cruised down the hall, unable to stand the suffering lining the hallways. The deeper we traveled into the hospital, the more sterile the air became. I vowed never again to complain about the smell of moldy books donated by retired Martin professors.

We dodged a crash cart. "You seem to know your way around, Bree; have you been to this hospital before?"

Without breaking stride, her voice floated back to me. "No, but I've been in a lot of hospitals."

Nearly toppling a food cart, I abandoned conversation.

After more turns than I could count, Bree halted abruptly in front of a heavy-looking forest green door. Through the door's small window, I caught a glimpse of Dr. Blocken and Kirk filling an overstuffed loveseat, each crowded against an opposite arm, apparently in an effort not to touch each other. Although I couldn't see her, I knew that Mrs. Blocken lay in wait, pacing the floor and undoubtedly accosting hospital staff anytime someone chanced by.

Bree eased open the door and entered the room, leaving it ajar for me. The occupants of the room glanced up expectantly, with equal parts dread and hope.

"Your coffee, Regina," Bree said. "I'm sorry I took so long. I met India in the emergency room."

Duly outed, I slid into the room. Dr. Blocken and Kirk blinked in disbelief. O.M., her hair now neon blue, didn't look up from the rock star biography she read in the corner, and Mrs. Blocken jolted from her seat.

After sputtering for a few seconds, she managed a profanity-laced version of, "What are you doing here?"

"I was worried about Olivia," I sputtered.

Mrs. Blocken pressed the heel of her right hand over her left eye as if blocking out my image and smearing her flawless makeup. Underneath her foundation, her complexion blotched. She removed her hand and seemed unable to speak. Dr. Blocken fidgeted, and then stood with phony assertiveness. A cuticle on his left hand was bleeding from being bitten to the quick. "India, we appreciate your concern for our daughter, but I think it would be better if you left." His voice shook.

Mrs. Blocken's naked anguish disconcerted me, and I merely nodded and backed out of the small waiting room. When the door clicked into the latch, I heard Mrs. Blocken's first sob. I hurried down the hallway, unsure if I was heading in the right direction. I followed sign after sign pointing me to some unseen exit. After confusing twists and bends, I found myself outside in the humid air and burning sunlight. I was outside but on the wrong side of the structure. Rather than go back into the hospital and risk becoming lost again, I circumnavigated the building until I reached the parking deck. As I walked around the building, the corners of my eyes itched, and I bit the inside of my lower lip.

Chapter Nine

After my visit to the hospital, I went straight home. Inside my apartment, I threw my shoulder bag on the couch beside Templeton, who didn't stir at the bounce. His black limbs splayed in front of the fan. The answering machine's blinking light stewed in a state of manic urgency. Sitting on the couch next to Templeton, I pressed PLAY.

The first message was from my mother. "India, call me when you get in. I want to know how the hospital visit went."

The second message was from Carmen. "India? I can never reach you. Mom told me about Olivia. What's going on? Why is Mark involved? Why was she at Martin? Why didn't you answer your cell?"

I had turned my cell off when I entered the hospital as instructed by the dozen no-cell-phone posters plastered throughout the building.

I did not recognize the third voice right off. "Miss Hayes, this is Detective Mains from the Stripling Police Department. I have some questions I need to ask you." About Mark and Olivia's relationship, no doubt. He ended with his phone number.

The final message was an especially cheery Bobby. "I hope Olivia's okay. By the way, I thought I'd help you out a little bit. I called the guys over in admissions about freshmen head count. Unfortunately, enrollment is down this year, only 554 incoming."

The machine signed off, and I fell back against the couch,

closing my eyes as I considered who to call back, who not to, and how to cause Bobby the most bodily harm.

The phone jarred me awake. It was still bright outside. I glanced at the green ceramic clock hanging above the kitchen counter. Three-thirty. My face felt grimy and my contacts had fused themselves to my retinas. The phone rang relentlessly.

I gave in. "Hello," I said, fully expecting my mother.

"This is Detective Mains. Did you receive my message?"

"Uh, yes, I was about to call you back," I lied.

"I see. I'd like to meet with you about Olivia's case."

"Okay," I mumbled, still waking up. "When?"

"How about right now?"

"Now?"

"I'm in your driveway."

I jumped. Templeton remained as prostrate as a slug. I rushed over to the peephole in my front door and peered out. Mains, leaning against a dark American-made sedan, waved at me. I involuntarily gasped.

Mains ignored the exclamation. "I promise I'll only take a few minutes."

I scanned the apartment for anything remotely embarrassing—stray underwear, trashy romance novels, regurgitated feline hairballs. As a woman living alone, any one of these was apt to be strewn in the oddest places. I stumbled down my abbreviated hallway and slammed my bedroom and studio doors. I glanced in the hall mirror. Dear God, I was a mess. The skirt and blouse I had worn to work were wrinkled beyond recognition, my hair was matted to my head like a flattened toy poodle. By the front door, I found a stray rubber band that Templeton would likely try to eat later. I threw my hair up in a haphazard knot.

As calmly as possible, I said, "I suppose I could meet with you now." I hung up the phone and opened the door.

My apartment consisted of the left half of a duplex facing the street. I chose it because of its low rent and its nearness to campus, imagining that I would walk to work. I could count on my left hand the number of times I had walked to the library. The resident of the right half of the duplex was my landlady, Ina Carroll, a self-professed bachelorette, never married because she hated to cook and claimed she didn't want some man to make her learn. In the late eighties, Ina received a letter from a former United States senator reminding her to remember her Irish heritage. Since that fateful day, painted stone and ceramic leprechauns had peppered every recess of her property. Lately, Ina had diversified and bought a couple pots of gold for the wee lads. I had made the mistake of telling Ina that a large portion of my family tree was Irish, as well. Ever since, she's forced corned beef and cabbage on me, despite my vegetarian protests.

Ina sat on one of the white resin chairs on her small stoop, watching Mains with raptor-like interest. Ina was four-feet-ten and never left the house without wearing lipstick. She had soft blue-white grandma curls and snappy green eyes. Her appearance deceived people into believing that she baked cookies and cooed over babies. Nothing could be further from the truth. Mains smiled at her. That was his first mistake.

Before we could slip inside, Ina's high, baby robin voice called, "India, dear, aren't you going to introduce me to your friend?" She leaned over the wrought iron fence that divided the stoop into hers and mine.

Mains looked at me expectantly with a hint of a grin.

Successfully trapped, I made introductions. "Ina, this is Richmond Mains," I said, purposely omitting *detective*. Not sure what to call Mains, I turned to him. "And this is my neighbor, Ina Carroll."

Ina reached over the railing. "Nice to meet you, young man. It's been such a long time since India's had a nice-looking male friend over. Of course, that Bobby is always here, but no need to worry. They're just friends, you see."

Mains produced a full-fledged smirk.

I think my heart stopped. "Well, I'll see you later, Ina," I said.

"Oh, I see." She gave me a dramatic wink. To Mains, she added, "Have India show you her studio. She's a real talent."

Safely inside, I leaned against the door. I fake laughed. "Ina's a character."

"I like the leprechauns. Yours?"

"Ina's." My face was still unbearably hot. "Please have a seat," I said, motioning to the couch.

Templeton was MIA. Mains turned from me and moved toward the couch but stopped dead when he saw my living room. As he gawked, I tried to look at it with new eyes. The living room was small, equivalent to the size of the master bath in the Blocken home. A half-wall separated the cubby kitchen from the room, and the back wall was a single sliding glass door. But I guessed that Mains was more intrigued by the decor than the dimensions. Nearly every inch of wall space and furniture was splashed with vibrant and combating colors. Batiks, textiles, paintings, prints, and photographs crowded each other for precious space. They all represented different artistic periods and different artists and crafters, some professional, most amateur, and a few of my own.

Mains stared to the point of embarrassment. More gruffly than I intended, I again asked him to sit. He settled on the couch. I perched on an ancient rocking chair that I'd recently refinished. The new cushion was a bright orange and red paisley print and matched nothing else in the room.

Mains didn't comment about my decorating prowess, but instead pulled a small notebook out of his jacket pocket. "This afternoon, I spoke with Dr. and Mrs. Blocken at the hospital."

Even with the floor fan aimed at him, he looked unpleasantly warm in his summer jacket.

"Oh," I replied, hoping to hide the true state of my frayed nerves.

"You failed to mention that your brother arranged to meet Olivia Blocken at Martin College this morning, just prior to her attack."

"Her attack? I thought it was an accident."

"She was pushed. A nurse discovered two hand-sized bruises on her upper back."

"Pushed?"

He nodded. "And with a lot of force. It takes a lot of strength or anger to cause that kind of injury."

I shook my head. "That's impossible. Olivia hasn't lived in Stripling in years. No one here would have any reason to hurt her."

"Not even your brother?" Mains watched my reaction with hazel-green eyes. Earlier at the fountain, I hadn't noticed his eye color as he'd worn sunglasses.

My flush undoubtedly morphed from red embarrassment to fuchsia anger. "Mark would never hurt Olivia. Ever. I can't believe that you're even suggesting it."

"But he did ask Olivia to meet him in his office," Mains said in quiet tones likely meant to pacify wife beaters and psychotics. It didn't work on me.

I began rocking. "Yes, he asked her to meet him. But he would never hurt her."

"So it is understood that Olivia was on campus to visit Mark. That's what her parents believe."

I folded my arm across my chest, waiting for the rest.

He didn't disappoint. "According to Mrs. Blocken, Olivia is kindhearted and wanted to smooth things over between Mark and her before the wedding."

With an unladylike snort, I held up my right hand to stop

him. "Let me finish for you, Detective Mains. Mrs. Blocken is convinced that when Olivia arrived on campus, she tried to reason with Mark who waited until her back was turned and pushed her into the fountain. Am I close?"

"That was her estimation."

I stood up, sending the rocking chair reeling on its rails. "In that case, I think we're done here. I'm sorry that you wasted a trip."

Mains stood as well. "Miss Hayes, the easiest way to end this is to prove whether or not your brother is responsible for the assault on Olivia Blocken. You're making it difficult for me to do that."

"I'm sorry, and if you wish to speak with my brother any further, I suggest you do so in the company of his attorney."

"And who would that be?"

"Lewis Clive."

"Have you thought of Olivia? Don't you care what happened to your friend?"

I mentally staggered. "Of course I care about Olivia." I held my voice level. "But Mark had nothing to do with her attack."

I stomped to the door and opened it.

Mains placed his notebook back into his jacket pocket. "Thank you for your time."

He smiled and stepped through the door. Black fur clung to his khaki-clad backside.

Ina waited on the edge of her chair. "Did India show you the studio?"

Mains glanced at me. "Not today."

Or ever, I thought.

"Your leprechauns are really sharp," Mains told Ina.

Ina preened. "Thank you. You wouldn't be Irish, would you?" She pushed herself up to lean on the wrought iron railing.

"I'm afraid not. I'm more English than anything else."

Ina jumped back as if she'd been stung by a yellow jacket. "Bloody English."

Oh, geez, I thought. Before Ina could leap into a full-blown tirade, I ushered Mains down the step. "I think you'd better go."

"Okay," he said, eyeing Ina, whose face blazed molten purple. "I didn't mean any harm."

I wasn't sure if he referred to his accusation of Mark or offending Ina.

After Mains's sedan disappeared around the corner, I asked Ina if she was all right.

After spurting for a few minutes, she managed, "You're dating an Englishman. Don't you know what the English did to our people? The suffering. He didn't give you any potatoes, did he?"

"I'm *not* dating Richmond Mains. He's a police officer. He asked me some questions about a case."

"A police officer to boot. The English are always looking for ways to bully," Ina said.

I rubbed my throbbing shoulder and felt the sharp fingertips of a migraine tickle my brain.

"Why would a police officer speak with you? Have you done something wrong?"

"No, I haven't done anything wrong. I'm not feeling too well. I think I'll go lie down."

As I opened the door, Ina leaned further over the railing so that her feet no longer touched the stoop. "I prefer Bobby Mc-Nally. Now, he's a fine-looking Irish lad."

"Aye, that he is," I remarked in a mock brogue.

Once inside, I looked longingly toward my shut bedroom door. All I wanted to do was go to bed and pretend the day had never happened, but I knew if I didn't show up at the obligatory Hayes Fifth of July shindig, there'd be heck to pay later.

For a brief minute, I contemplated skipping the whole thing, but if I didn't appear, my mother would come looking for me or send Carmen to do the job. I headed toward my bedroom, not for a well-deserved rest, but to get ready for the inquisition at my parents' house. I made a mental note to wear running shoes instead of my standard flip-flops, just in case I needed to make a quick exit.

CHAPTER TEN

My parents' house was only five minutes from my duplex, the long way, and I found myself there much sooner than I liked. Once in my parents' driveway, I sat for a few moments admiring my mother's cosmos and snapdragons and gathering my strength.

The front door to the ranch sprang open, and my father flew down the ramp in his titanium wheelchair. "India, stop moping in that heap of metal and greet your poor old dad."

I slipped out of the car. "Happy Belated Fourth, Dad." I leaned down to kiss his cheek. "Are Carmen and Chip here already?"

"That they are, my girl. Don't tell her I told you so, but your sister is as big as a triple-wide trailer."

I laughed. "No promises."

He made a three-point turn and sailed up the ramp with little effort. Before the accident, my father was an active man, an avid jogger and recreational athlete. His thin runner's body was long gone, now replaced by the thick chest and broad shoulders of a wheelchair racer.

I trudged up the ramp, dreading with each step my mother's unavoidable questions about Olivia. Her first concern would be how all this affected Mark. She would look to me for answers. I couldn't blame her because I knew we were all wondering the same thing. "Will Mark have a relapse?"

After Olivia's ill-fated graduation party and her subsequent

71

departure for points south, Mark had fallen into a state of severe depression that had lasted months. My mother had been convinced that he would do something to himself. She'd sent him to counseling and had found a doctor to prescribe anti-depressants. In the end, it wasn't the hours of counseling, or the drugs, that had pulled Mark out of his self-made pit, but mathematics. During much of that time he'd retreated to his apartment to write new theorems, which was his idea of self-comfort. When he'd finally created a new one, he'd been so excited that he'd showed one of his math professors, who had helped him get it published in a prestigious math journal. While hiding away in his apartment with math books and his calcula-tor, Mark had missed the first quarter of his junior year of col-lege, but since he was such a genius, most of his professors had let him make up the missed classes with extra assignments. The following fall semester one of his professors had talked him into applying to graduate school. Since then, Mark had thrown himself into the study of math and little else.

The front door led directly into the family room. Atop the hardwood floors, the furnishings were tasteful, but inexpensive, and the only embellishment to the minimalist style was a wall of crosses that my mother had collected in every size, color, and medium, along with a few choice paintings by their favorite lo-cal artist.

As I stepped inside, a high-pitched voice exclaimed, "Dia!" and my four-year-old nephew Nicholas catapulted himself into my arms. My nephew was a miniature replica of his father, with dark hair and eyes, and tan, southern Italian skin. Nicholas rambled on about attending kindergarten in the fall and the other kids in his playgroup. Apparently, a little tyke named James was a real pill. When Nicholas first began to talk, he learned quickly in our family that you had to speak loud and fast or risk interruption.

"Okay, Nicky, let Aunt India sit." My sister's calm voice preceded her into the room.

Nicholas continued to talk and cling to my neck.

"It's fine, Carmen," I said.

I sat down on the couch, Nicholas on my lap. Carmen frowned at me. She hated it when anyone undermined her authority in any venue, especially in Nicholas's case.

There was no mistaking Carmen as my sister. We both had fair skin and changeable gray eyes, gifts from our father. Although my dark hair was long and wild, Carmen had hers in a no-nonsense mom cut. My mother had been known to mix up our baby pictures.

As I sat, I noted that my sister was, as my father adeptly described, as big as a triple-wide trailer. Carmen was pregnant with twins, in accordance with her life plan. Nothing screwed up Carmen's life plan: At thirty-one, she'd have three kids, a house, a guinea pig, and a loving husband. After graduating high school, she had attended one of the half-dozen Presbyterian colleges that cluster in western Pennsylvania, a choice that had thrilled my mother, a Presbyterian minister, to no end. As intended, Carmen had met her future husband, Chip Tuchelli, while there, and they'd married right after graduation. They had moved back to Stripling and established their careers as teachers: Carmen, high school, and Chip, elementary. They'd borne Nicholas, and now my blessed sister was pregnant with twin girls. It was all very disgusting.

Before Carmen could remind me that Nicholas was her son, my mother entered the living room. She wore a long patchwork skirt and a lime green T-shirt. Her gray hair was pulled back into a high ponytail.

"Oh, good, you're *finally* here," my mother said. "How's Olivia?"

"She's in surgery, or she was. She might be out by now."

Carmen sat down beside me on the couch. "Mom told us what happened. Mark really pulled Olivia out of the fountain?"

I nodded.

Carmen shook her head. "I just read about her upcoming wedding in last week's paper. The announcement was the entire front page."

My mother gave me a beady stare. "Yes, the paper was the first that I had heard of the upcoming wedding. Why do you think that is, India?"

I hid my expression behind Nicholas's head, which was a challenge as it wove back and forth. "You don't use the Internet."

"What's that, India? I didn't hear."

I peered around Nicholas. "Maybe you need a better news source."

"Like my daughter, perhaps?" Glowering, she adopted the same tone she used with church parishioners to encourage them to cough up something extra for the offering plate.

Carmen changed the subject. "How are the Blockens holding up? Mom said that you went to the hospital after you dropped off Mark. Will Olivia be all right?"

"Of course, she'll be all right." I looked around. "Where's Mark anyway?"

"Outside with your father," Mom said. "You should have come directly from the hospital. Mark hasn't said three words since you left. Maybe you can get him to talk."

"What do you want me to do? Beat what happened out of him?" The all-too-familiar knife of guilt twisted in my chest.

"I don't like your tone, Miss. You can't let him bottle it all up inside again. Like last time. If you had been here then . . ."

Carmen watched us from the corner of the room as if preparing herself to break up another fight. Nicholas looked bored with the pointless adult chatter, jumped from my lap, and ran outside. "I'm gonna help Grampa and Pa cook."

"Pa?" I asked my sister, happy for the change of subject.

"I'm sure it's only a phase. He's fascinated with the wild west," she answered me.

I laughed. Carmen frowned. Our reactions summed up our relationship. I followed my mother and sister to the backyard where my brother-in-law and father scorched veggie burgers and tofu hot dogs on the grill.

Chip waved at me with his spatula and continued a debate with my father about the best way to skewer tofu. I sat at the picnic table, set and ready for the meal, and shaded my eyes. The afternoon temperature and humidity rose in tandem.

Mark sat in a lawn chair not far from the grill, staring into space. I waved at him, but he looked through me.

I shook off the foreboding feeling creeping up my spine. "Can't we eat inside with the central air?"

My mother huffed. "Do you want to be dependent on a conditioned environment for the rest of your life, India, like an unfortunate lab rat?" She stalked to the barbecue to instruct my father and brother-in-law in the obvious method to skewer tofu.

I took that as a no.

My sister lowered herself slowly to the bench seat.

"Whew. I don't remember being this hot when I was expecting Nicky."

"He was born in January," I remarked.

Carmen fanned herself with a plastic plate. After a minute of creating Hurricane Andrew force winds, she asked, "What do you think happened to Olivia?" She glanced at Mark. "How do you think Mark is? Really?"

I picked up my own plate and fanned myself. "How does he look? Why does everyone think that I know Mark so well? He's your brother too."

"Yes, but you two are so much closer in age."

"Carmen, you're only three years older than Mark." Carmen always thought the three years separating her and Mark, not to mention the five years separating her and me, were the equivalent to four eons. Mark and I were born only eighteen months apart.

Carmen shrugged.

"Food," Dad declared and wheeled over to the end of the table.

Chip followed with a platter of fake meat. Mark got up from his lawn chair and went into the house. My mother moved to follow him.

Dad grabbed her arm. "Leave him alone, Lana, he'll come out when he's ready."

Mom looked uncertain, but sat at the table with the rest of the family. After passing the pasta salad, Mom raised an eyebrow at me. "India was just about to tell us how she learned about Olivia's wedding."

I pulled the piece of watermelon away from my mouth. "I was?"

"Yes, you were," she said, spearing a piece of tofu with her fork.

When Carmen wasn't looking, Nicholas grabbed the watermelon from my plate.

It took all my power not to roll my eyes. "She called me a few months ago to let me know. Happy?"

"Why didn't you tell anyone?" Dad asked.

I took a new piece of watermelon. "I was going to—"

"I've decided to eat more protein during the third trimester of the pregnancy," Carmen interrupted.

I smiled my thanks at her.

"That's a good idea," Dad said.

Mom was suspicious. "What kind of protein?"

Carmen forked a cucumber from her salad. "Oh, you know,

beans, nuts, a little chicken, peanut but—"

"What?" my father bellowed.

I thought I heard the Stripling High School bell tower, three miles away, echo at his cry. But it could be my imagination. My mother followed with a more colorful exclamation that would turn the church elders' heads.

"I have to think about the girls," Carmen defended herself.

"I can't believe this. Alden, do we even know our children anymore?"

Did you ever know them? I thought to myself.

"Mother, be reasonable," Carmen said.

Good luck.

"Don't you want the babies to be healthy? They need protein."

Dad's face was turning an impressive shade of red. "Hello, soy. It has a higher—"

"I never ate meat during any one of my pregnancies," Mom said.

"I know, Mom," Carmen said sensibly. "And maybe that shortage of animal products contributed to Mark's depression and India's fear of commitment."

I did roll my eyes that time, and Carmen gave me an apologetic smile.

"I understand your concern, Carmen, but you've never eaten chicken yourself. How do you know how it will affect you, let alone your fetuses?" Mom asked.

"Well, I . . ." She paused and then confessed, "I have had chicken before, and fish, too."

Shock registered on my parents' faces. Chip slouched down on the bench. I was willing to bet he was her chicken and fish supplier. My quiet brother-in-law hid a grin behind a napkin, and Nicholas—weaned to these types of shouting matches—chomped on a carrot. I, however, knew it was a matter of milliseconds before I was enlisted to support one side of the argument or the other.

"Nicholas," I raised my voice over the indignant declarations flying across the picnic table. "Let's play tetherball!"

"Yeah," my nephew agreed, and we ran away to a far corner of the backyard where a tetherball pole stuck out of the ground. We whacked the ball around the pole. I took care not to hit it too hard and hurt little Nicholas. He, unfortunately, was in a competitive take-no-prisoners state of mind and whipped the ball and rope back at me, nailing me in the forehead.

I was sitting on the grass and Nicholas was rubbing my forehead, saying, "Sorry, Dia," when Mark and Theodore ambled out of the house. My parents, momentarily distracted from their lecture, watched Mark with apprehension.

Nicholas abandoned me when he spotted the mammoth feline. "Teo," he cried and raced across the yard. Before Nicholas reached him, Theodore lay down on the grass in slug position beside Mark.

I stood, still rubbing my forehead. Carmen deflected my parents' attention by asking Mark what he did on the Fourth.

"India didn't tell you where I was yesterday?" Mark asked.

My mother whirled around.

"Mark, geez," I replied, unable to stifle a whine. I shot him a warning glare.

"I was at the Blocken house, visiting Olivia. India was there, too," Mark said.

I wondered if Carmen could think of something worse than eating chicken to distract my parents.

"What's this?" Mom asked me.

I ground my teeth. "I was invited to a picnic there."

"You were?" She sounded dubious.

"Olivia invited me. She was here . . ."

Mark piped in, "For the wedding. Right?"

"Why didn't you say that earlier?" Mom's blood pressure was

getting a workout.

"It would've upset you."

She scowled. "I wouldn't get upset." She started piling dishes on a tray to take back into the house. She stopped cleaning up and squinted at Mark. "And why were you there?"

"I wanted to see Olivia. I just wanted to talk to her," Mark said, barely above a whisper.

Carmen got up and wrapped an arm around Mark's shoulder.

Mom was wise enough to let Mark's comment go. I wasn't so lucky. "What's your reason, India?"

"I'm a bridesmaid," I muttered.

"What's that?"

I gritted my teeth. "I'm a bridesmaid. There. Happy?"

"Why would you agree to that after how Olivia treated your brother?" she asked.

"Because she asked me. Because she was my friend long before . . ." I trailed off, afraid to finish the sentence. Before Mark lost it over her.

"He's your brother."

"See? You're upset. Can I call it, or what?" I took a breath. "Let's drop it. I was there—so what? It doesn't change Olivia's condition now." I didn't add what Mains had told me about Olivia's accident, or that *attack* would be a better word for it.

Mark stared at me with barely contained tears in his eyes. I glanced down at the spongy grass. More than ever, I regretted my agreement to be part of Olivia's wedding. The childhood memories that had led me to say yes were so far away in the presence of my brother.

Dad rolled over to Mark. "Everything will be fine. Olivia will recover, and you will get your chance to talk to her."

"I just wanted to talk," Mark said.

Carmen directed Mark to the table.

"Come get something to eat," Dad said. "We have plenty of

tofu dogs left, your favorite."

Mark slid onto the bench. Dad asked Mark about his latest mathematical discovery. My mother opened her mouth as if to ask me another question.

"Nicky, do you want a rematch?" I asked.

"Okay," he shouted, and we raced to the safety of the tetherball.

As Nicholas and I played, I remembered playing the same game many times with Olivia. I wondered how she was in the hospital. I hoped well on her way to recovery.

CHAPTER ELEVEN

I had trouble falling asleep Saturday night. I tossed and turned with worries for my brother and for Olivia. I finally drifted off at five in the morning, but my sleep was tortured with dreams.

Mark and I raced through our parents' house, the old one, the one of our childhood. We careened through the dining room, kitchen, family room, and living room in a continuous loop around the stairs until we were silly with dizziness.

Carmen sulked in her upstairs bedroom, listening to the same annoying pop song on her boom box over and over again. Occasionally, she yelled at us to be quiet.

Heedless of Carmen's threats, I hounded Mark who held my beloved stuffed wolf, Humphrey, for ransom. I changed directions, hoping to trap him in a corner, and swung open cabinet doors in an attempt to hit him on the head. An old hand at our game, Mark fell for none of these tactics and whooped at my near misses.

Frustrated, I felt hot tears prick my eyes. "Come on, Mark. Just give 'im to me. Please. I didn't mean to trip you in front of Olivia."

We both knew this was a lie. I had purposely snaked my left foot out in front of my brother as he'd run out the front door to see Olivia that morning. While Mark brushed dead leaves and dirt off of his blue jeans and red sweatshirt, Olivia and I dissolved into giggles.

Mark yelled something back, but it escaped his mouth in a

cacophony of bells, loud and insistent. He yelled again, in the kitchen now, shaking Humphrey over his head and enticing me to pounce, but the harsh bells overpowered his cries . . .

I opened my eyes and arched out of a tight ball. The clock on my nightstand read ten 'til nine. I cursed its existence. The phone continued to ring with mounting urgency.

Unable to ignore the clatter, I grabbed the receiver.

"Good morning, India. I hope that you're up," a voice filled with reproach said. "I'm ready to leave for the service."

"Ina?" I rasped. My mouth tasted like something akin to a week-old litter box. Not that I had ever tasted one; I just imagined that it tasted that bad.

"You are awake, aren't you? I hate to be late for service."

"Yes, yes, I'm awake. I'll be out in a minute."

"I will be waiting by the car." She hung up.

I dropped the phone back on its cradle and fell back into the bed. After a few seconds of staring at my ceiling and tickling scant images of the dream from my mind while debating how to weasel out of church that day, the awful taste in my mouth forced me to my feet.

Grappling for my glasses, I stumbled over castoff shoes as I struggled to the bathroom. When my teeth were brushed and other urgent matters attended to, I flew back to my bedroom and threw on a lame outfit that clashed horribly with my shoulder bag and five-dollar flip-flops.

Ina fidgeted by my car, wearing a prim polyester suit complete with pill hat. Green, of course. Nearly tripping in the gravel driveway, I debated telling Ina that being one of my mother's flock and a Protestant she should wear an orange suit, but thought better of it—she'd set an Emerald Isle hex on me for sure.

"Ready to go?" I asked.

The question didn't deserve a response, and I didn't get one. On the way to Stripling Presbyterian Church, where my mother officiates as pastor, Ina blathered on without my encouragement or involvement.

"I've been thinking of becoming Catholic, you know. All good Irish people are Catholic."

I grunted a response, hoping it was a coffee hour Sunday, heavy on the donuts, low on the coffee.

"But on the other hand, it's a little late now. Catholics have so much more to think about. I really don't think I could fit confession into my schedule. Plus, think of all the bingo you have to play to be accepted. You know, I'm always on the run. Busy, busy. And the kneelers. I don't think I can kneel that long anymore. Nope, these old bones couldn't take it. Of course, you can be Catholic. You're young and have a lot of kneeling in you yet. You're sharp enough for bingo too. And"—she added the *coup de grace*—"the Catholics on West Avenue have a twelve o'clock mass."

I ignored her and spun the car around the town square and into the church's parking lot.

A couple of dozen sedans and minivans sat in the lot. Attendance dropped in the summer months with lawns to mow and barbecues to stoke. Add in a holiday weekend and you had a ghost congregation. Ina scampered out of the car and into the building without waiting for me.

The church, consisting of three stories and the standard bell tower, is located on Stripling's central square. Constructed in regimented Western Reserve architecture, the building has sharp corners, red brick, and leaden windows. The congregation's elderly janitor tended the lawn and gardens with fatherly devotion. Deciding I'd dawdled long enough, I stumbled through the heavy wood doors into the church. The morning ushers were already gone.

I walked into the sanctuary in the middle of the prayer requests. A parishioner raised his hand.

"Yes, Lester," my mother called on him from the pulpit.

"I think we should all keep the Blocken family in our prayers. Their daughter's in the hospital," Lester said.

A murmur fluttered through the church as I grabbed an empty pew near the back.

My mother held her composure even though she knew the congregation must know about Mark's part in Olivia's accident. Gossip was Stripling's favorite pastime. "Yes, of course. We will pray that she makes a full recovery. Olivia is a close friend of India's, and we are all concerned for her well-being."

Members of the congregation glanced at me. I gave a weak smile. Ina flashed me a beady look.

During the sermon, I shredded my church bulletin into hundreds of tiny pieces.

After the service, it was indeed a coffee hour Sunday. I wove my way to the church's fellowship hall, trying not to shove unobservant churchgoers into the walls—especially those who stood between me and a maple crème stick. Pastors' kids must always demonstrate the highest levels of restraint.

As I made my way, the congregation's Mesozoic parishioner, Melba, a young ninety-seven, asked me if I had decided where I was planning to attend college in the fall. Rather than tell her, for the one hundred and second time, that I had already commenced from college and graduate school, I said that I was contemplating a school on the East Coast, knowing full well that my flippant comment would reach my mother.

With donut in hand, I moved to the outskirts of the room. I was savoring my donut when a pair of small arms wrapped around my knees.

"Hi-hi," Nicholas said.

An oversized bite of donut lodged halfway down my throat.

Bending over, I began coughing. Nicholas patted my back.

His high voice chimed, "Hold up your arms, hold up your arms."

I did as instructed and created a spectacle. Several parishioners eyed their own pastries with concern. With my arms in the air like a street punk caught shoplifting cigarettes, I hacked.

Carmen, the ever-nurturing mother, handed me a glass of water. "Drink."

Nicholas watched as I guzzled the liquid. His voice trembled. "Will Dia die?"

Carmen patted her son's dark head. "She'll be fine."

"I'm fine, Nicko," I croaked.

"See, she can talk. If she was really choking, she wouldn't be able to speak," she said.

I massaged my throat.

My mother entered the fellowship hall, free of her robe and stole. As she passed, she shot a pointed look at my neck. No doubt, she had already heard about my near-death experience by oversized pastry. My father wheeled in after her and winked. A church elder accosted him, lamenting the pinched building fund.

Carmen grabbed my arm. "How's Mark?"

"How would I know?" I said warily. Somehow, I had irritated Carmen. Again. I decided to try an evasive maneuver. "You know the detective handling Olivia's case turns out to be your old boyfriend Ricky Mains."

That got her attention. "Ricky? Really? Does he still have that awful laugh?" Carmen shuddered.

"Yeah, he does. Anyway—"

"I haven't seen him in a couple of years. How does he look? Did he get fat or anything?"

Nicholas squinted at his mother.

"No, he's neither fat nor deformed," I said.

Carmen looked disappointed. "He was my last boyfriend before Chip."

"I remember."

Carmen looked down at her stomach and sighed. "He had nice hair, really dark and smooth. Is he balding?" She sounded hopeful.

"Nope." Church members turned their heads. I glanced around the room. "I think you're right; we have good reason to worry about Mark. Your old boyfriend told me that there were bruises on Olivia's back. Looks like she was pushed into the fountain."

Carmen gasped. "I thought it was an accident."

"It doesn't look that way anymore."

The room thinned as churchgoers snatched the last of the donuts. I watched the donuts disappear with deep-seated remorse. One was never enough.

Carmen held a protective hand to her belly. "Do you think— could Mark have anything to do with . . ."

I looked directly into my sister's eyes in surprise. "Do you think so?"

She bit her lip.

Nicholas tugged on his mother's skirt. "Dad says it's time to go. The baseball game is about to start."

Carmen's brow smoothed. "Okay, tell Daddy I'll be there in a minute."

Nicholas wove through the remaining parishioners.

"Mark wouldn't hurt anyone, Carmen. You know that. He can't kill a honeybee."

"I know. You're right." She paused. "But he was behaving strangely yesterday."

"Give the guy a break. He just found out that Olivia was getting married and had been seriously hurt within the space of a few hours. Carmen, I know that Mark didn't do it. And if you don't know the same, you don't know your brother."

The kitchen ladies, cleaning up the last of the donut crumbs, glanced at us in surprise, their ears on high alert.

"Keep your voice down," Carmen said. "What does Ricky think about all this? Did you ask him?"

"Carmen, would you forget about Ricky Mains?"

Carmen had the decency to flush. "Chip and Nicholas are waiting." She fled the room.

I turned my back to the kitchen ladies and took three deep breaths. My parents chatted with a young couple. I rudely interrupted and asked Dad if I could talk to him for a minute. Happy for the chance to escape his pastor's husband obligations, he followed me into the hallway.

Without preamble, I asked, "Where's Mark?"

"Mark went back to his apartment last night. He needed space. He'll be fine, India. And so will Olivia. Don't fret."

My father was so certain.

After church, I dropped Ina at a chain restaurant with a group of blue-haired church ladies for Sunday brunch before heading home. When I saw Mains's dark sedan parked obstinately in front of the duplex, I knew it wasn't good news.

Chapter Twelve

Mains stepped out of the automobile when I slammed my car door. Without salutation, I marched across the lawn. He leaned against the passenger-side door and waited.

I kicked the right rear tire of his car lightly. "Nice car."

Mains was subdued. "I'd like to speak with you for a few minutes, Miss Hayes."

"I really don't think I have time today, Detective Mains, but thank you for asking."

"It's important."

"No doubt," I said. I stumbled over one of Ina's leprechauns as I made my way toward the duplex.

"Olivia Blocken is dead."

I whipped around. His statement had sucked out a piece of my lungs, leaving a gaping hole in its place.

"She died earlier this morning. She never woke up from the surgery. She was brain-dead before the end of the operation. Her family decided to remove life support."

I forced my brain to process his words. Dead? Brain-dead? Life support? His lips continued to move, but the sound didn't reach my ears. My breath shortened.

"I think we should go inside to discuss this," Mains said.

"We will not go inside. I don't want you in my house again." I managed to lower my volume by a half decibel. "Now, tell me why I wasn't told of Olivia's condition yesterday. You were here, why didn't you tell me then?"

Mains removed his mirrored sunglasses and placed them in his shirt pocket. "I wasn't aware of it until after I saw you." He held up his palm. "And—"

"They didn't want me to know, did they?"

He nodded.

As I suspected, but that didn't make it hurt any less. The hole in my chest grew larger and threatened to swallow me piece by piece. It would start with the heart and work outward. Suddenly, all the anger I projected onto Mains dissipated into the white-hot atmosphere, and I was exceptionally tired. I bumped into yet another leprechaun, and it fell face down in the grass. My lack of sleep was catching up to me. Mains held up his arm, as if to catch me. I wouldn't allow it and waved him away.

"Is there anything I can do for you, Miss Hayes?" His cop-look was gone, replaced with an expression of concern.

"You can stop calling me Miss Hayes," I muttered as I bent down, ostensibly to right the leprechaun, but really to hide my face.

"I can do that, India."

I nodded, then turned and walked toward the house.

Mains moved from the sedan and followed me. "I'm sorry. I have to ask one more thing."

I stopped but didn't turn around. The grass needed mowing and impatiens watering.

"Do you know where your brother is?"

I forgot the lawn and garden. I turned to face him. "He doesn't know?"

He removed his sunglasses from his shirt pocket and restored them over his eyes. "He knows, I'm afraid. Mrs. Blocken called his apartment about nine-thirty this morning and told him the news."

That jolted me. "Oh, no."

Mains nodded.

Looking up the quiet street, I rubbed my eyes with the heels of my palms, pushing my glasses far up into my hair. The frames scratched my forehead. "Have you spoken to him since then?"

"That's the problem. We can't find him. He wasn't at his apartment or his office at Martin. We tried your parents' house as well. Is there anywhere else he might have gone?"

The anger that abandoned me earlier reignited. "Do you want to know so you can help him or to arrest him?"

Mains's expression altered from concern to frustration. "No one is arresting anyone. Yet."

"I have no idea where he is."

Mains handed me one of his business cards, the third he had given me in the last twenty-four hours. Was the accident really only yesterday? I wondered.

"If you see your brother, call me, or ask him to do so."

I dropped the card into my shoulder bag along with the other two that languished there.

"As of right now, this is a homicide investigation." With that, he was gone.

My key wouldn't fit; it repeatedly missed the lock in the brass doorknob. I kicked the wooden door with my flip-flopped foot. Pain shot through my toe and up my ankle. A black scuffmark marred the door's paint. I held one shaking hand with my other and forced the key into the lock. I dumped my keys and shoulder bag on the hardwood floor just inside the doorway. I shut, locked, and bolted the door. Hobbling to the kitchen-cubby, I opened the freezer and grabbed an ice pack. On the living room couch, I elevated my foot with the blue-gelled ice pack.

I wrapped the remainder of my body in the orange bed sheet. Silky black fur clung to the bright cotton. Head under the light sheet, I felt entombed, distanced, but not completely safe from the terrifying world on the other side of the cotton. The bright summer sun dripped through the kitchen window and penetrated the cloth. My pale skin gleamed in the hot ocher light. The determined sunrays fought through my clenched eyelids, and the shadows alternated red hot and bright black. Second by second my foot released hold of its pain.

I felt Templeton's body alight on the back of the couch. Walking the sofa's length, he butted my shrouded head with his own. My acute memory replayed every slight, every remark, every hurtfully cruel word or deed I had ever committed against Olivia, a lifetime's worth, until she was the princess and I was the mustachioed villain.

And then I thought about Mark.

I threw off the sheet and catapulted up. Templeton flew across the room, his expression astonished. I ran into my bedroom and changed into a T-shirt and long men's shorts with a few flecks of indigo paint on the right hemline. In the bathroom, I washed my face, damp with tears I could not recall. After scooping my heavy hair into a tight knot, I scooped up my keys and shoulder bag and ran out the door.

As I turned the car off quiet Calvin Road, Ina and her blue-haired friend Juliet careened onto the street in Juliet's vintage compact automobile. Ina waved wildly. I didn't wave back.

CHAPTER THIRTEEN

Mark's apartment was in a low-rent district just inside Akron's city limits. A few miles from downtown and the state university, the apartment complex was a haven for financially strapped college students. Martin students, courtesy of their parents, lived in the nicer buildings found in Akron's compacted suburbs such as Stow, Tallmadge, or Stripling. Mark moved into the apartments as a Martin undergrad, wanting to pay his own way and choosing all that he could afford. Even as his educational and financial levels rose, he never mentioned moving. The apartment complex was a tight cluster of wood-sided structures, maybe twenty in all. Each building held nine apartment units on three floors. My brother's building sat in the middle of the complex, next to the swimming pool.

When I parked my car in front of Mark's building, pulsating rap music from poolside shook the windows. On this hot summer day, the pool crawled with late teens and early twenty-somethings. The high-pitched chatter from the female sunbathers competed with the rap in volume and pitch. A mid-summer sheen of suntan lotion and dirt glazed the improbably blue water's surface.

Mark's apartment was on the first floor. I knocked, scraping my knuckles on the coarse wood. After several minutes, hearing nothing from inside, I used my key. The door opened into a small great room that functioned as his living and dining space. The back wall consisted of his kitchen, not much bigger than my own. The apartment was a sty. Papers, books, clothes, aluminum cans, and plastic wrappers littered the floor and furniture.

Even on such a beautiful day, the shades were tightly drawn. I turned on a light. I called his name, but I knew that he wasn't there. Out of habit, I picked some of the junk off the floor and tossed the cans into the recycling bin. I leafed through a pile of mail that I found by the front door. It was postdated the previous year. I dropped it on the ground—if he wanted to live like a slob that was his choice to make. I snooped through his papers on the kitchen counter to see if I could discover where he had gone, but they bordered prehistoric.

An enormous thud sounded in the bedroom. I yelped. The tip of Theodore's tail flicked over the kitchen counter.

"Hey, Theo." I patted his head. He squeaked at me and pointedly glared at his empty food dish. I rummaged around the kitchen for cat food and placed a handful in his bowl. His expression plainly said, "More." Feeling sorrier for Mark than Theodore, I placed two more handfuls in the dish. I hoped animal rights groups wouldn't picket me for contributing to feline obesity. I asked Theodore where Mark was, but his face was too deeply ensconced in his turkey-flavored cat food to reply.

Before leaving, I scanned my brother's bedroom—surprisingly clean—and the small bathroom—which decidedly wasn't. I found Theodore's leash draped over the secondhand sofa. I wrestled him into his harness and clipped on the leash. I couldn't bear to leave him in Mark's drab apartment alone. I scribbled a note to Mark telling him where Theodore was should he come home. Using the lead, I tugged the cat away from the bowl. His thick pads flattened out to the kitchen floor, and his nails dug into the brown linoleum. I tugged again. He didn't budge nor miss a beat in his chewing tempo. I hefted the great cat into my arms. He yowled and hissed. I picked up the half-empty dish, holding it to his mouth so he could eat, and carried the cat and meal out of Mark's apartment.

A couple tankini-clad girls watched me manhandle Theodore into my car. They looked about eighteen and were the walking poster children for the benefits of tanning beds. The sportier of the two wore a silky pageboy haircut; the other had long, blond locks.

"Man, that's a big cat," Pageboy called out.

I pushed flyaway hair out of my face and readjusted my glasses. "He's a Maine Coon cat. They're generally a big breed, but he might be a little too big."

I slammed the door before Theodore could escape, not that I thought he'd move as long as he was in the vicinity of a well-stocked food source.

Blond Locks smoothed her swimsuit over her flat stomach. "You shouldn't let your cat get that big, you know."

I mentally snorted, no one *lets* Theodore do anything.

"The cat's not hers," Pageboy said.

Before they could accuse me of cat-napping, I said, "He's my brother's cat."

"You're Mark's sister?"

"Uh, yeah," I said.

She snapped her gum. "We live next door to him. I'm Brit. This is Karen."

"I'm India. Have you seen Mark today?"

Brit and Karen consulted each other with a look.

Apparently spokesperson for the duo, Brit said, "Saw him this morning, when we were heading to the pool at about ten."

Karen nodded in agreement.

"He was acting really weird," Brit added.

I stepped closer to the aluminum fence. "Weird?"

"Yeah, like he was crying really hard, and when we asked him if he was okay, he didn't even look at us."

My shoulder began to throb as it always does when I'm upset. "So he didn't say where he was going or anything?"

"Naw," Brit said and wrapped a bright towel around her waist. "But after he left, this older guy pulled up and banged on his door. Me and Karen were talking to Kev at the time, he's, like—well, we're kinda dating or will be. The only reason I noticed is because this old guy showed up with a couple of cops. Kev, he's going to the police academy after he graduates; he said it was, like, a takedown."

Mains and reinforcements.

Karen finally spoke up. "Is Mark in trouble?" Her eyes sparkled hopefully.

"No," I said. "Best of luck with Kev, Brit."

After rolling down the windows in my car for Theodore, I hurried back into Mark's apartment.

Certainly, my brother wouldn't be so distraught that he'd—of course not. I yanked his portal phone from the kitchen wall where it hung next to a three-year-old calendar. I dialed my parents' number. No one answered, and the machine picked up. I didn't leave a message. My parents were having Sunday lunch at some parishioner's home or trapped into some type of meeting with the church elders. I contemplated calling the church office but thought better of it.

I tapped the portable phone into the palm of my right hand. Where could he have gone? Then, it hit me. No, he couldn't be that stupid, I thought.

But then again, I knew he could.

CHAPTER FOURTEEN

For the second time that weekend, I directed my car down my childhood street. Several homeowners along its length were mowing their lawns or gardening through the oppressive afternoon heat. The Blocken house remained rooted and stone silent. Several cars speckled its long driveway. The blinds and curtains at every window were sealed tight. I discreetly passed the house, searching for my brother's car.

Childishly, I directed my eyes forward as I rolled beyond the Blocken home, believing that if I couldn't see them, they couldn't see me. I drove the street's length, and I didn't see Mark's car or any other sign of him. I exhaled with relief and guilt. How could I think that he would have come here? Oh, me of little faith. Maybe Mark was smarter than I gave him credit for, I thought. I looped around the block for a second pass—just to be sure—and headed home.

I parked the car in my driveway and sprinted into the apartment, while awkwardly managing Theodore and his now-empty food dish, before Ina could burst out of her unit and harangue me with questions. Slamming the door, I bolted it behind me. I dropped the cat. He landed with a resounding thud.

Templeton hissed and arched his back at the intruder. The two felines knew each other socially, but weren't best pals. Theodore stomped across the room to examine Templeton, who jumped off of the couch and dashed out of the room faster than the speed of sound, no doubt to stew under my bed while contemplating the most inconvenient place to deposit a hairball in revenge. Theodore leapt onto the couch and settled into Templeton's favorite spot. I showed Theodore where the litter box was in the tiny utility room.

"Use it, or you'll make a very nice fur collar," I told him.

For the first time in days, I entered my studio. My shoulders sagged. I hadn't painted in weeks. It was so easy to simply accept mediocre failure in place of lifelong ambition. I mentally excused myself, considering the circumstances of late, but my guilty conscience would not forgive me.

The studio was a small second bedroom that I had converted into an art den when I had rented the apartment. The flooring was slab-cement stained with acrylics, paint thinner, and every other possible substance a painter can spill, drop, or knock over while at work. Ina, upon hearing that I was a painter, allowed me to remove the carpet under a three-finger Girl Scout swear that I would replace it if and when I moved out. The room contained one window flanked on either side by metal shelves holding all the essential trappings of a painter's arsenal: brushes, blank canvases, pigments, and remnants of rejected works. My easel faced away from the door and dominated the middle of the room. Across from the easel sat a decrepit sofa I'd salvaged from a Martin dorm and splattered with every shade of oil paint in the rainbow.

On the colored cushions, someone lay prostrate.

Startled, I cried out. The other person released an equally girlish squeak.

Mark.

"What are you doing here?" I gasped.

He clutched a throw pillow to his chest. "I was looking for you. You weren't here, so I let myself in."

"What are you doing in this room?" I demanded, to cover up my relief at finding him.

"I was looking for you, and then, I saw . . ." He gestured to my easel, which held a nearly complete twelve by fourteen portrait of a young girl. The girl was about ten, had cropped brown hair, startling blue eyes, and small features. She wore a bright T-shirt and ratty jean shorts. She perched on the edge of the front steps that led into her home. Her knees touched, and she hinged forward at the waist. The gaze held intensity and concealed amusement.

Olivia. A forgotten wedding gift.

"I haven't slept in two days, but I was able to sleep here." He stared at the painting and avoided my eyes. He laughed mirth-lessly, bitterly. "She's dead. Her mother called me this morning. She accused me of killing her. Is that what you think?"

I froze in the studio doorway. "Of course, I don't think that." Like Mark, I avoided using Olivia's name. "Mrs. Blocken's searching for a scapegoat. No one could seriously think you'd hurt anyone." My conversation with Mains that morning came to mind, but I pushed it away. He might suspect Mark, but he didn't know my brother.

Mark nodded, staring at his feet. Then he started to cry, powerful sobs that shook his entire body. I remained frozen, again wishing my more compassionate and maternal sister was with me. Something soft grazed my leg. Theodore. He walked across the room and crawled into Mark's lap. Mark clung to the cat and wept into his thick fur. The cat purred in reply. Mark didn't question the cat's presence.

After several tense minutes in which Mark wept, Theodore comforted, and I idled, Mark wiped his face on the pillow that would never be quite the same. With his mission accomplished, Theodore deserted his master.

"Is there anything I can get you?" I asked.

He ignored the question. "I can't even believe it, you know. Can you?"

"No." Tired from standing but not wanting to move any closer to my brother, I sat on the cool cement floor.

"I knew that she didn't love me and never did. I was just someone she used to pass the time," he muttered. "But when I found out that she was engaged, I lost it. I thought I was over her. All those equations and theorems I put in my head pushed her out. But now, I know I wasn't over her, I was just distracted from thinking about her. With her face splashed on the front page of the paper announcing the wedding, I couldn't be distracted. I didn't expect to feel that way when I heard about her wedding. I'm not a total idiot; I knew she was bound to get married some day. I wish I didn't feel this way about her."

"I didn't think—"

"You didn't think at all, India. You knew that I'd find out about the wedding, the social event of the summer." His teary voice didn't veil his anger. He stood up. "You should have told me, to at least prepare me. You could have done that much."

I was fixed to the floor.

"So, I went to the Blocken house, the last place in the world I'd ever want to go, only to find my sister there, laughing and socializing with the family that I was never good enough for, that she was never good enough for."

"Maybe I shouldn't have agreed to do it when she asked. I wasn't thinking about you and her. I was thinking about her and me. She is my friend . . ." It was all I could say. Mark would not understand how Olivia pulled me in with childhood memories, why I didn't think of him before agreeing to be a bridesmaid. He wouldn't understand why Olivia's use of creepy Brad Coldecker had changed my mind.

Mark stepped back and laughed hollowly. "You mean she *was* your friend. She's dead, India, dead. Do you understand that? She's not marrying anyone now."

My stomach dropped and tears welled in my eyes. "Mark, no.

You didn't."

"I didn't what? Tell me what I didn't do."

I stood. "I'm sorry. I didn't mean—"

"Did I kill her? Isn't that what you want to know? No. But thank you for your sisterly faith. Did I see her on campus yesterday? Yes. I couldn't believe that she actually came to see me. But she wasn't alone."

"Who else was there?"

"I didn't see anyone. I only heard her talking to someone. Since she wasn't alone, I went back to my office and waited for her to come to me. After a half hour, she never showed, and I went to the fountain and found her." His voice trailed off.

"What were they talking about, Olivia and this other person?" I said Olivia's name for the first time since I'd found Mark in my studio.

Mark swallowed hard. He walked directly to my easel and kicked it over. Both easel and canvas clattered to the floor. We both looked at the damage. The sharp edge of the metal easel had torn a five-inch gash into the canvas just above Olivia's head. With a moan, Mark pushed past me and fled the room.

After a moment of paralysis, I followed him. At the front door, he struggled with lock and bolt.

"You have to tell the police what you heard," I said, frightened by his behavior but also terrified for him. "You have to. If you don't, even if they can never prove that you attacked her, people will still think you had something to do with it. You have to prove them wrong."

He continued to wrestle with the door. His mania made it impossible for him to manipulate his hands correctly.

"Don't you want to be cleared, Mark?"

I heard the mechanical click as the bolt recessed into the wooden door frame. Mark threw open the door and was gone.

CHAPTER FIFTEEN

I tried Carmen's cell phone number but only got her voice mail. A quick rap battered my door. I peered through the peephole and saw just the crown of Ina's white permanent.

"India Veronica Hayes, you open this door to an old woman." Her head bobbled aggressively. "I'll get louder. I'll wake up the whole street from their Sunday naps." More quietly, she added, "And anyway, Dearie, I'm your landlord, so I have a key." She waved my apartment key over her head where she knew I could see it. It dangled from a three-inch-wide blue-glittered shamrock.

I opened the door. "Home invasion, Ina?"

She sniffed. "What's that unbelievable racket I heard through my wall?"

Ina had changed from her Sunday morning green suit into pink capri pants and matching tank top.

The loose skin under her upper arm waved as she shook her index finger at me. "What on earth is going on over here? First, I see you peel out of the driveway without waving hello, when Juliet is in the car with me of all things. Then, I overhear you screaming like a crazed banshee. It was all I could do not to come busting in here when all that yelling was going on."

Ina shuffled further into the room. I shut the door behind her. Wouldn't want to wake those Sunday nappers. She perched on the edge of the rocking chair, feet dangling above the floor.

"Spill it," she ordered. "Man trouble got you, honey? I

tangled with some of that in my day. Tell me the problem, Ina has the answer. I've been on this earth a lot of years, and I've learned a thing or two about handling a man. How do you think I managed not being saddled with a husband and a screaming brood of my own?"

Ina took a breath, and I jumped in. "It's Mark."

"Oh, I see. It's about Olivia, is it? The accident was a terrible thing. Juliet had all the juicy gossip about it. And did she ever lord that over me, seeing how my tenant was at the scene of the crime yesterday and neglected to tell me the biggest news flash since Stripling got city-wide sewer."

The migraine threatened to resurface. "I didn't deliberately not tell you."

Ina blinked, probably trying to digest the double negative. She'd placed me on the defensive and retarded my grammar.

"Is that why that bloody Englishman was over here yesterday? About Olivia?"

"Yes. I don't have time for this. Mark ran off."

Ina cocked her head to the side and her face softened. "I'm sure he's fine, lassie. Maybe he went over to the hospital to visit Olivia."

"Olivia's dead."

Ina covered her mouth like a heroine in a silent film. My phone rang. Irritation replaced the horror etched on her face. She scowled when I picked up the phone.

It was Carmen. "I've had about enough of your cryptic voice messages, India. What's this about Mark?"

With Ina listening openedmouthed, I told Carmen about Mains's visit after church and finding Mark in my apartment. For once, Carmen listened without interruption.

"Okay, first relax. Mark's probably at his office taking his frustration out on that five-hundred-dollar calculator of his. Try not to worry."

"He was livid."

"He needs time to cool off. You can't canvas Stripling trying to find him. He wouldn't—he won't do anything stupid. Mom and Dad are at the Chaulkers for the afternoon. Wait until they get home. The last thing Mark needs right now is them on his case. He obviously wants to be alone, and you know as soon as Mom finds out she's going to be all over him. I'll call Mom and Dad later in the afternoon."

Carmen's strategic planning provided me the illusion of safety.

"How are you?" Sisterly concern inflected her words.

I choked for a second and turned away from Ina, who was still on the edge of her seat. Her expression was equal parts concern and barely contained excitement.

"I'm fine."

"Do you want me to come over?"

"No, don't bother. Ina's here."

Carmen laughed. "I'm sure she's doing her best to comfort you."

"Of course."

An hour later, when Ina realized I wasn't going to rush out the door in search of Mark or take her other suggestion and visit the mourning Blockens, she stomped out the door, claiming that she was missing a program about Irish folk singers on the public television station.

The remainder of the day, I floated around my apartment, starting a multitude of pursuits, but finishing nothing. I tried to read a novel, but the words blurred on the page. I started to tidy my bedroom, but after making my bed, I dropped a pile of dirty laundry on the floor and gave up. I picked up one of the dozens of half-full sketchpads that decorate my apartment and etched thumbnail sketches on the thick paper. The poor renderings frustrated me. I ripped the page out of the wire-ring notebook and threw it into the small hallway. It bounced off my studio's door. I didn't enter the studio or upright the toppled easel and painting. I'd simply shut the door.

I hoped all afternoon and into the evening that Mark would call. He never did. My mother eventually rang and chastised me for not calling her at the Chaulkers. She agreed with Carmen that Mark needed time alone, although I knew she was dying to counsel him. I went to bed early, hoping that Olivia would call in the morning to tell me she'd found a miracle self-tanner or a ridiculous hat for me to wear during the wedding. Or even a golden dress.

CHAPTER SIXTEEN

The next morning at Ryan Memorial Library began with a staff meeting and with Jefferson Island complaining about the Dewey Decimal System. Even when I was in top librarian form, I wasn't up to hearing one of Jefferson's cataloging speeches, and with events of the previous day still fresh in my mind, I wanted to run screaming from the room.

"If Martin College is going to transform itself into a university within the next ten years, it is imperative that we find another way to organize our resources that allows for growth," Jefferson said.

It was a diatribe we'd heard countless times before.

Lasha interrupted him, "We will consider your recommendation, Dixie. Are there any other issues that should be brought in front of the entire group?"

Jefferson frowned. "I made a slideshow to illustrate my argument."

Lasha's expression looked pained. "I think it would be best to e-mail it to the staff, so each librarian can review it as he or she has time."

Beside me Bobby snickered. I bet he wasn't going to be watching Jefferson's slideshow.

"Well if you think that that's best. However—"

"Excellent, I think this meeting's over, people," Lasha declared and rose.

"But," Jefferson began. "I brought it with me . . ."

However, it was too late—the room emptied before he could boot up his laptop.

Behind the reference counter, Bobby slipped into one of the high chairs.

I took the other. Seeking a distraction from my thoughts, I studied Bobby's get-up. "What's with the suit, Bob-o? Have an afternoon dalliance planned in the stacks?"

Bobby adjusted his perfectly straight collar. "Regrettably, no, but thank you for the idea. I'm having lunch with Bree and have to exude some level of professionalism."

"Really?"

Bobby gave me a sideways glance. "Yes." He paused. "I'm sorry about Olivia."

"How'd you hear?" I asked. I slapped my forehead in mock surprise. "Duh, Bree told you. Over breakfast, maybe?"

Bobby ignored my acid tone. "She called me after they removed life support yesterday morning. She was with the family and Kirk when they made the difficult decision. It's been hard for her."

"I'm sure. I'm glad you're there for her."

I booted up my computer and logged on to the library's E-mail account. There were a couple of messages from professors with research requests and the College president's secretary reminding us to renew the president's overdue books.

"She doesn't know anyone here. She's from Virginia and only here for the wedding." He paused. "Now, for the funeral."

"Wow, and here I was only thinking about myself, having heard about my friend's death from police hours after it happened," I said as I renewed the president's books. "But I have plenty of people in this town to comfort me, don't I?"

Bobby's brow wrinkled. "Would you stop playing with your mouse and look at me?"

I shut the E-mail account and turned my chair to face him.

He looked confused and a little hurt. I felt a twinge of guilt for mistreating him. I knew that I should feel sorry for Bree. Her closest friend had been murdered, and now she was stuck in a strange town miles from home. Despite knowing this, I couldn't bring myself to feel sorry for her. I hadn't liked how she'd fawned over Olivia at the picnic, nor did I like that she had moved Bobby's sympathy from my family to her and the Blockens. I knew from dealing with Bobby and his past girlfriends that he would repeat anything I said to his current love, so she had effectively stolen my best friend when I needed him most.

"Why didn't you call me?" I asked.

Before Bobby could answer, Nasia, Lasha's thirteen-year-old daughter, sashayed to the desk. She wore a skimpy tank top and shorts covered by her mother's mammoth red cardigan. Lasha had mentioned that Nasia was in a "rapper's hoochy mama" stage.

"Good morning, India," she greeted, adding a sophisticated tone to her still-juvenile voice.

Lasha and her daughter lived just off campus, so Nasia was a frequent visitor to the library during the summer, especially when there wasn't anything good to watch on television, or so she said.

"Hi, Looker," she said, using her mother's pet name for Bobby.

"Good morning, Nasia," Bobby said reservedly. He looked panicky.

She batted her blue false eyelashes in response.

Lord, I thought.

Nasia batted her eyelashes again. A stray lash poked her in the left eye. She winced and looked away as if she spotted something else of interest. She oh-so-casually rubbed her eye. Bobby shot me a pleading look. I hopped off my chair and walked around the counter, situating myself in between Bobby and Nasia. She rubbed her eye furiously.

"Nasia, I want to show you something in my office," I said.

She nodded and let me steer her toward the back room. I glanced back at Bobby. He flashed an appreciative grin.

In the staff bathroom, I dampened a paper towel and handed it to Nasia. "You are going to have to take those ridiculous things off."

Nasia sniffled. "Do you think he saw?"

"Who?" I asked, handing her a second paper towel.

"Bobby. I'm soooo embarrassed."

"Bobby? Naw," I lied. "He was too busy reading his horoscope on the computer."

"Really?" She met my eyes with one-and-a-half of hers.

"You know, Nasia, Bobby's a little old for you."

She bristled. "I was just practicing for eighth grade."

"I went to Stripling Middle School for eighth grade too, and I know, for a fact, that you won't be allowed to walk through that door dressed like this."

"Times have changed." She patted her hair. "And how would you know what it's like there, anyway? You're old."

Ouch.

After I parked Nasia in front of a computer terminal where she immediately logged onto her online profile and would be happily entertained for hours, I lost the rest of the morning helping a tearful August graduate with a paper on *The Fall of the House of Usher.* I gave the senior every book relating to, critical of, and written by Poe in reference to the short story. Her thin arms strained under the weight of the texts, and I helped her carry them to the checkout desk where Erin stood.

"I can't thank you enough," the girl gushed. "You really saved me. I wasn't finding *anything.*"

I smiled, feeling quite smug.

The student added, "If I hadn't gone to college, I think I

would really have liked to be a librarian too," the student said.

I glanced at Erin, who smirked.

I had returned to the reference desk when Bree walked in.

CHAPTER SEVENTEEN

Bobby met Bree at the door and kissed her on the cheek. A student worker rearranging the volumes on the new bookshelf dropped a heavy stack of textbooks on his left foot. He hurried around the checkout desk to the workroom, presumably to walk it off. It's little wonder, though. Bree was stunning in a form-fitting tailored tank top and slim-fit chinos. Bobby and Bree spoke for a moment before approaching the desk.

I looked up at the last second.

Bree's face was drawn, and her eyes bloodshot. She smiled nervously. "I'm sorry I didn't call you and tell you about Olivia. Bobby told me that you learned about it from the police."

I couldn't think of anything to say. I wouldn't allow myself to look at Bobby. Bobby, my friend, should have told me, not Bree, who I hardly knew.

"It all happened so fast. She was in surgery, and then her family had to decide what to do. I don't think any of us slept the night after the surgery," she said in a rush.

I swallowed. "I'm glad that you were there to help them. I'm sure it meant a lot to the family and to Kirk. How are they doing?"

Bree made a pained expression. "As well as can be expected."

"Has the family made any arrangements?"

Bree shifted her weight. "Not yet. The detective, May, I think it is . . ."

"Mains," I said.

"Right, Mains, he said the . . . the body should be released tomorrow afternoon, or the next morning. He seems confident the case will be closed soon."

"He does?" I asked, surprised.

"He has a suspect."

My shoulder ached. I bit the inside of my lip. "A suspect?"

Bobby placed a hand on Bree's arm. "We should go. I've only half an hour for lunch."

"Right, of course. I'll let you know when the service is," Bree told me.

"I'd really appreciate that."

She turned one last time. "I'm sure it was an accident. He didn't mean to hurt her."

Openmouthed, I watched them leave the library. When they reached the door, I jumped off my chair and hurried after them. Outdoors, the afternoon heat hit me like a heavy curtain.

I caught them in the staff parking lot. "Wait."

Bobby turned around. "Did I forget something?" He patted his pockets.

"Who? Who did you mean when you said 'he didn't mean to hurt her'?" I was breathless.

A group of students playing a scrap game of touch football in the library's courtyard stopped and watched us.

"I'm sorry for saying that, India. I shouldn't have—"

"Who?"

She gave me a pitying smile. "Your brother, of course. Olivia talks, talked, all the time about him being obsessed with her. He sent her flowers and candies, begging her to come back."

"Maybe at first, he . . ." My face flushed.

"Olivia never thought Mark would hurt her. And I know that he didn't mean to do it. It was a horrible accident. The police believe the attack wasn't planned."

"The attack wasn't planned?" I screeched.

The football players mumbled to themselves and moved closer. Bobby stepped between us, opening the passenger-side door of his aged but well-cared-for car. Bree slipped inside.

He shut the door. "India, please go back inside."

I gasped. "Did you hear what she said? She thinks Mark's responsible for Olivia's death."

"You're making a scene. How is that going to help Mark?"

I was dumbstruck.

Bobby blew out a breath. "Can we talk about this when I get back?"

When I didn't answer, he shook his head and walked around the car. I watched them roll away.

"That shows how loyal you are," I shouted at his brake lights.

The football players gaped.

"What are you looking at?" I demanded.

They snickered and resumed their game, this time as tackle.

When my shift ended, I rushed out of the building at the fourth chime of the bell tower. The afternoon had trickled by. A handful of patrons had stopped in, but none of them had needed guidance from the reference desk. When Bobby returned from his lunch with Bree, I refused to talk to him. I knew it was childish, but I was too hurt by the scene in the parking lot to trust myself to speak.

When I reached my car, I stood back from it and examined the rusted tire wells and dented, multicolored fender. I kicked the rear tire hard. The tire bit back through my thin-soled sandals. I dropped my shoulder bag and danced in place, holding my foot. Thankfully, the early afternoon football game had long since dispersed.

I hobbled toward the driver's door.

"Ms. Hayes?" a refined voice called.

I spun around. Provost Lepcheck approached me at a fast trot.

Without pausing, I scooped up my bag. Thankfully, it had been zipped tight for once in my life. "Sam," I replied, using his first name to irk him.

He scowled, making his jowls more pronounced. A chin lift lay in the near future. Lepcheck looked office casual in a pressed polo shirt, polo with a big P, and corresponding charcoal slacks.

"Do you know the current whereabouts of your brother, Mark Hayes?" His manner was grave.

As opposed to my other brother, Mark Hayes, I thought. "I would think he's in his office."

I squinted into the glaring sunlight. Maybe it would rain and cool the evening.

"I'm afraid he isn't. I've rung him several times throughout the day and just now stopped by his office. He was not present."

This was bad. Lepcheck had walked over to my brother's office to speak to him, instead of sending one of his minions.

"Your brother has placed the college in an awkward position with both the community and the local authorities. The president is not pleased."

He pronounced "president" as if declaring the name of a powerful warlord.

"Both my brother and I are aware of the situation. I'm sorry I don't know where Mark is. I've been working at the library since eight this morning. If you want to make certain of that, you're welcome to speak to Lasha."

Lepcheck stiffened with obvious dislike of Lasha, who through some impressive finagling had secured tenure her third year at Martin. "The situation is urgent. The administration is not amused with the disregard that Mr. Hayes has shown for the college community on this matter. He has not contacted my office, or the office of the president, regardless of the numerous requests to do so by both. Because of this, and other questionable matters, a decision has been made. Mr. Hayes has been suspended from the college without pay, effective immediately, until these unfortunate circumstances are rectified. His two classes will be divided between Dr. Roth and Dr. Ames."

"You—" I began angrily.

"I will warn you, Ms. Hayes, that we are also concerned with your behavior. Please, remember that Martin College is a respected and historic institution, and its faculty is not exempt from treating it as such."

The tips of my fingernails cut into the heels of my palms. I couldn't think of anything to say that wouldn't get me immediately fired, suspended, or guillotined, so I clamped my teeth hard onto the inside of my lower lip.

Done with the unpleasantries, Lepcheck brushed his hands across each other twice. "Please, inform Mr. Hayes of our decision."

CHAPTER EIGHTEEN

I reached my apartment in two minutes and headed directly to the phone. When my father picked up on the other end, I told him about Mark's suspension.

Dad's first outburst was, "Outrageous," followed by a few choice words and declarations about the Bill of Rights.

"Don't worry," he advised. "I'll call Lew. He'll have a lawsuit on Lepcheck's desk tomorrow morning."

Lewis Clive was the attorney my parents kept on retainer in case they ever have the urge to be arrested. My parents' tangles with the law usually were the result of tethering themselves with steel chains to old growth forests or dilapidated historic buildings.

"Have you seen Mark?" I asked.

"No. Your mother's a wreck. She figures the Blockens blame Mark for Olivia's death. I finally persuaded her to go to work today. It wouldn't do any good for her to pace the floorboards here, not when there are people at the church who need her."

"Oh."

He recognized my tone. "I know Mark can be difficult and . . . er, emotional sometimes, but we need to support him the best we can. Your brother is tougher than you think. But the Blocken family . . . oh, to lose a child. I can't think of anything worse in this life."

My eyes teared when I allowed myself to remember.

"Will Mom visit the family?" My mother, in her capacity as

minister, often calls on Stripling families in times of tragedy.

"She thought it wise if she didn't under the circumstances. She did call Bill Myer over at the Lutheran church, and he promised to drop in on them. The Blockens are members of that church, if you remember. Bill had planned to officiate at Olivia's wedding."

And now he will officiate at her funeral, I thought.

"I'll talk to Lew," my father said. "I'll ring you back when I hear from him."

After I hung up, I called my brother's apartment. No answer. I had left a message on his voice mail to call me immediately, using the word "urgent" an excessive number of times. I couldn't leave a message about Lepcheck's announcement.

Hanging up the phone for a second time, I hovered beside it, trying to decide if I should call my sister on her cell phone or my mother at work or the Pope at the Vatican about Mark's suspension. Maybe Ina was right, and I would make a good Catholic. I thought better of any more calls. My mom and sister—though probably not His Holiness—would learn of the situation soon enough. I wasn't in the mood to discuss it, especially when I had yet to tell Mark.

Templeton was suspiciously MIA. I perched on the couch next to Theodore, who had made himself quite comfortable in my home, when the phone rang.

"India," the voice rasped as consequence of two packs of cigarettes a day for forty years. "Lewis Clive. I just got a call from your old man and said that I'd call you myself. I'll get the ball rolling on my end to take legal action against the college on Mark's behalf. It's unreasonable for the college to suspend him when he hasn't even been officially charged by the police." He paused, and I heard him inhale deeply through the end of his unfiltered cigarette.

"Legal action?" I asked.

He chuckled. "Nothing too serious, only making noise about contract and compensation violations to let them know that we mean business."

"I see. Is there any chance that Martin could suspend me too?"

Lew barked another laugh that turned into a ragged cough. He cleared his throat noisily. "They wouldn't dare. They cannot dismiss you for something your sibling allegedly did. Martin may be a private college, but they take state and federal money like everybody else for scholarships, grants, and the like. They're susceptible to state and federal law."

I nodded before remembering I was on the phone. "I understand."

"Terrific, terrific. When I'm done with those patsies, they won't have a leg to stand on," he said with unmitigated glee. "However, without Mark's consent, I can't move much further in this case except to become an irritant in the backside of Martin's admin. It is imperative I speak to him ASAP. Your father implied that you know where Mark is most of the time. I need to find your brother, the sooner the better. Can you do that?"

"I'll try."

"Terrific," he rasped. "I should be in my office until eight tonight." He gave me his office and cell phone numbers. "Remember, the sooner you find Mark, the sooner we can nip this thing in the bud."

After hanging up, I called my father back to tell him that I had heard from the lawyer and planned to look for Mark. Dad agreed to stay home in case Mark called, but his tone implied that he would have preferred to actively search for his son. He promised to call Carmen and Mom.

I changed out of my skirt and blouse into an outfit more conducive to a suburban manhunt, as it were. It was a little past five when I left my apartment, and the sun was still well above the horizon.

When I turned onto campus, I envisioned Lepcheck behind every stately oak and under every overpruned shrub with a fresh pink slip in hand—though the logical side of my brain argued that Lepcheck wouldn't be on campus after five during the summer. I drove through Martin's grounds without incident and parked in the Dexler lot.

Dexler Math and Science, a squat two-story brick building, held few of the Western Reserve airs as the other structures scattered around campus did. When Martin's board of directors vowed to improve Martin's math and science reputation in the 1970s, they did so with half-hearted intentions. Martin trustees tended to be elderly alums, who had majored in pretentious subjects like Latin.

The building was quiet, the result of summer campus hours, but unlocked. I tiptoed past a classroom with a lecturer waxing on to a classroom of drone-faced undergraduates. The mathematics department resided on the first floor of the building, but my brother's office was on the basement level, the result of constant overcrowding. In addition to Mark's office and an astounding number of cobwebs, the basement level housed the boiler room, chemistry lab, and offices of other low-ranking faculty. The cement-walled hallway was dark and the air was damp and musty.

No light showed underneath Mark's door, but I knocked anyway, I didn't get an answer, nor had I expected one. Thinking maybe I'd leave a note, or pick up a clue where he was, I tried the doorknob—locked. Security has never been first and foremost in the Martin mindset, and the lock appeared flimsy enough. Taking a cue from television cop shows, I removed a spare library card from my wallet and slipped it in between the doorjamb and the lock. With a *click*, the lock gave way.

Inside the tiny room, I shut the door behind me, elated with my exploit. My smugness evaporated when I turned on the light. On the desk sat an overturned picture frame, which immediately struck me as odd. Mark wasn't one to decorate his office with personal items. The only bit of his personality he'd ever displayed in the room was an old classroom slide rule that he'd bought at a sale of out-of-date school supplies held at Stripling High School several years ago. The slide rule hung on his wall beside a College-issued calendar. I was happy to see that the calendar in his office at least displayed the current year.

I walked around the desk and turned over the eight-by-ten picture frame. The sound of broken glass clattered as I moved the gilded frame. The glass was cracked, but I recognized the photograph immediately. It was Olivia and Kirk's engagement picture, the one that had appeared in the Stripling newspaper. The matte photograph showed the couple looking at each other. They were wearing matching sweaters.

Why does Mark have this? Where did he get it? I thought.

My stomach turned. I thought of Lepcheck's threats and the Blockens' accusation against my brother. Wasn't it my job to protect him? Wasn't that what was drilled into me by my family? It was those thoughts that spurred me to do what I did next, even though the more logical side of my brain begged me not to.

I picked up the frame and stuffed it in my oversized canvas bag. As I tucked it away, I heard the sound of feet thundering down the basement steps. I turned off the overhead light.

Seconds later, someone pounded on Mark's office door. "Mr. Hayes, Mark Hayes, this is the police. Open up. We have a warrant to search your office."

My heart dropped into my shoes. I had nowhere to hide. The tiny subterranean office didn't have a window and the only sizable piece of furniture was Mark's desk. For a millisecond, I thought of hiding underneath it. In the dark, I felt for the tiny space, but discarded the idea when I remembered the cobwebs in the hallway. Who knew what lurked under his desk.

"Open it." A key slid into the lock. Before the key could complete its turn, I opened the door and pasted a polite smile on my face as if I had every right and reason to be there. Which, of course, I didn't.

Two uniformed police officers, one a woman, a Martin maintenance worker, and Detective Mains faced me. They'd jumped in surprise when I whipped open the door. "Yes?" I asked.

Mains found his voice first. "India. What a surprise."

His voice was dry, and I didn't think he was really surprised at all.

CHAPTER NINETEEN

I swallowed. My mouth had gone dry. "Why are you surprised, detective? This is my brother's office."

He said nothing and stepped inside. I backed up.

He flipped on the lights. "Your brother's not here."

"Afraid not," I said. My heart was beating so hard, I was surprised that he couldn't hear it.

"We have a search warrant." He handed me a folded document on legal-sized paper. I read it carefully.

My shoulders twitched. "Okay," I said as if they needed my permission.

Mains motioned for the two officers to enter the office. The maintenance worker, eagerly watching the cops' every movement, remained in the hallway, but peered through the door. The room was cramped, but I couldn't abandon Mark's office under the circumstances. Unfortunately, that wasn't my decision.

After instructing the officers where to pry, Mains turned to me. "Would you join me out in the hallway?"

Walking through the door, my bag brushed up against the doorjamb, and I became acutely aware of the engagement picture resting at the bottom. What if I hadn't found it before the police arrived? What if they asked for my bag? I worried. The shoulder strap cut across my body; I adjusted it to hide the bag behind my back.

The maintenance worker, whose name tag read Pat, looked

at us eagerly, undoubtedly thinking he was about to witness his first untelevised pistol whipping. Mains also seemed to notice Pat's excited expression and asked the maintenance guy politely, but firmly, to wait in the stairwell.

The two officers rooted through Mark's desk, muttering to each other.

Mains redirected his attention to me. "Could you tell me what you were doing in your brother's office? Alone, at this time of day?"

"I was looking for Mark."

He appeared unconvinced. "How did you get inside the office?"

"The door was unlocked," I lied. "Mark often forgets simple things like locking doors."

"Why were the lights off?"

"I turned the lights off. I was about to leave." I counted that one as a half-truth.

Mains made a note in the tiny vinyl-bound memo pad he had taken from his jacket pocket.

"Did you notice anything out of the ordinary in his office?"

The frame weighed heavily inside my shoulder bag. "No." No half-truth there.

He snapped the memo pad shut. "You are free to stay if you like, but outside of the office."

I nodded. A loud crash escaped Mark's office door, followed by an even louder curse from one of the officers. Mains sighed heavily.

He and I peeked through the doorway and found one of the officers picking up the broken pieces of Mark's prized slide rule from the floor.

"Make a note of the damage," Mains said.

Red-faced, the youngest officer nodded.

I slipped back out of the doorway. "I need to make a call. I'll be upstairs. There's no reception down here."

Mains barely gave me a nod in acknowledgment.

I hurried to the exit. When I reached the stairwell, I found Pat had abandoned his post. I broke into a trot. In Dexler's parking lot, I hurried to my car. I unlocked the car and grabbed a T-shirt from the backseat. Like a fugitive, I glanced around before unlocking the trunk. I opened it and shifted the junk around until I could pull back the carpeted bottom to expose the empty tire well. Currently, the spare tire was on the right front wheel. I pulled the frame from my bag and wrapped it in the T-shirt. Carefully, I placed the wrapped frame into the tire well, rolled the carpet back, and slammed the trunk shut. The bag was thinner, but I had to hope that I was the only one who would notice.

I was breathing hard as I stuck my hand in the bag again, this time for my cell phone. I scrolled through my phonebook for Lew's number.

"Baxter and Clive, attorneys," a woman's voice chimed. I told her I'd like to speak to Lew and gave my name. Within seconds, he came on the line. "Did you find Mark?"

"Um, no, but I'm at Mark's office, and the police are here searching it. They had a warrant, so I let them."

Lew sucked air through his gaped front teeth. "I better come down there."

I paced outside Dexler's entrance until Lew arrived in his imposing SUV. Before we entered the building, I handed him the warrant that Mains had given me. He mumbled to himself while he read. Only five feet five inches tall, Lew was a stocky man with flaming red hair and beard and a perpetual sunburn. I didn't know where he stood on the numerous left-wing causes that my parents chained themselves to, figuratively and literally, but he was an excellent lawyer. He'd bailed them out of lockup within hours of arrest and had helped them tap dance their way out of convictions.

Lew dropped his cigarette onto the pristine Martin walk, crushing it with his tasseled loafer. "The warrant does mention that the search is in connection to the Olivia Blocken case," he said to himself more than me. I nodded anyway.

I fidgeted. My conscience nagged me about the purloined photo in the trunk.

In the dark stairwell that led to the basement level, we met the two uniformed police officers. One said that Detective Mains would like to speak to me. Lew and I continued down the steps. Aside from Mains sitting in Mark's desk chair and the slide rule that sat in pieces on the file cabinet, the office didn't appear disturbed. Mains frowned when Lew followed me into the cramped office space.

I introduced Lew as the family lawyer, and he rose to his full height. "I represent the Hayes family and, at this time, am providing legal counsel to Mark Hayes and his sister India pertaining to the untimely death of their good friend Olivia Blocken."

"I see." Mains stood up from Mark's chair. "It would be wise if you'd advise Mark to come down to the police station."

"Why?" I asked.

Lew waved my outburst away. "When I next speak to Mark, I'll discuss the matter with him. Can I ask why you'd like Mark at the station?"

"I have some questions for him."

"Such as?"

"You can hear them at the station. I assume that you plan to be there."

"Yes, I'll be there."

"India, if you see your brother, ask him to come down to the station. It's for his own good," Mains said.

In my estimation, when something is for someone's own

good, it's always bad news.

"I'll try," I promised.

Mains left the office. Lew followed him into the hallway, demanding to know if Mains's officers had confiscated anything. Mains said that it would be in the report. I heard their heated voices travel further down the hall until they disappeared with the slam of the stairwell's door. I sat at Mark's desk and wracked my brain for an idea of my brother's whereabouts. As far as I knew, he wasn't close with anyone in his department or at Martin in general, aside from me, and I even suspected that had more to do with genetics than personal preference. I tried to think of people outside of Martin who Mark was friendly with, but no one came to mind. Mark never offered information to me about his friends or activities outside of his schooling and job. Was that because he really didn't have any outside interests? Or was it because I never asked? I wondered

The door to the stairway slammed again. "India," Lew's raspy voice called down the corridor. I met him in the hall.

"What?" My nerves were shot.

He waved his cell phone. "Your father just called. Your brother's at your parents' house. Let's go." Not waiting for my reaction, he ran up the stairs like a warrior running full-tilt into battle. I got the distinct impression that Lew was enjoying himself.

I certainly wasn't.

CHAPTER TWENTY

Lew sat on the edge of my father's favorite armchair, insisting that Mark confront Mains at the Justice Center. My mother and sister paced the living room on individual but intersecting orbits. My father observed the hysteria from his wheelchair under the picture window, adding bellowed advice into the fray. Mark cowered on the couch alone, saying only that he had been at a park all day thinking. What he'd thought, he didn't share. His shorts and T-shirt were speckled with dirt and dust as if he'd spent many of those thoughts rolling across a sandy baseball field. His left knee had a bloody scratch. He refused to explain it, regardless of our mother's innumerable entreaties to do so. I skirted the fringes of the room, close to the front door—whether to block the exit or reserve myself a clean getaway, I hadn't decided.

"For God's sake, Mark, talk to the police," Carmen said as she made her hundredth pass by Mark and the sofa. "We all know that you didn't do anything wrong."

"Don't swear, Carmen," Mom reprimanded from her loop. "Mark, honey, I understand how much you cared for Olivia, but you have to face these accusations."

"Your mother's right." Lew gave an uncomfortable laugh. "Nip this thing in the bud, son." He was certainly fond of that particular cliché.

"If you all would be quiet, maybe the boy would have a chance to speak," Dad said.

Mom rounded on Dad. "He's had plenty of opportunity to speak, Alden."

"It is doubtful that you could hear him if he did, the way you and Carmen are behaving."

"How we're behaving? This is serious, Dad. Mark is really in trouble, but, as usual, he's completely unconcerned," Carmen said, as if insulted.

"Does he look unconcerned to you?" Dad said.

As one, we assessed Mark's level of anxiety. He stared resolutely at his folded hands. All the anger he'd spat at me the day before was gone as if it had been drained from his body. In my eyes, he was thinner, paler, and utterly weak.

Tears welled up in my father's eyes, and I suspected he saw the same. My mother and Carmen were less sympathetic.

Mom directed her next question to Lew. "Could the police question Mark here?"

"Possibly," Lew remarked, "but wherever Mark meets the detective, he better be willing to talk. And before he can talk to them, he must talk to me. I cannot represent him if I don't know what he knows."

"He'll talk," Carmen said. She stood over Mark. "You have to talk. Don't you want to end this? You almost lost your job today. They might not be able to fire you for being a suspect, but they have every right to do it if you don't show up for class and spend the entire day doing God-knows-what at some nameless park."

Mom folded her arms. "Don't swear—"

"I know, Mother!" Carmen shouted, cutting her off.

My mother recoiled.

Carmen became positively unhinged. Pregnancy hormones no doubt. Under different circumstances, I would've enjoyed the spectacle.

I spoke up. "Screaming at each other isn't helping."

Big mistake. Carmen turned on me.

"Maybe if we all leave, Mark will feel comfortable enough to talk to Lew about, um, whatever happened," I hastened to defend myself before she struck.

I leaned against the wall, satisfied that I had settled the entire matter. I was wrong. Mom and Carmen both sputtered in an attempt to be the first to correct me. Whoever yells loudest wins, and Mom won.

"India, we need to know what happened, why Mark is in all this trouble."

"He doesn't have anything to hide, so why can't he talk to Lew with us in the room?" Carmen asked.

I thought of the framed engagement picture lying at the bottom of the trunk. He doesn't have anything to hide? Is that really true?

If possible, Lew's burnt skin had deepened into a darker shade of red. "I think that India has made an excellent suggestion, and, as your attorney, I encourage you to give us some privacy."

Carmen stopped mid-stride in her circuit. "Fine."

I jumped out of the way as she stomped out the front door. I hoped the twins didn't inherit their mother's temper.

"You'll have to excuse her. She's due in the fall," Mom said to Lew, as if he hadn't noticed.

She followed Carmen out the door. I wondered what her excuse was.

My father murmured quietly that he'd be in the study if needed. He left the study door open half an inch.

It was fast approaching seven, and I was thinking of adjourning to the kitchen where I could find some peace, and possibly a snack, when Mark spoke. "India can stay."

"Fine, fine," Lew said, beaming, apparently relieved Mark hadn't completely lost the use of his tongue.

"I really don't think I should," I argued. "I mean, shouldn't this be confidential?"

Lew pointed to an empty armchair. I sat.

"Are you willing to speak to Detective Mains?" Lew asked.

"Yes," Mark said. "Can it wait until tomorrow?"

The lawyer thought for a minute. "I don't see why not. It's already late in the day. It won't hurt to sit a few more hours. You're not under arrest. But I have to add, Mark, you're not under arrest right now. I haven't had much time on your case, so I do not know all the particulars, but I do know the Blocken family has fixated on you as the main suspect."

"Was Olivia murdered?" I asked. I still couldn't fathom that possibility.

"Undoubtedly. The coroner is a tennis buddy of mine. After your father called me and told me the situation, I gave her a ring. She explained that the pronounced bruising on Olivia's back is consistent with other injuries she has seen when the victim is shoved hard. The coroner believes that Olivia was deliberately pushed into the fountain. There are also bruises on the front of her calves, probably sustained when she collided with the low rim of the fountain as she fell in. She must have been caught by surprise, because there were no marks on her hands indicating that she reached out to catch herself. In addition to the head injury, she had a pretty serious case of whiplash from the impact. Whoever did it had to be mighty angry. To have back bruises that pronounced, she was shoved with tremendous force."

I shuddered.

"However, the coroner said the cops don't believe that the murder was premeditated."

Mark whispered something I couldn't make out. Apparently, neither could Lew. "What's that?"

"It's my fault," he whispered hoarsely.

"Your fault?" Lew asked. "Are you saying that you are responsible for Olivia's death?"

"Yes."

It was as though a lead rock had slammed into the center of my chest; my lungs constricted. Mark had killed Olivia? I felt lightheaded and longed to place my head between my knees, but I was afraid to move. I allowed my mind to play with the idea, but then rejected it like I did my paintings if they amounted to nothing more than wasted paint. Breath reentered my lungs.

"Did you kill Olivia Blocken?" Lew asked, calm as ever.

"Yes."

"How?"

"I could have saved her," Mark said. "I could have been with her. I heard her talking to somebody at the fountain, but I went back to my office to wait for her to come to me. I was always the one to take the initiative in everything. For once, I wanted her to come to me first." Tears rolled down my brother's sunken cheeks. He said, barely above a whisper, "If I hadn't been selfish, if I hadn't had to prove to myself that Olivia would look for me, I could've protected her from whoever did this to her."

Regardless of my parents' rule of no smoking in the house, Lew shook a cigarette out of a crumpled pack and lit it with a yellow plastic lighter. "Did you push her into the fountain?"

Mark looked up from his folded hands, startled. "No, of course not."

"Then, it's not your fault that she died. Don't take responsibility simply because you have some misguided white knight fantasy."

"Not my fault?" Mark leapt from the couch. "Of course it is my fault. She came to Martin to see me. If I hadn't asked her there, she wouldn't have come. If I'd left her alone. . . . If I'd met her at the fountain when I heard her voice. . . . If I—"

"Son, sounds to me like you have a lot of ifs, but not a lot of sense."

Mark collapsed back onto the couch.

The dramatics wore out my last nerve. I bit the inside of my lip, and the taste of blood stopped me from screaming at my brother like my sister and mother had. How dare he let me think even for a minute that he killed Olivia? How dare he indulge himself in wails and lame guessing games when he was in real danger of being fired or even arrested? I thought angrily.

Still gnawing my lip, I left the room. In the kitchen, I filled a glass with water. I rinsed out my mouth and into the sink's steel basin. Bloody water spiraled down the drain. I wondered how this could get any worse.

CHAPTER TWENTY-ONE

Around eight o'clock, Lew came in to tell me he was going home. My brother would be spending the night at my parents' house at Lew's urging. He thought Mark shouldn't be alone. My brother had agreed to visit the police station early the next morning; Lew would drive him. The lawyer had also agreed to pursue a lawsuit against the college; the paperwork would be on Lepcheck's desk by tomorrow afternoon, although Mark hadn't seemed to care about his jeopardized position at Martin.

Tuesday, I was the poster child of denial. I had the evening shift at the library. I spent the daytime feverishly cleaning the apartment and, for the first time in a long time, painting in my studio. Around ten, Mom called to tell me Mark had returned from questioning at the police station. She withheld any other details, and I didn't ask. At the library, I passed my shift in a daze and four cups of coffee. Looking for distraction, I volunteered to help Jefferson catalog the new books and had little contact with people, either patrons or staff. It was Bobby's day off. I gave my mind the day off thoughts of Mark and Olivia, as well.

The next day was my day off, and I ran out of stall tactics. My apartment sparkled from the ceiling corners to the bathroom tile. A completed oil painting solidified on my easel, but I couldn't motivate myself to start a new one.

I picked up the morning paper off the front porch. *The Stripling Dispatch,* owned by some huge media conglomerate in

Albuquerque, appeared every Wednesday and Saturday on the townspeople's doorsteps regardless of whether they actually read it.

While the Akron paper had made a small mention of Olivia's death in the local section, the *Dispatch* gave the story full coverage. Front page, above and below the fold. Never one to withstand the seduction of print, I read.

MARTIN PROFESSOR CHIEF SUSPECT IN BLOCKEN MURDER

—Maribel Smythe, Dispatch staff writer

—Stripling. The day after the Fourth was a dark one for one local family. While other families were enjoying the extended holiday weekend, community leaders Donald and Regina Blocken received a frightening phone call a little after ten Saturday morning informing them that their daughter, Olivia, was in an ambulance enroute to the hospital. Olivia Blocken, Stripling High School graduate and recently of Newport News, Va., suffered from brain and head injuries after falling into the fountain outside the Dexler Math and Science building on Martin College's campus. The fountain is a well-known landmark on the campus entitled "Empowerment."

I skimmed down through the full-page article as Maribel Smythe waxed on about the details of the fountain. No wonder she couldn't find a job at a large daily, I thought uncharitably. In the third paragraph, she wrote,

Due to an extensive brain injury, Blocken's surgery was unsuccessful. Dr. Andrea Maddox stated, "Olivia's impact with the fountain was severe. The sculpture cracked her skull and punctured her frontal lobe. My team and I did everything we could for her. We told the family that permanent brain damage was likely."

Sunday, doctors determined that Blocken was indeed brain-dead, and the family removed life support early that morning.

The police are investigating Blocken's fall as the coroner suspects Blocken was a victim of foul play. Detective Richmond Mains, the lead detective on Stripling's police force, well known for solving the mailbox baseball case last April . . .

I skimmed again.

During the interview, Regina Blocken stated, "I heard that the Hayes boy was found near my daughter. He's been obsessed with Olivia for years."

I paused in my reading. Mrs. Blocken's accusation again of my brother was clear.

Mark Hayes, son of politically active Alden and Rev. Lana Hayes of Stripling, and a member of the mathematics faculty at Martin College, dated Blocken during high school. Blocken and her fiancé, Kirk Row, were in Stripling this week preparing for their wedding, to be held at St. Jude Lutheran Church on Saturday. On the Fourth, Hayes crashed the Blocken family gathering, reportedly to ask Blocken to meet him the next morning, the morning of her attack, at his office on Martin's campus.

My arms dropped the newsprint from my sight while I conjured the courage to keep reading.

The police are investigating Hayes, but stress he is not under arrest at this time.

Dr. Samuel Lepcheck, provost at Martin College, stated in a press conference yesterday afternoon that the college is in "full cooperation with the police." He refused to comment on the involvement of Hayes in the case. However, a college source confirmed exclusively to the Dispatch *that Hayes has been suspended indefinitely from his position as assistant professor of mathematics at Martin College.*

The article ended with a request that anyone with information about the case contact Mains or the Stripling Justice Center. Theodore had watched me pace as I'd read the article. He yawned enormously, allowing me to view his full range of sparkling white teeth. Templeton, persistent in his war for dominion, was MIA, probably doing undercover work. However, I didn't have time to worry about their feline domestic dispute. All 20,000-plus Stripling residents and the entire Martin community were hungrily reading the Smythe article. The paper had committed irretrievable damage to Mark's reputation, to my family's reputation. Innocent or guilty, public opinion would hang my brother.

Knowing that my parents read the *Dispatch* religiously, I called their home. The answering machine picked up. "You have reached the home of Alden and Rev. Lana Hayes," my mother's preacher voice announced. "We are unable to come to the phone right now and encourage you to join us at Martin College in support of our son, Mark, who has been unjustly suspended from employment there. If you have an emergency to share with Rev. Hayes, please contact the church office. Have a blessed day and may the peace of Christ be with you."

Oh, hell.

CHAPTER TWENTY-TWO

I circled campus with the windows down, hoping to locate my parents. Not much of a challenge. At the south end of campus near Dexler, I heard them.

"Hark, Hark, bring back Mark! Hark, Hark, bring back Mark!" A militant's call that wrote itself, I thought. I still couldn't see the protest from Dexler's lot but heard it clearly. The chanting increased in volume and ferocity. "Hark! Hark! Bring back Mark! Hey! Hey! We want Hayes!"

My father's specially-equipped van dominated the lot. Massive and olive green, a barely readable SAVE THE AMAZON sticker decorated its tarnished bumper.

I jogged around the corner of Dexler with escalating dread. Then, I saw them. My mother marched in front of a small band of protestors as they circled the fountain. My father was stationed in front of the marchers, bullhorn in hand, leading the chant. Nicholas sat on his lap, covering his tiny ears with his palms. I didn't see Carmen or Chip. A small group of students and faculty congregated to the side of the spectacle. The dozen or so marchers carried chalkboard-sized placards that read, UNLAWFUL SUSPENSION!, INNOCENT UNTIL PROVEN GUILTY!, and my personal favorite, MARTIN COLLEGE: EQUAL OPPORTUNITY EXECUTIONER! Mom toted that one. I suppose I should be relieved that they hadn't strung an effigy of Lepcheck from the fountain.

Beyond the small cluster of Martinites, a TV van from Akron

136

Canton News parked on the science quad. The finicky grounds crew would love that. A cameraman zoomed in on the protestors as the petite correspondent recorded a sound bite.

Not yet eleven, the day was already scorching in the low nineties. The marchers' energy began to wane. Most participants were elderly parishioners from my mother's church and associates from my parents' liberal causes.

I proceeded across the brick walkway. Nicholas spotted me before I reached them. He jumped off his grandfather's lap. Running full tilt, he flung his small frame into my arms.

"Ufh," I uttered.

"Dia!" Nicholas's cry was barely decipherable over the commotion.

"What are you doing here?" I asked, stalling the looming confrontation with my parents.

"Mommy and Daddy had to teach today."

"They did?"

He nodded importantly. "They're helping people get their graduate equalizer degree."

"Ahh. GRE is probably easier to say."

He thought about that and nodded. "I'm helping Gram and Granpa."

"You are?"

"I'm learning to use my First Amendment right to peaceful protest."

Dad bellowed through his bullhorn, instructing the protestors to continue their chanting, then wheeled over to Nicholas and me. Zealous and sheepish looks fought for control over his expression. The zealot won.

"Dad," I said, the weight of my disapproval heavy in the name.

"That horrible article was in the paper this morning, and your mother and I had to do something to support our son."

I shifted Nicholas off my hip and put him down. He un-shouldered his HUGS-NOT-GUNS backpack, a gift from his grandfather, and poured its contents of action figures, markers, papers, and plastic blocks on the brick walk. He squatted on the walk and began constructing an intricate fortress.

"The article upset me too, but you don't see me marching on Martin. This isn't just about Mark. I could lose my job."

"Is it more important to keep your job than support your brother?"

I wiped both my hands down my face.

"Hey! Hey! We want Hayes!" the chanters shouted.

"Why would you want to work for an organization that condemns your brother?" He sounded disgusted.

The late morning sun burned my dark head. I wished I'd worn a hat like all good militants do. "All of Martin isn't against Mark. Good people work here too. This is Lepcheck's work. He's wanted to boot Mark for years, because Mark never finished his PhD."

"After everything settles down," my father argued, "Mark will complete his doctorate. He needs more time."

I wouldn't be dragged into a debate about Mark's perpetual dissertation. "Fine. Whatever. All I'm trying to tell you is it's not the entire school. It's Lepcheck."

"Who has the most power?" He spat like a true patron of proletariat. "Individuals rise to the level of their incompetence."

Under my breath, I counted to ten backwards. I don't know why I thought my parents would retreat because it put me in an awkward position. They've been marching on something or other, motivated by sheer principle, since the Summer of Love.

Several of the elderly protestors sat on the knee-high stone wall that surrounded the fountain to catch their breath. They limply held their signs, every so often jerking them upright in a half-hearted wave.

I decided to change my tactic. "Your troops are exhausted. Why don't you give them a break for at least a half an hour or so?"

"We will not break ranks," he bellowed. Nicholas looked up from his blocks. "But I see what you mean," he added in a normal tone. He fished into the Velcro pouch of his carpenter pants, which he wears for the endless amount of pockets. He'd said once that if his legs couldn't carry him, at least they could hold odds and ends for him. He handed me the keys to the van. "I have a cooler of water in the van. Can you go fetch it for me?"

Who was I kidding? I took the keys. I played with the key ring, swinging it around my index finger as I walked back to the Dexler parking lot. The key chain was a palm-sized plastic ornament that declared, SAVE THE KOALAS.

I unlocked the van and opened the sliding door. More placards about Mark's suspension lay across the bench seats. My parents expected more walkway warriors than those who had shown up. A box of bright poster paints and brushes sat on the floor next to the cooler. If I were in a more forgiving mood, I would've remembered that I have my parents' activism to thank for my early interest in art. At a young age, I helped my father paint posters and pickets for different protests that he spearheaded across the country. Carmen and Mark took no interest in the activity, so it became my father's and my own. When we painted those placards for AIDS awareness, gun control, and library levies, he noticed a talent that I hadn't known I had and enrolled me in art class at a local studio. Three days a week for twelve years, I took classes from that studio, honing my skill. It was understood that I would one day be a famous painter that those outside of the art world would recognize.

I pulled the cooler out of the van. It ka-thunked onto the

blacktop. Many *understood* things never happened. That was never truer than when I thought of Olivia, and what her life might have become.

On the sidewalk, I opened the lid to the cooler. It indeed held water. A lot of water. I tightened the lid, then hefted the container into my arms and waddle-walked back toward the fountain.

I was passing a cluster of evergreen bushes when I heard, "Psssst. Psst. India."

Alarmed, I dropped the precariously held cooler. On my foot.

CHAPTER TWENTY-THREE

"Shh . . ." I exclaimed.

"India?" the bushes asked with concern. "Are you okay?"

Because the bush was not engulfed in flame, and I recognized the voice, it was safe to assume that I was not having a Mount Sinai moment.

"Mark?" I barked.

My right big toe, which had been creamed by the falling cooler, was already turning blue. I may never wear flip-flops again, I thought forlornly.

The bushes rustled as Mark crawled out of his hidey-hole. His glasses sat crookedly on his face, and dead leaves and twigs snarled in his hair and beard. He brushed the majority of the dirt and underbrush from his T-shirt and shorts.

"Is this what you did Monday? Roll around in the bushes while you ditched work?" I asked.

Mark pulled a large twig out of his hair. "Huh?"

"Never mind. What are you doing here?"

"I've been staying with Mom and Dad. I heard them prepare for a rally this morning. It didn't take a genius to guess what the rally's for. What are you doing here? You could get fired if Lepcheck sees you."

"Supporting you is more important than my job," I said quixotically, although I'd shared that exact sentiment with my father.

Mark shook his head. The remaining twigs flew back into the

hedge. "This suspension is the least of my worries."

I thought of the picture in the trunk of my car, and I silently agreed. The perfect opportunity to confront him about it presented itself. "The police searched your office Monday."

"You told me that already."

"What I didn't tell you is that they didn't find anything incriminating."

"Of course they didn't."

"Not even that engagement picture."

"Engagement picture? What are you talking about?"

"I reached your office a few minutes before the police. There was a framed copy of Olivia and Kirk's engagement picture in the middle of your desk. How did you get it? Why was it there?"

"Why would I have that? It's not mine. That's the last thing that I would want to have."

"I saw it with my own eyes," I insisted. "I have it, if you don't believe me."

"You took it from my office?"

I crossed my arms. "You do know about it."

"No, I don't. But you stealing, well . . ."

"You wanted me to leave it in your office for the police to find? You should be thanking me you're not in jail right now. Tell me where you got it."

"I'm telling you, it's not mine." His voice cracked like an eleven-year-old boy's. "I have no idea what you're talking about. And that you would accuse me of hoarding a picture of Olivia, like, like some psycho. You're—" he stopped, apparently searching for the most scorching epitaph. "An idiot."

Having called myself worse in the Monday morning mirror, his insult didn't faze me. "I don't think you're a psycho."

"Yes, you do."

"No, I don't."

"Yes, you do. You think that I had something to do with . . .

with . . . Olivia's death. Just like her family, just like Lepcheck. My own sister."

"No, I don't," I protested.

A pair of students walking by paused at my outburst. Contrary to national folklore, librarians have been known to yell now and again. Feeling disgruntled, I gave the students a nasty mind-your-own-business look that I had mastered behind the library's reference desk.

Mark's hand went to his mouth. "I know. I know what happened."

I watched him wearily. "What?"

"Someone planted it in my office. They wanted the police to find it because then they would have some real evidence."

"Planted? Come on. Who would do that?"

"Anyone could have done it. Security on campus is down in the summer, and any nimrod with a credit card could break into my office."

"Maybe not any nimrod," I said under my breath, thinking of my own B&E.

Mark's eyes shone. "Whoever was with Olivia at the fountain planted that picture. I just know it."

Now that Olivia's death was a puzzle, a mystery, a tricky logarithm that he could possibly unravel, he could see it as a mathematician, with scientific detachment. He used the same gusto when teaching quadratic equations. When he turned off his emotions, Olivia's death was like arithmetic, and Mark was very good at arithmetic. His idea was logical if not provable.

"Tell me about the other person. Male? Female? White? Black? Asian? Anything?"

"I already told you, I didn't see anyone."

"What did the person sound like?" I persisted.

"I didn't hear the other person speak."

I threw my hands up in the air. "Then how do you know

anyone was there?"

"I heard Olivia's voice; she was talking to someone."

"This is the twenty-first century, Mark; she was on a cell phone."

"You're wrong. I felt that someone else was there."

Terrific, now he's receiving psychic inklings.

I tried to keep my voice at a quiet level as more students strolled by between classes. In the background, the chanters continued their mantra, "Hark! Hark! We want Mark! Hey! Hey! Bring back Hayes!" My father would be wondering what happened to me and the cooler.

"Did you tell the police this?" I asked.

"Yes, and they said the same thing you did about the cell phone."

"You're sure someone was there?" I shifted, trying to ignore my throbbing toe.

Mark looked me directly in the eye for the first time, his eyes as wide as dinner plates. "Yes, I swear."

I believed him, just like I believed him when we were kids and he'd told Mom that he hadn't stolen all the figurines from the church's nativity set and hidden them in odd places throughout the church. The janitor had found the frankincense-bearing wiseman inside the church's industrial tub of orange punch mix the following July. Okay, I had believed him then because I'd done it—the manger kidnapping, anyway, not the blackmail. Olivia and I had done it, to be exact, but when faced with the angry accusation from our mother, Mark had had the same face he wore at the moment. If he could wear that earnest face when confronted with Mom's full-on fire-and-brimstone persona, he had to be telling the truth. And for the record, it had been Olivia's idea to put the wiseman in the punch.

"Okay. I believe you."

Mark's despondent face broke into a weak smile.

"Promise me you won't do anything about this. You're in enough trouble as it is. I'll handle it."

"Handle it? What are you going to do?"

"Well, I can't tell the police about the photograph, because I swiped it from your office just before they arrived, now can I?"

"Where is it?" he asked, his tone hushed.

"Safe," I answered evasively. "I'll find out where that picture came from. Maybe you're right, maybe it will lead to someone who knows who—what—happened to Olivia."

He nodded. "What are you going to do?"

I shook my head. "Never mind. There's something else." I had to ask him even if it sent him back into a black mood.

Mark waited and I gathered my courage.

"It's something Bree said to me. She said that you sent Olivia flowers and candy long after Olivia moved to Virginia."

Mark's pale face flushed with embarrassment.

"You actually did? I thought she was making it up. I thought you had no contact with Olivia."

Mark looked down at the sidewalk. "She called me."

I blinked. "When?"

"Every now and again when she was having problems or just needed someone to talk to."

"What exactly does every now and again mean?" I felt my agitation grow.

"Every six months or so. I hadn't heard from her in the last year or so, though. I know now that's because of Kirk," he said sadly. "That's what I wanted to talk to her about: why she hadn't been calling. I wanted her to know that I would still be there for her." He looked like he was about to cry.

"She led you on," I whispered.

Mark's face hardened. "She didn't promise me anything."

"She called you. She shouldn't have. She didn't let you get over her. That's wrong. It was selfish and wrong."

"I know she cared about me."

I gritted me teeth. "Why didn't you tell me?"

Mark looked up from the sidewalk and met my gaze. "She asked me not to. She said you wouldn't understand."

"Damn right, I wouldn't understand. She led you on for years, and you let her." My anger at Olivia burned within my chest. How could she treat my brother so poorly? How could the both of them keep it from me for so long?

"I'm sorry," he whispered.

"Sorry, what are you sorry for?"

"You're right; I let her lead me on. I loved it when she called. Now look what's happened because of it. She's dead, and I'm the number-one suspect."

My anger deflated, and I patted his arm. "You're not responsible for what happened to her. I will figure this out. We have the picture to go on now, remember?"

He nodded.

"Go home, if Lepcheck sees you here, he'll have one of the rent-a-cops throw you in a janitor's closet. Or worse."

After a little more prodding, Mark agreed, got into his car, and drove away.

I picked up the cooler and shuffled to the fountain. Nicholas was still on the ground with his pile of blocks, now deconstructing the fortress, but my father was in front of the protestors waving what appeared to be a permit to protest in Lepcheck's face. Lepcheck's complexion blazed maroon under his bottled tan.

Putting the cooler down next to my nephew, I crouched beside him and whispered, "Hey, Nicko."

He looked up from his blocks. "Dia!" he shouted at top voice.

I winced and peered up to see if we had attracted Lepcheck's glance, but my father had his undivided attention. I held a finger to my lips. "Shhh."

He mimicked me. "Shhh."

"I have to go. Can you tell Grandpa that after he's done talking to that angry-looking man?"

"The one with the purple face?" whispered Nicholas.

"That's the one."

I beat a hasty retreat.

I knew I was being a coward, but I couldn't hang around with Lepcheck in sight. No need to tempt fate with the status of my employment.

CHAPTER TWENTY-FOUR

Something nagged at me about Olivia's death, aside from its occurrence and the general suspicions against my brother, of course. After stopping at my car where I kept a candy stash for just such an occasion, I made a stop before I left campus. I jogged to the east side of Martin, past the gymnasium and into the thick of the dorms. I stopped in front of a small modular building tucked away between the gym and the end of fraternity row: the safety and security office.

I didn't come to this part of campus often, only when I had a dire need to bribe the real powers-that-be on campus.

The modular's door was unlocked, and I stepped in. The reception area was empty. Lucky for once, I caught the safety and security secretary on her smoking break. I slipped around the desk and scurried down the hall to the office at the very end. After a deep breath, I knocked once and opened it. The room was absolutely freezing, but the man sitting behind the desk looked like he'd recently marched the Mojave Desert at high noon. The lights blinked, but the tired window air conditioner labored on.

"Well, hell's bells," he said by way of greeting. "They caught you again."

"Really, Mutt," I said. "I'm completely innocent."

"Uh-huh. First things first." He drummed his fingers on the desktop.

I slid a king-sized chocolate bar onto the metal desk that

divided the tiny room. The candy bar was a little worse for wear after spending the morning in my smoldering car, but Mutt didn't seem to mind. He chuckled softly and made a gimme sign with his hand. I rifled through my shoulder bag, pulled out another bar, and slapped it down next to its mate. Mutt gestured that I could sit.

I settled on the lone metal folding chair, grimy from decades of dust and chocolate.

"Well, lovely India, what can I do for you today? Fix a no-parking zone ticket? Speeding?"

I shifted uncomfortably on the frigid metal. "Not this time."

"Hmm." Mutt worried his chin, seemingly enjoying torment-ing me. Then he snapped his fingers. "I know you're here to save your brother from a murder rap."

I jumped. But, then again, I didn't know why Mutt's com-ment surprised me. Lee Mutton, head of safety and security, had intimate knowledge of every rumor that pulsated through Martin's campus, and none came bigger than Olivia's murder.

Mutt unwrapped a chocolate bar and finger-combed his mustache in preparation. His navy uniform was opened to the navel, displaying the unseemly view of his signature beer belly barely restrained by a white T-shirt. Appearances couldn't be more misleading. Mutt ran the entire campus from his little of-fice where security monitors lining the walls flickered from scene to scene with an efficiency of an iron hand. Mutt was Jabba the Hut in navy cotton blend. And if Mutt ever found a reason to rise from his abused desk chair, look out. Rumor had it that the three-hundred-plus, six-three security lord once threw a frat boy out of a second-story window while breaking up a rave. Of course, it was probably all rumors. He couldn't pos-sibly still be head of security after chucking Martin's bread and butter out of a window, could he? Another rumor claimed that Mutt wasn't fired for said chucking, because he has some dirt on Lepcheck so horrible that he's virtually untouchable. I considered all of this as Mutt polished off the first candy bar and chugged a sweaty can of cola before moving on to the second.

"So?" he asked between bites. He wiped chocolate from his lip with the back of his hand.

I took a breath. "You're right. I haven't broken any of Martin's hallowed traffic laws—at least not lately."

He smirked. Chocolate clung to his mustache. "Hallowed, huh? My, you professor-types and your big words."

"I'm not technically a professor."

"Excuse me, you librarians," he amended.

I plunged in. "Have you been involved in the Blocken case?"

Mutt finished the second bar and became officious. "Not so much. The police are salivating over this one. And the whole situation has more Lepcheck than I can stomach."

"What do you know?"

"You know," he said philosophically. "This isn't really like fixing a parking ticket. It's a little more complicated. Lepcheck would put me on the curb if he knew I was even speaking to you about it."

"I thought you were un-fire-able."

"That's the word on the street."

I opened my bag and slapped two more chocolate bars on his desk. I'd need to restock after this visit.

Mutt smiled. "Like I was saying, I don't know that much. But my boys were some of the first ones on the scene."

"Boys?" I arched my brow. At least three female security officers patrolled the campus.

Mutt grunted. "My boys and girls, then. Happy?"

"Very." I nodded for him to continue.

"One of them, Mike, found your brother sobbing over Olivia at the scene. Mark had already pulled the girl out of the fountain and was holding a shirt to her head wound. Mike said Mark was a scarier sight than the girl. Mark wouldn't let anyone close to her until the EMS arrived."

I shuddered, envisioning the scene: Mark cradling Olivia's bloodied head, blood and water ruining her designer sundress. The image of Mark's tortured face, even in my imagination, was more than I could stand.

"Hey, you okay?" Mutt asked, halfway concerned. The third chocolate bar was long gone. He patted the fourth as if to say, "I've got something special in mind for you."

"I'm fine." I pushed the image deeper into the recesses of my mind to fuel future nightmares. "Did you catch the mur—the accident on video?"

"Of course that Mains hotshot asked me the same thing the morning it happened. If I had, this case would be an open-and-shut deal, but we don't have any security cameras on that side of campus. Low traffic."

"Aren't low traffic areas the most attractive to crime?"

"Don't preach to the choir. I bring the same point up at my annual budget hearing. I have a feeling the board'll spring for it this year." He paused. "We do have one camera, the Dexler lot, that shows your brother walking toward the fountain at about eight-thirty, back to Dexler, and then again to the fountain forty-five minutes later."

"He's already explained that. He went to the fountain, heard Olivia talking to someone, and left to wait for her in his office where he asked her to meet him. He got tired of waiting and walked back to the fountain, again, and found her."

"Why'd he go to the fountain in the first place?"

"I—he probably was pacing around campus. He walks when he's nervous, and I know he was nervous about seeing Olivia again."

Mutt looked doubtful.

I changed the subject. "What happened to Olivia's car?"

"What car?"

"Well, she'd have to have a car to drive to campus from her parents' house, and she certainly didn't drive it out of here."

"There wasn't any unknown car on campus for any extended period that I know of, and trust me, I would know. I offered a free personal day off work to the officer that writes the most tickets this summer."

"Can you do that?" I asked, thinking of the campus' strict attendance policy. You had to have your mother's fresh death certificate in hand or be in intensive care before the college would give you an extra day off.

"No, but they don't know that. I'd watch those yellow lines if I were you."

"There's no way that Olivia walked to campus. Her parents live over ten miles away, and she'd rather die than take public transportation." I blanched at my poor choice of words.

Mutt ignored the *faux pas*. "I'm telling you, there was no car here long enough to get a ticket."

"But, a car could have been here for a shorter period, not giving your boys and girls time to whip out their ticket pads and pencils. Just enough time to shove Olivia in the fountain and leave."

Mutt inched the last chocolate bar closer, but did not open it. "All I know is that your brother's car was in the lot the whole time."

CHAPTER TWENTY-FIVE

I stopped at Lula's Flowers on the town square and bought the most expensive arrangement that my meager budget could bear. I might not eat for a few weeks, but the arrangement was worth its price. It was a cluster of yellow roses, orange lilies, and fragrant herbs in a blown glass vase. No carnations or baby's breath. I signed the card simply "India."

I drummed my fingers on the steering wheel as I drove the ten minutes to the Blocken home. I hadn't seen a member of the family since they chased me out of the hospital on Saturday afternoon. I knew that I wouldn't be welcome, not as long as they suspected my brother, but visiting them was the only way I could think of to find out how that photograph got into my brother's office. Logic told me that one of the Blockens must have been involved because they were so certain that Mark attacked Olivia. Nostalgia told me that the family would never do such a horrible thing despite how they felt about Mark. Spite told me that Lepcheck planted the photos. As the three points of view fought for dominance, I found myself directly in front of the Blocken home.

I knocked on the door several times, but there was no answer. Either no one was home, or they saw me and refused to answer. I stepped off the Victorian's elaborate porch and returned to my car with the flowers. I hesitated on the stone walk, then I meandered around the house to the wooden gate between the garage and house. I peered over the gate and saw O.M. sitting alone on a picnic table butted up to the side of the garage, smoking a slim cigarette and rifling through a box of chocolates. Her short hair was the startling neon blue hue that I'd seen at the hospital.

I tapped on the gate. Chocolate flew out of the box and onto the chemically treated lawn. She stubbed her cigarette on the underside of the tabletop. "You nearly gave me a heart attack."

"I didn't mean to scare you. Can I come inside the gate?" I asked.

She shrugged.

I hung my arm over the gate to unlatch it. The gate was tricky, it had to be jiggled and jerked to cooperate. Although I hadn't opened it in several years, I had no trouble. The gate saddened me.

Seeing that I was alone, O.M. picked up her half-smoked cigarette and fished a lighter out of her oversized dark denim jeans.

I set the flowers on one of the umbrella tables, remnants of the Blocken Fourth of July picnic that seemed so long ago. "Care if I sit beside you?" I asked.

She shrugged. I climbed onto the picnic table next to her and leaned against the garage. We didn't speak for a few minutes. O.M. smoked, and I secondhand smoked. Her pixie-like face was devoid of makeup and expression.

"Want a cigarette?" She held the pack out to me.

"No thanks."

She shoved it back in her pocket and turned her face away. I wished I smoked.

"Those chocolates look good."

She handed me the box. Moon-shaped thumbnail prints indicated ninety percent of them had been investigated and passed over. Chocolate encrusted O.M.'s right thumbnail, creating a muddy swamp color with her poison-green nail polish.

I chose a piece that was free of nail marks. I popped it in my mouth. Apricot. Yuck. "You know there's a guide on the box lid, so you don't have to mutilate all the candies."

"When they get all mixed up, the guide's shot to hell."

She had a point. I swallowed the apricot candy. At least she was talking to me, even if belligerently.

I tried to soften her further. "I like your hair."

She ran her hand, the one free of chocolate, thankfully, through it. After a full minute of silence, she whispered, "I dyed it for the wedding to make Mom mad. She hasn't noticed yet."

"I'm sorry."

"Yeah."

"When is the funeral?"

"How would I know? They don't tell me anything." She took one last drag of her cigarette and stubbed it under the picnic table. She carefully placed the butt in her pocket. "My parents and Kirk are fighting over the arrangements and stuff. He wants her to be buried in Virginia. If he thinks that Mom's going to let that happen, he really is psycho."

"He did lose his fiancée," I said in Kirk's defense.

"I lost my sister, and I didn't go crazy. He was so angry yesterday. I thought he was going to hit my dad."

"Over the funeral?"

"Yeah, I guess. I was upstairs in my room with music on when he came over. I couldn't really hear them until Kirk started yelling at Mom and Dad. By the time I got to the stairs and could see them, Kirk was so bonkers, I couldn't understand what he was saying with that Southern accent of his. After Kirk left, I asked what happened, but Mom acted like I wasn't even there."

Looked like I had my first suspect: the furious fiancé.

I saw an opening. "Have you been missing any photographs of Olivia?"

She seemed surprised by the question. "No. I mean I'm not missing any. But if my parents are . . ." she shrugged. "Why?"

"Uh," I began. I didn't want to tell her about the engagement picture, but I didn't want to be another exclusive adult. "Things get misplaced."

O.M. frowned. Before she could persist, we heard a car roll up the driveway. A car door slammed, and a moment later, Mrs. Blocken stood by the gate I'd left opened.

I jumped off the picnic table.

"Olga!" she called. "Have you seen—" Mrs. Blocken stopped when she spotted me. Her face reddened to the shade of her coif. "What are you doing here?"

"I—"

"Leave my house at once. How dare you come here?"

O.M. pulled her knees to her chest and looked away, out into the yard.

"I didn't mean to upset you, Mrs. Blocken." I felt like a five-year-old.

Her eyes blazed. Her attention transferred to the bouquet of flowers I bought. "Where did these come from?" She picked up the vase and read the card. "Do you know why Olivia chose you as a bridesmaid?"

I blinked, struck dumb by the question.

"To get back at me."

"At you," I managed to say.

"She wanted to get married in Virginia, and I said absolutely not, that her father and I would only pay for a Stripling wedding." She spun the vase in her hands. "I didn't know about the wedding party until a month ago when it was too late to replace you. You should have heard the glee in her voice when she said your name."

Mrs. Blocken looked me directly in the eye and dropped the vase onto the cement walk. The beautiful hand-blown glass shattered into a thousand pieces.

"I'm sorry to bother you," I whispered and fled, trampling the lilies and roses as I brushed past her.

CHAPTER TWENTY-SIX

I told myself that I didn't care about Mrs. Blocken's hostility, but my tear ducts thought differently. Wiping my eyes and muttering, I drove to the duplex. I pulled into the drive and spotted Ina sitting on the front porch, Theodore in her lap. I rubbed my face vigorously before getting out, so it'd appear I only had a nasty sunburn.

"India," Ina called. "I read the *Dispatch* this morning. It doesn't look good for Mark, does it?"

I waved away her question. "How did Theodore get out here?"

"Who? This little mite?" She scratched him under his double chin. He purred with the ferocity of a jet engine.

"I don't think *little* is the right adjective, but yes, the cat in your lap."

"Well." She settled in for a good tell-all.

I sat down on the glider beside my door. This could take all afternoon.

Theodore purred.

"I was out in the yard, rotating my leprechauns," Ina said.

I glanced at the yard; the leprechauns were in a different configuration.

"You know they get tired of being in the same place all the time."

I nodded and wondered if I had anything in my duplex suitable for lunch.

"I was trading Blinky with Petunia."

"What?"

"India, you really should learn their names." At my blank stare, she added, "The leprechauns' names." She shook her head in disgust.

I rubbed my left shoulder. "Ina, what about the cat?"

"Right. I was out here moving the gang around, when I heard a terrible ruckus from your apartment. I mean really terrible. Banging. Screams and yells. It was awful. I thought for sure you were being murdered. You know the town's homicide rate skyrocketed this week."

Yeah, from zero to one.

"I broke into your apartment with my key, and Templeton was beatin' the stuffing out of this little guy. Your wildcat was in a rage. He was biting and scratching. Just awful. I clapped my hands, and Templeton ran into your bedroom, but poor little fella just lay there. I felt for sure he was half-dead. I picked him up as gentle as could be and brought him over to my place to care for him. He didn't make a peep while I tended him and brushed his fur back into place. Templeton might have rabies. Won't that be sad if you have to put him down?"

"Templeton does not have rabies," I enunciated each syllable.

Ina looked doubtful. Theodore hung over her thin arms like a swooning maiden. It really wasn't the best day for me to referee cat wrestling. "Can you watch Theodore for the rest of the afternoon, until they both settle down?"

"Why of course. I'd hate for anything to happen to this little fella."

Little. I snorted mentally. "Do you need a litter box or anything like that?"

"No, no, I have everything I need for Fella, left over from Archie."

Archie was Ina's prehistoric feline who floated to the big catnip garden in the sky three years ago. The cat had lived to age twenty-five.

"I'll wash Archie's things down real good for the fella." Glumly, she added, "They've been collecting dust for so long."

"I better check on Templeton." I hurried into my apartment. I shut and locked the door behind me. For whatever that was worth. Ina had a key.

Tufts of black and gray cat fur littered the living room and kitchen. I followed the line of fur puffs down the short hall into my bedroom, where the real battle had raged. Fur covered the bed and the fitted sheet had innumerable tears. My laziness had paid off. If I had made my bed that morning, the cats would have shredded my grandmother's quilt.

Templeton slept in a tight ball in the middle of the bed. The slumber of the triumphant. I sat on the bed next to him, and he opened one yellow eye. A tuft of gray fur hung from his mouth.

After checking the cat over for injuries and finding none, I carried him to the kitchen where I presented him with a peace offering in the form of a can of tuna.

Even with the unwelcome distraction of Feline D-Day, I couldn't chase the image of Mrs. Blocken and the vase of flowers from my mind. I had to think of a better plan of attack to find the origin of that photograph. Only I, and now Mark, knew that I'd stolen the photo from his office. If I continued to ask about it, suspicions would rise. Even O.M. had asked me why I wanted to know if they'd misplaced any photos of Olivia. I could easily imagine what her mother would say. I would have to be subtle. I laughed in spite of myself. My parents had not set any example in subtlety.

A tap on the door knocked me out of my reverie. Ina. Theodore was draped over her right shoulder, covering her entire torso.

"Why is the door locked?" she asked.

"I didn't want Templeton to get out and wreak havoc in the

neighborhood."

Ina ignored the transparent lie. "In all the excitement, I forgot to tell you that that filthy Englishman stopped by earlier."

"Filthy Englishman?"

"That detective fellow."

"Detective Mains?"

"Yeah, that's right." Ina adjusted Theodore higher on her shoulder.

"What did he want?"

Ina thought for a minute. "Let me see," she paused. "He showed up when I was breaking Fella and Templeton apart. I'd left the door open, and he waltzed right in. Isn't that like the English, always invading something?"

"What did he want?" I repeated before she could travel too far off track.

"I'm getting to that," she said. "Of course, I'd remember better if Fella and I had a place to sit."

Mutely, I let her in. She sat on the edge of the velvet sofa and placed Fella, aka Theodore, next to her. In my peripheral vision, I watched Templeton streak to my bedroom. I wanted to tell her to get on with it, but Ina does everything according to her own sense of timing, so I waited.

"He asked if you were home, and I said no. Then, he asked if I knew where you were, and I said that you do not consult me concerning your schedule." She bestowed me with a look.

"Is that all? Did he say why he wanted to see me?"

"No, he didn't. Normally, I would have asked, but I was so worried about Fella here, I didn't. I thought Fella was a goner, for sure. But you're made of stronger stuff; aren't you, boy?"

The cat purred agreement.

"Thank you for telling me, Ina, but I have to be off again . . ."
Ina cocked her head at me, not picking up on the obvious hint.

"I don't think that Templeton and Theodore should be

together for a while, so if you could take Theodore back to your apartment, I'd really appreciate it."

"I see your point." She rose and hefted Theodore back onto her shoulder. "Where are you off to, in case you get any more surprise visitors?"

I ushered the two to the door. "Tell them, I'm at the dentist."

If Mains was looking for me, I knew I needed to find out about the engagement picture fast before he figured it out. Dr. Blocken was the next obvious person to talk to, and I was betting that he was at his office. When Olivia and I were kids, that's where he'd always gone after a fight with his wife. I just hoped that he'd talk to me.

CHAPTER TWENTY-SEVEN

Dr. Blocken's dentist office angled onto the square, a circle of manicured grass and centennial sycamores surrounded by pavement and flat-faced store fronts. The Presbyterian and Lutheran churches indicated east and west, respectively. The square's real estate is a coveted commodity in Stripling and parking on the square even more so. However, at one-thirty on a summer weekday afternoon, I easily found a space two buildings down from Dr. Blocken's office, which butted hips with a beauty parlor on the right and a CPA on the left. A tanning salon leased the second floor of his building. Meticulously renovated with Western Reserve airs, the building shone as if it existed at the turn of the twentieth century. A large white wooden tooth declared DR. DONALD BLOCKEN D.D.S. over the main entrance.

A woman smoking a filter cigarette stood under the tooth. Blond, burly, and busty in office casual dress, her head appeared to sit directly on her bosom like a basketball on a lopsided shelf.

The basketball rolled left to right as I approached the door. "Closed." She took a long drag from her cigarette and added, "Family emergency."

I felt my shoulders droop.

"If you have some type of dental emergency, all of Dr. B's patients are being referred to Dr. Keller over on Darcy Avenue." She spoke with rapid-fire precision like a woman too busy to relish her words. "We don't take walk-ins anyway. You didn't have an appointment, did you?"

I shook my head.

"I didn't think so. I would've known."

"I'm a friend of the Blocken family and was wondering if I could speak to Dr. Blocken on a non-dental matter."

She picked stray bits of tobacco ash off her tongue. "You're not a reporter, are you?"

"No."

"There was one from the *Dispatch* here earlier today, salivating at the doorstep. If you are a friend of the Blocken family, you certainly know why."

"Olivia."

She nodded. She looked me up and down, starting at the crown of my head and stopping at the tip of my toes. "What happened to your toe?"

"Cooler fell on it."

She grunted. "Dr. Blocken's here. What did you say your name was?"

"I didn't. I'm India." I omitted my last name.

She followed suit. "Nance. I'm Dr. B's office manager." She held out her hand. I shook it.

She dropped her cigarette on the walk and crushed it with her flat foot. "Wait here while I tell him." Nance dug a key out of her hip pocket and unlocked the office door, shutting it behind her. For the next ten minutes, I witnessed downtown Stripling loll through the long July afternoon. A handful of pedestrians shuffled by, and the garden club, grouped on a nearby corner, argued over the cause of the drooping petunias fringing the edges of the square. Some members decried too much water; others claimed not enough.

The door opened, and Nance peeked out. "He'll see you."

She led me through a mauve and walnut waiting room and

past sterile, white-blue examination rooms to an inner sanctum. Dr. Blocken's office was much like his home, expensive, tasteful, with artfully-selected décor: conspicuously manly, dark, and intimidating.

Dr. Blocken hunkered at an expansive mahogany desk. My parents would suspect that the wood was stripped from a virgin African forest. The desktop was clear of files, papers, and all the other usual office trappings. Its only decorations were a green-hooded desk lamp, a telephone, and a broken plaster mold of a painful-looking underbite.

Nance's eyes boggled when she saw the broken mold.

Dr. Blocken looked apologetic. "I dropped Nella Perkins."

Nance bustled out of the room and returned a minute later with a dustpan and small dust brush.

"Nance," Dr. Blocken said. "Schedule an appointment with Mrs. Perkins to create a new mold. Sometime next week. Inform her that the visit will be free of charge."

"Of all the molds to drop. The old bat. She's a gagger. The last time I fitted her for a mold she spit the compound into my eye. On purpose too." Nance brushed the last of the mold dust into her pan and marched out of the room.

With Nance and what was left of Nella Perkins's underbite gone, he invited me to sit. I chose one of the two armchairs flanking the desk. The buttery leather would give my father heart palpitations. The chair nearly swallowed me.

Dr. Blocken, resembling a bear with a particularly tricky pinecone, fumbled with a pen in his hands with ragged fingernails, and I could imagine how the mold had ended up in pieces.

I placed my bag on my lap, using it as a shield. "Thanks for seeing me."

"Seeing you reminds me of Olivia as a little girl. Back then, it was hard to see one of you without the other," he said.

I shifted, trying to think how to start. I was facing a broken man who just lost his daughter. My own losses in life were so much smaller by comparison. I didn't know what to say. How does anyone know what to say at times like these?

I took a deep breath and tried my best. "I'm very sorry for your loss. I want you to know that. Olivia was a good friend, and I'll miss her."

"Thank you." He turned the pen over and over in his hands. His reading glasses slipped further down his nose. He removed them and tossed them onto the desk. They skittered across the glossy surface and came to rest next to the phone. He laughed. "I haven't cried. Do you think that's wrong?"

I folded and unfolded my hands in my lap. "We are all still in shock." After a pause, "Have arrangements been made for the funeral?"

He laughed, hollow and short. "My wife's taking care of all of that, just like the wedding. I don't know anything about it. I only know the place and time."

"And what is that?"

"Tomorrow. Afternoon. At the Lutheran church. It should be quite a production. Regina will get her event of the season after all." His tone was bitter. "Everything will be picture perfect for the funeral and the wake afterwards. She was nearly hysterical this morning because she couldn't find the engagement picture that she'd ordered."

My pulse quickened. "Engagement picture?" My voice sounded impossibly high. I hoped that Dr. Blocken would not notice.

"A framed copy of Olivia and Kirk that she'd planned to put by the guest book at their wedding reception. She wanted to report it missing to the police, even though I said it was nonsense to bother them with things like that. Of course, things will be misplaced at a time like this."

"The police?" My heart skipped a beat.

"She's convinced the missing picture has something to do with Olivia's death. She thinks everything has something to do with . . . the murder." He clutched the pen tightly in his hands as if brandishing a knife.

"Maybe Kirk has it," I said, hoping to throw suspicion somewhere else. In my mind, I apologized to Kirk.

"Kirk? Regina already asked him. He denies taking it."

"When did Mrs. Blocken talk to him about it?"

"Yesterday. Our meeting was not a pleasant experience. Olivia never picked a man worth his salt."

I ignored the implied slur against my brother, knowing that he hadn't been thinking about Mark—at least not at that moment.

"Kirk's successful," I excused. "He owns a pretty successful business."

"Don't defend him. If he was so wonderful, he wouldn't be causing problems over where Olivia's buried. She wasn't married yet; it's our right to decide what she'd want."

There was no way to ease into my next question, so I just asked. "What about Olivia's car?"

He blinked at me. "Why would we bury her car?"

"No, I mean, didn't she have some type of car to get around Stripling while she was here?"

"Why do you want to know that?"

"I'm wondering how she planned to get around town while she was here. I'm sure there were a lot of last-minute errands for the wedding."

"She and Kirk flew from Virginia, and we picked them up at the airport. She could've borrowed one of our cars if she needed one."

"Do you know where Kirk is staying?"

"The Cookery Inn. I'm sure it's costing me a fortune."

I wasn't surprised that Kirk was staying at the Cookery. It was the best hotel in Stripling and not far from the square and the Lutheran church where the wedding was to have been held. It was also the place where Mrs. Blocken had been planning to hold Olivia's lavish reception.

Dr. Blocken's eyes narrowed. "Why? Are you looking for him?"

"I just wanted to give him my condolences. I'm sure he must be devastated."

Dr. Blocken snorted. "I hope you didn't come here to petition on his behalf."

"I didn't."

"Good. In fact, I'm glad you came here. You're the only one who can convince Mark to turn himself in. You have to do that, and if your friendship with Olivia meant anything to you, you will. You can spare all of us, my family and yours, the grief of a long, drawn-out trial."

I bit the inside of my lip, thwarting a smart-mouthed retort. "Dr. Blocken, I know that my brother is innocent. He never would have hurt Olivia."

"I was afraid you'd say that. I was hoping that you'd listen to reason. Your brother was angry, upset. Maybe was an accident, but it happened. We both know how he was about Olivia. The thought of her upcoming marriage made him snap . . ."

I shook my head, unable to speak, hoping that my head shake was enough.

"I see that you are wearing blinders where your brother is concerned. You always have." He hit the intercom on his phone. "Nance, can you show India out?"

I stood. "I am truly sorry about Olivia, but my brother is innocent."

Dr. Blocken looked away from me, out the window that gave him a scenic view of the square. A tear slid down from the corner of his eye.

My heart broke for him, and tsking about Nella the Gagger the whole way, Nance led me to the door.

Hurrying to the car, I planned to unlock my trunk. I pushed the carpet back and exposed the tire well.

"India," someone called.

My head connected with the trunk's lid.

Ann Barnard, my mother's long-time secretary, ran toward me from across the square. Her tight brown poodle curls and wide hips bounced in tandem with her awkward stride. "Thank goodness I caught you."

"What's wrong?" I slammed the trunk shut.

She doubled over, hands pressed to her knees. She gasped, "The reverend called and said if I heard from you, I should tell you—and, while I'm on the phone, I spotted you, standing right across the street, plain as day." She took three more gulps of air.

I held her shoulder. "Tell me what?"

"Mark," she gasped. "He's been arrested."

CHAPTER TWENTY-EIGHT

I fished a water bottle out of my car and instructed Ann to drink. She chugged the twenty ounces like a salty seaman. After some coaxing, I convinced Ann to follow me back to the church. I was afraid she would pass out from the heat.

When we entered the church office, Ann moaned when she saw the flashing red light on the answering machine and sank onto a small loveseat in the corner of the room.

The church office was a testament to Ann's abilities. Or lack thereof. Piles of office paper and old service bulletins indicated the location of her desk. The telephone tipped precariously atop the mound of files and memos; all incoming lines had lit up.

She held the water bottle in a viselike grip; the plastic crackled in her grasp. "I can't take it anymore. I love your mother, you know that. She saved me and my family, but I can't take it anymore. Not one more thing. Not one more thing," she mumbled to herself. "I know she cares, but I can't work under these conditions. Not without her here to help me."

I put my hands in the hip pockets of my shorts before the urge to slap her overtook me.

"I'll resign today." She sniffled.

I watched without feeling any sympathy. On average, Ann vowed to resign twice a month. I knew the routine. My mother would console her, and Ann would agree to stay a little while longer.

I took three giant steps away from the loveseat, putting myself out of smacking range. I wasn't in a mood to be gentle. "Tell me what she said about Mark."

She rocked in her seat and tapped the empty bottle on the side of her head.

"Ann," I said sharply.

She jumped.

"Tell me," I said, trying to mimic the voice of God—or at least that of my mother.

"I'm sorry, I'm so sorry. Here I am, worrying about myself, and your poor brother's in trouble. I'm a horrible person. I'll resign today."

I knelt down in front of her, shooting for the compassionate deity. "You're not a bad person. Please, tell me what my mother said."

She blew her nose. "Mark was arrested at the Reverend's house about an hour ago. A neighbor saw the arrest and called your father's cell phone."

"Where are my parents, do you know?"

"At the Justice Center. Protesting. Reporters have been calling left, right, and front. I'm sure they'll be mobbing me here any moment."

"Is that all she said?"

"I should have asked more questions. I'm horrible. I should've asked."

I was losing her again. "Ann, listen to me, I'll have Saul drive you home. You can have the rest of the day off."

"But the Reverend!"

"I promise you, my mother won't mind. You've had a rough day. Will your daughter be home?"

"I think so."

I stood up. "I'll be right back."

I found Saul Mellon, janitor, in the sanctuary dusting the pew seats. With headphones on his ears, he jived down the aisle.

Before Ann and Saul left, I called Ann's daughter to make sure someone was there to monitor Ann and administer the correct dosage of antidepressants.

Running on adrenaline, I double-checked the church's locks, then ran three blocks in my sandaled feet to the Justice Center, figuring it would take me longer to find a parking place than to get there under my own steam. As I trotted that last half block to the building, I could hear my parents' faithful troop. "Hark! Hark! Bring back Mark!"

I skidded to a stop when I had the building in sight; the soles of my sandals slapped my heels. A crowd of forty or so townspeople had gathered outside Stripling's municipal building, grandiosely named the Justice Center. It held the police department and the mayor's office.

The demonstration blocked the walk and spilled over into the public library's parking lot next door. Gathering my courage to enter the fray, I elbowed through the spectators, until I had a full view of the scene. Carmen was at the top of the stone steps that led to the large white doors of the police station, getting into Mains's face. He looked pained. The commotion swallowed her words that she punctuated with sharp finger jabs into the detective's chest. Having been on the receiving end of one of Carmen's rants more often than I could count, I felt a twinge of sympathy for the detective.

Below on the crowded sidewalk, my parents and cohorts decried injustice and waved their placards at the bottom of the steps. The placards' sayings were the same as those I'd seen at Martin that morning. The troops, abuzz with the excitement of the arrest, stood erect in their orthopedic shoes and grasped their signs proudly. A half dozen uniformed officers stood between the protestors and the spectators. A TV van procured a corner of the Justice Center's lawn, the same crew I had seen that morning at Martin. It appeared they had *carte blanche* to park on the grass all over town. The reporter stood outside the van jotting down some notes.

"Dia!" a tiny voice called in the crowd behind me. My brother-in-law Chip carried Nicholas through the mob to stand beside me.

"Where's Mark?" I asked without preamble.

"Uncle Mark got arrested like Saint Paul," Nicholas said.

Chip shook his head, his eyes on Carmen the entire time. "I promised the midwife that I wouldn't let her get overexcited and look at her."

"You should know by now you can't make Carmen do anything," I said. "Tell me what happened. I want to know everything."

Chip gnawed on his lower lip. "Carmen and I just got here. Your mom left a message on my voice mail that we were to pick Nicholas up at the Justice Center. No further explanation. We rushed here. I found Nicholas, and Carmen went berserk when she saw that guy she's talking to now."

Talking was a euphemism.

"And?" I prompted.

"That's all I know, I swear."

Nicholas copied his father. "That's all I know, I swear."

"Who is that guy anyway?" Chip asked.

"That's the detective on the case. Rick Mains." I didn't add that he was also Carmen's ex-boyfriend. Chip didn't need the extra anxiety that that bit of information would bring. The guy was a saint for voluntarily marrying into our family as it was.

"I'm going to try to talk to Mom and Dad."

"Good luck," Chip said. The worried look was still plastered on his face as he watched Carmen rip Mains limb from limb.

During our short conversation, the crowd had grown around us. Again, I elbowed through the crush. At the picket line, I had a clear view of my parents. Both were flushed with chivalry and the cause. I glanced around for any windmills.

"Can't let you through, Miss. Orders of the detective," the burly officer explained. His nameplate read, Officer Knute.

I pointed at my parents. "They're my parents. I'm Mark Hayes's sister."

Officer Knute looked doubtful and shook his head. "Sorry."

"I have ID." I rifled through my oversized shoulder bag. Like a faithful pet, it rested on my hip.

He looked at my driver's license, but shook his head. He did that a lot. "The detective said, no one gets through."

I pointed to Carmen who had given up skewering Mains with her index finger and was now waving both her hands erratically in his face as she continued to lecture him. "How did she get through?"

Officer Knute grimaced. My sister was not one to take no for an answer.

"Couldn't pistol whip a pregnant lady, could you?"

He turned pink. "Watch your mouth."

In my peripheral vision, Kirk strained to break through the police line ten feet to my left, and was stopped by a female officer who was a few years younger than me and had an impossibly straight nose and beautiful, thick, curly black hair. He roared at her. She roared back, towering over Kirk by half a head. His body pulled taut. His biceps and shoulder muscles bulged against the thin cotton of his blue T-shirt. When the officer rebuffed him for a third time, he clenched his jaw.

I stopped pushing against the barricade. "Thank you for following your superior's orders so thoroughly."

Officer Knute gave me a look I suspected that he reserved for funny farm pickups.

I allowed myself to be swallowed into the crowd as I moved closer to Kirk. When I got within five feet, I saw a face behind him. Bree.

Bree placed her hand on Kirk's shoulder. "Please let me take you back to the inn."

He rounded on her. My heart jumped into my throat when I saw his face contorted by anger and driven by grief. He glared at Bree. "You can leave if you want, run off with that pansy librarian. Do you even remember Olivia? I'll stay here and make sure that bastard gets what he deserves."

Bree recoiled, but the crowd trapped her beside Kirk. Furious tears poured down his face. Seeing Kirk like that I could believe that he was capable of pushing Olivia into the fountain hard enough to kill her. I looked away.

To get the image of Kirk's expression out of my mind, I focused on an elderly protestor marching in his own circle, and maybe to the beat of his own private drummer. The gentleman's bifocals bounced on his nose with the rhythm of his steps, and a sprinkling of resilient hairs blew in the light updraft he created with his swaying placard. Of the contingent, he marched the closest to the police line. He proudly carried his banner by Kirk and the female officer.

At that moment, with reflexes honed by countless hours of heart-pumping aerobics, Kirk threw out a fist. Missing the officer completely, he punched the elderly protestor in the eye. The shocked officer faltered. Taking advantage of her weakness, with a tribal yell, Kirk barreled into the demonstration.

The crowd surged back and forced me away. I couldn't see who Kirk pummeled next, if he pummeled at all. The roar was deafening. Above it all, I heard my father through his megaphone, "Turn the other cheek. Turn the other cheek. Passive resistance." His voice was pitched high with excitement.

Mains rushed down the stone steps in the direction where I'd last seen Kirk. Carmen hobbled after him.

My father continued to shout encouragement. "Do not re-sis—" His voice broke off, and my heart skipped a beat. If Kirk hit my father . . . I didn't complete the thought.

Mains's voice called over the megaphone, "Show's over folks. Clear out. Or you'll be arrested for loitering."

No one moved.

"Now!"

The throng broke apart. Excited gossip flew threw the air as people scurried back to their cars. The TV reporter spoke closing remarks into the camera.

Free of the crush of excited townsfolk, I was able to see my parents and their bedraggled crew of merry men and women. My mother attempted a last stand.

"We have a right to protest. Have you ever heard of the Bill of Rights? You're the same pigheaded boy that you were in high school. I should have never allowed you to take Carmen to the prom," she told Mains.

"You're welcome to protest but not within five hundred feet of this building. If you don't move, I'll be forced to arrest you."

She held out her wrists. "Go ahead. I have been in worse jailhouses than this. I marched on Washington in Seventy-Two."

Lord, I thought.

I walked up to the line of the police and found myself eyeball to eyeball with Officer Knute again. "Excuse me?"

Officer Knute's face was flushed and his hair ruffled. "No one's allowed to pass."

"Don't you think that's just a formality now?"

Officer Knute should give glaring lessons at the academy. His were especially heartfelt.

Mains glanced at us while dodging my mother's insistent index finger. "Let her through," he told Knute.

"Detective—"

"Do it."

I flashed Officer Knute an angelic smile.

The officer Kirk had dodged had him on his stomach with

her knee on his spine. She grabbed his arms and pulled them together behind his back.

"Don't do that," the punched protestor exclaimed. He sat on the Justice Center's lawn, his hand over his already blackening eye. "I don't want to press charges."

The officer ignored him and handcuffed Kirk.

"But I don't want to press any charges."

My father wheeled over to his side. "What Christian charity. That's very kind of you, Stan."

Stan got up slowly and clapped my father on the shoulder. "Alden, I don't know when I've had such a time. How exciting!" He beamed at my father.

Mains left my mother's objections and joined the small crowd gathering around Stan.

"Take him in," he told the arresting officer.

She yanked Kirk to his feet. Dirt and specks of asphalt peppered his T-shirt and khaki pants. Kirk spotted me as the officer lifted him from the ground. He didn't speak; he didn't have to speak. Perhaps he was the one who should be giving out glaring lessons.

Stan's face fell. "But I don't want to press charges."

Mains nodded to the officer, and she frog-marched Kirk up the department's stone steps. He didn't resist. Stan's declarations of goodwill became louder.

Mains cut him off. "Mr. Row's under arrest for disturbing the peace, even if you don't press charges."

The tone of command silenced Stan. My father whispered to his protégé.

Mom picked up where she left off, pointing at Mains's chest, "Furthermore—"

I stepped in front of her. "For goodness sakes, Mom, call it a day. None of this is going to help Mark."

"India Veronica Hayes, you will not interrupt me when I'm in the middle of a private conversation."

I flushed with embarrassment and anger. Before I could make a smart remark—and I had a few beauties in mind—my father wheeled over. "Lana, she's right. We must regroup."

"I want to see my son. I demand that I see my son," Mom said.

Mains stood his ground. "You can't visit Mark right now. He's in the middle of being booked."

Booked, I thought. My stomach felt queasy. Mains glanced away from my mother, who had planted herself squarely in his line of sight, and met my gaze. "If it's any comfort, his lawyer is with him," he said. For a second his hard look softened, but it was so quick I wondered if I'd imagined it.

My mother scowled. "It's not."

After a few more minutes of arguing, Mom seemed to realize that Mains wasn't going to change his mind and agreed to go home. As their small band of players dispersed, the television correspondent shouted questions. Well trained by my parents, nobody would comment to the press. A uniformed officer walked over to the news crew. The show was over. After several minutes, they left. My parents loaded their placards into the van. Chip buckled Nicholas into the back seat of his hatchback. I watched their activities carefully, making certain every member of my family intended to leave the Justice Center.

Carmen threw a parting shot at Mains as she walked to her husband's car. "I expected better from you, Ricky. I'll remember this."

Mains watched her walk away with a bemused expression. He left his officers to supervise and entered the station. My sister and her family drove away.

"India, do you need a ride?" my father asked.

"No, I'm parked on the square."

He nodded. "Meet us at the house. Lew will be over after

he's done here."

I nodded, but dreaded another family council of war.

Before climbing into the van, my mother looked down at my feet. "My word, India. What happened to your toe? Did one of those hooligans crush it during the tussle?"

I sighed. Seemed everyone was thinking about anything and everything . . . besides Mark. I looked up at the imposing building. Somewhere in there, my brother sat, alone and scared. I hoped Lew could get him released.

CHAPTER TWENTY-NINE

Lew shook a smoke and a lighter out of a crumpled pack of cigarettes. He lit up, ignoring my parents' complaints. The scene in my parents' living room was eerily similar to the one that occurred Monday evening. My father sat attentive and anxious in his wheelchair, Lew sat in my father's armchair, my mother and Carmen paced canyons into the floorboards, and I stood off to the side with my arms folded.

One glaring absence disturbed the reenactment: Mark.

"The police searched Mark's apartment this afternoon and found evidence that links him to Olivia Blocken's murder," Lew said.

Carmen gasped, stopping dead in her tracks, and I wrapped my arms more tightly around myself.

"That's impossible," my mother said with a fierce mother lion look on her face.

"What was that?" Carmen asked.

"A scarf that matches the sundress Olivia was wearing the day she was killed."

"That doesn't mean he killed her, for goodness sake. Maybe he picked it up at the scene when he found her. He was in shock," Carmen said.

"Mark insists that he's never seen it. Honestly, I'm surprised they haven't searched his apartment before now. I have a friend at the department who said Mains got an anonymous tip this morning, suggesting the police check out Mark's home." He took a long drag of cigarette. "Lana. Carmen. Sit down. I can't think with you marching around me like a damned German battalion."

Carmen perched on the arm of the sofa, but my mother continued pacing, but more slowly. Lew shrugged, apparently resigned. "Because Mark was arrested late, I can't get a bail hearing until tomorrow morning at the earliest. Let me tell you, the district attorney is salivating over this whole thing. It's the biggest case of his career, and he was not impressed with the little stunt you pulled in front of the Justice Center this afternoon."

Mom frowned. "We have every right to—"

"Lana, I'm well aware of your constitutional rights, thank you. I'm afraid Mark will spend the night in jail."

Carmen stood. "We can't let that happen. Mark didn't do anything wrong." She resumed her march around the sofa.

"I understand your concern. But I've been to the jail many times. It's small, cozy even. There are only a few cells. Stripling isn't exactly Gotham City, nor is Stripling's jail Grand Central. First thing tomorrow, I'll post Mark's bail. I'll request it, but there's no way the judge is going to release him on his own recognizance. However, the D.A. cannot refuse a bond settlement with Mark's history in the community. I'll warn you that the price for his release may be fairly steep." Lew removed a sheet of paper from his breast pocket. "Traditionally, the district requires ten percent of the bail be paid up front, or you could make arrangements through a bail bond company. This is a list of bondsmen in the county that I trust, in case you need help coming up with bail. Like I said, I expect it to be rather high."

Neither of my parents reached for the paper. Lew finally placed it on the coffee table.

"We won't be posting bond," my father spoke.

"What?" Carmen squawked.

"We won't be posting bond. Mark's innocent, and I won't be contributing my money or any of our money to a justice system that's set to condemn him."

Lew's face fell, but he quickly regained control. "Alden, I understand and respect your principles, but, all lawyer-talk aside, that's a plain stupid decision. The trial could be months away. The DA needs the time to build a case against your son, and, frankly, I need the time to build a worthwhile defense. Under those circumstances, the Stripling PD cannot keep Mark in their tiny holding cell. He'll be moved to a county jail or even a prison for the time leading up to and during the trial." Lew inched forward in his seat. "The men that he'll meet in these places could be hardened, Alden. Hardened criminals. God knows what they'll do to a sensitive kid like Mark."

My father flinched. "This is not up for debate."

There would be no prison time in my brother's future. I spoke for the first time. "I'll get the money you need, Lew."

"India, that is neither your responsibility nor your decision," my father said.

"It shouldn't be," I said with heat. "It should be yours, but you choked. You'd rather let Mark rot in prison for your ideals than consider his well-being."

"We've all had a long day. We'll discuss this in the morning," Mom said in the tone she usually reserved for times when budget meetings with the church elders turned sour.

"There's nothing to talk about," Dad said.

"Damn right," I agreed.

"India," my mother warned.

Carmen looked at Lew. "How much time do we have before he's moved to one of these other places?"

Lew thought for a minute. "That really depends on the prisoner transfer schedule, but I have some favors I can call in at the station. I can buy Mark a couple of days at the jail. He'll be out of there Friday, though, at the latest."

"Do that, Lew. We'll discuss this again before Mark's moved," my mother decreed.

I stormed out of the house.

CHAPTER THIRTY

I stopped at Mark's apartment to pick up a few of his things, then headed into town. Police cruisers and a few automobiles speckled the Justice Center's lot. I parked near the library. I grabbed my shoulder bag and the canvas sack I had brought from Mark's apartment.

I jogged up the stone steps. The front room of the police department was deceptively small. A glass wall and doors behind the front desk closed the majority of the department off from the public. The room resembled a waiting area in a family doctor's office. Two groupings of uncomfortable chairs book-ended the desk. The four side tables held collections of back issues of magazines. A ficus plant languished in the far corner beyond the reaches of natural light. The department was not the typical Stripling-chic to which most public buildings in the town aspired. It is one of the few town structures where function trumped form. The Stripling Historical Society bemoaned this fact.

The front desk was a four-foot-high counter bolted to the linoleum floor, similar to the reference desk at Ryan Memorial Library. Behind the desk sat Officer Knute, who didn't appear pleased to see me.

"May I help you?" he asked, offering nothing of the kind.

"I'd like to speak with Detective Mains, please."

He raised an eyebrow. "Don't you think it's a little late to be speaking to the detective?"

I glanced at my wristwatch. It was just after nine. I hadn't realized the time. Mains had probably gone home hours ago. But maybe he hadn't. Maybe Officer Knute just didn't like me.

I narrowed my eyes at him. "Is he here?"

Officer Knute grumbled that he was.

"Then may I speak to him?"

"Your name, please."

"India Hayes. I'm Mark Hayes's sis—"

"Yeah, yeah," he interrupted. He'd heard it before. Knute made an in-house call. "This is Knute at the front desk. . . . There's a woman here to see you . . . about the Hayes case. . . . She claims that she's his sister. India. . . . If you're sure, sir. . . . Right-oh." He hung up the phone. This time when he addressed me, he was much more polite. "Please take a seat, it could be a few minutes."

I sat on one of the chairs on the desk's right flank. It was as uncomfortable as it looked. I shifted on the hard plastic surface, so that it didn't hit me directly on my tailbone.

I didn't wait long.

Mains stepped through the glass doors. His tie and jacket were gone, his shirt collar open at the throat, and his brown hair stood on end as if he'd been pulling on it throughout the day. He raised his eyebrows at me.

"Hi," I greeted him as if it was ten o'clock in the morning and we were old pals.

He stood waiting for me to continue.

I stood up and hefted my bag to my shoulder. "I'm sorry to bother you so late."

Knute snorted from his station at the desk.

"I want to apologize for any problems my parents and Carmen caused today."

He laughed. "I felt like I was back in high school. Your sister hasn't changed a bit."

"I'm afraid not," I replied.

"I appreciate your apology, but I doubt that you came all the way down here just for that."

"I, um, I—"

"Spit it out," he said.

"Can I see Mark?"

For a half second, I thought Mains looked disappointed, but it must have been my imagination. Whatever his first reaction was, it was immediately superseded by doubt. "We don't usually allow a suspect's family member to visit our jail cells this late in the day."

Knute clicked manically on his mouse, probably playing Solitaire. The clicking slowed as he eavesdropped.

"I won't take long. I want to make sure he's okay."

"I can assure you that we take fine care of our wards here," he commented, as if offended.

"I'm not implying that you've mistreated Mark in any way."

Mains scratched the stubble on his chin. "I suppose a few minutes can't hurt. I'll take you down."

Knute stopped clicking altogether.

Mains slipped a magnetic key card through the scanner bolted to the glass door's frame. A buzzer sounded, and I followed him through the door. Through the glass wall, I glanced at Knute. I was wrong. He wasn't playing Solitaire; it was Free Cell. He glanced from my gaze to the screen and back. I winked at him.

The duty room was a conglomeration of green and beige metal desks placed in islands like a fourth-grade classroom. Mains and I were the sole occupants. I rubbed my eyes; the lights were grotesquely bright. Mains stopped at a desk. Unlike the other work stations about the floor, which were sprinkled with personal possessions and family snapshots in inexpensive frames, Mains's desk held a soup can of pens and pencils, an ancient black telephone, and two large stacks of file folders. The bottoms of the file folders ran perfectly parallel with the edge of his desk. If the cop thing didn't work out, Mains would make an excellent librarian.

Mains made a call. I was pretending not to overhear when I spotted Mark's name on one of the files. It took all my will power not to grab the manila folder and flee the building. Mains told whoever was on the other end of the line, "We'll be down in a minute. . . . Uh-huh. . . . It's his sister . . . the other one . . . right." Mains laughed, and then glanced at me. He followed my line of sight to Mark's file and stopped laughing. "Ten minutes tops," he said and hung up. "Find anything of interest?" Mains asked me.

"Nope," I replied with a sweet smile.

"You'll see your brother. I can only give you a few minutes."

Mains walked across the room to a secure steel door leading to the stairwell. I followed him down steep steps. Our footsteps echoed in the hollow space, and the stairwell smelled like the inside of a freezer.

As a Western Reserve municipality, Stripling connected itself with civilized New England and distanced itself from its Midwestern-ness. The small city had a three-volume tome of building codes that emphasized Western Reserve construction, a mishmash of nineteenth-century New England architecture carried west by Connecticut businessmen. The city council enforced the building codes with an iron fist, which forced the jail level of the Justice Center to be built underground. I thought about Mark shivering deep in the pit of the building. My stomach tightened. He was alone and scared, wondering why no one had gotten him out of there yet. Mark was far too sensitive to be angry about the injustice of it all. It was my job to be angry, and I felt myself become more furious by the minute as we walked down the stairs. I was glad that I was following Mains, and he couldn't see my face. I didn't want him to know how I felt. I needed to be on his good side to help my brother.

We walked down another flight of cement stairs, and the temperature plummeted.

"Is Kirk down here?"

Mains glanced back to me. "We let him go."

I stopped dead. "What?"

"Regina Blocken and the mayor's wife are on the Garden Club, the library board, and the Women's League together. If that guy he clocked wouldn't press charges, I couldn't hold him without the department's backing."

"I didn't know the Blockens even liked Kirk."

"The family is not one for scandal of any kind. I got the impression that she plans to send Kirk back to Virginia as soon as possible."

We reached a third steel door. I wondered if it was inlaid with lead or maybe kryptonite. The stairwell emptied into a damp hallway. The temperature dropped another twenty degrees. Goosebumps crawled across my bare arms. I touched the tip of my nose; it felt like an ice cube. At the end of the hallway was another steel door that had a card scanner. Who did they have down there anyway? King Kong? I wondered.

Mains swiped his card through the scanner. The officer who had arrested Kirk at the protest waited on the other side of the door. Her name plate read V. Habash. Her curls were barely restrained into a ponytail at the nape of her neck.

"Evening, Detective," Officer Habash cooed. Maybe I imagined the cooing.

Mains gave the officer a broad smile and a wink. I hadn't imagined anything. "Officer Habash." Mains nodded.

Mains turned to me. "India, Officer Habash will search you. It's protocol."

"Uh, right, of course," I said as if I was an old hand at this.

"Step over here, please," Officer Habash directed. "Hold out your arms."

She worked swiftly, starting at my armpits, and patted down the length of my body.

"She's clean," Officer Habash told Mains. As if I could hide anything in a tank top and a pair of nylon shorts, I thought.

I was carrying my shoulder bag and the canvas bag from Mark's apartment. "I'll have to search those too, ma'am," Officer Habash stated.

Ma'am? Come on, I thought.

I reluctantly handed her the satchels. She rummaged through my shoulder bag.

She then moved to the canvas bag, unzipping it. "Huh?"

Mains sidled over and took a peek inside the bag. "What are these for?" he asked.

"Well, I—"

"I know you're a librarian, but . . ." He dumped the bag on a metal tabletop with a succession of muffled thuds. Half a dozen paperback books fell out of the bag, some were mathematics texts, but most were mystery and fantasy novels. A half-realized smile played on Mains's lips.

"He's stuck in that cell with nothing to do. With nothing to read. I hoped I could give him some of his books to take his mind off things."

Mains's face broke into a full-fledged smile. "So having nothing to read is the worst punishment you can think of?"

"Just above Chinese water torture and thumb screws," I remarked with, what I hoped, passed for an endearing smile.

Officer Habash watched our exchange with a bemused expression.

"Officer Habash, search the books, please. Make sure she's not hiding any box cutters between the pages."

I stopped just short of rolling my eyes.

Officer Habash flipped through the books.

I watched her with a sigh. I was anxious to see Mark, and I was becoming colder by the minute. "I don't know what I could possibly hide in those books."

Mains looked at me. "You'd be surprised. With your upbringing, I'm sure you have a lot of tricks up your sleeve."

"And what is that supposed to mean?"

Mains grinned. "I dated your sister, remember?"

Like I could forget.

"They're clean," she said. I wondered if Officer V. Habash watched a lot of crime show reruns.

"I'll allow the books, Miss Hayes, but only three. Pick three," Mains said.

I looked down at the titles scattered across the desktop. The request was similar to, "If you were stranded on a deserted island and could only take one thing, what would it be?" But the scenario was worse. "If you could only read three books for the rest of your life, what would they be?" I chose Mark's favorites: a calculus book that he'd owned since he was eleven, *The Two Towers*—don't ask me why that's his favorite fantasy novel—and *Travels with Charley*.

"Fine," Mains said after I had made my selection. "Leave your other things here."

I followed Mains into the holding block with the books clenched tightly to my chest.

CHAPTER THIRTY-ONE

The cell block's outer walls were smooth and steel-plated. The room held three cells. The first was empty; the other two were occupied, one by an intoxicated man and the other by my brother.

The drunk clung to the bars of his cell. "Well, well, if it ain't Mister Big Time Detective Mains. And who do you got there?" He leered at me, making me wish I was wearing thick snow pants, a heavy parka, and stout working boots. "Is she your girlfriend?" To me he added, "Looking real fine today."

Mains wrapped the metal bars with the flashlight in his hand. "Shut up, Phillip, and sleep it off."

"Now, how am I supposed to sleep in the same room with a murderer? What if he goes ape shit and attacks me in the night?" Phillip slurred.

"I said, shut up," Mains growled.

Mark cowered on the bottom half of a metal bunk bed, behind silvery bars, each an inch in diameter. Mains set a folding chair in front of Mark's cell.

A thin gray blanket wrapped around Mark's head and shoulders. His cell contained a relatively clean sink and a toilet, though I didn't inspect them at length, and the cell's two walls were painted a redundant gray.

Mains rapped on the bars of Mark's cell with his knuckles. "Hayes, you have a visitor."

Mark jolted and peered out of his cotton cocoon. His glasses sat precariously at the tip of his nose. "India?"

He jumped up and banged his head on the bunk above him. Catching his foot in the blanket, he toppled onto the floor. "Ow," the crumpled heap moaned.

"How's anybody able to sleep with that racket," Phillip complained.

I stood up from my chair. "Mark, are you hurt?"

Mains stood alert, his back pressed up against the bars of the opposing cell.

Mark stumbled up. "I'm all right." He rubbed the back of his head.

I swallowed a hysterical chuckle. I slid the books through the bars. "I brought you something to read."

He took the books from my hands. "Thank you," he whispered. He lovingly placed the books on the bottom bunk.

Mark still wore the same T-shirt and shorts that he'd had on when he'd popped out of the bushes that morning. "Are you sure you're all right?"

"Yeah. Maybe I can sue the police for damages," he joked mirthlessly.

Mains remained silent.

"Not a good idea under the circumstances," I said.

"I suppose you're right." Mark walked up to the cell's bar with the blanket wrapped around his shoulder like a wizard's cloak. "It's freezing down here, though." He rubbed his hands together.

"Could he get another blanket?" I asked Mains.

"Hey! I want another blanket too," Phillip remarked.

Mains replied a noncommittal, "I'll see what I can do."

Mark rubbed the knot on his head. "Lew said I should get out on bail tomorrow morning. It's only for one night, right? And now I have something to read."

I bit the inside of my lip, afraid to tell Mark of my parents' no-bail policy and, until I had the bail money in my hand, I didn't want to tell him about my plan to get him out of jail. Luckily, Mark changed the subject himself. He dropped his voice. "The police showed me the scarf they found in my apartment. I've never seen it before." He lowered his voice further, and I leaned my ear to the bars. "It's like the you-know-what."

Mains cleared his throat, and I jerked back. Subtlety is not a tradition of high regard in my family, and Mark was particularly bad at it. He gave me an exaggerated nod and look.

"Time's up," Mains said.

"Right, I'll bring it up with Lew. Well, if there's anything else you need, tell Lew, and we'll try to get it to you," I told my brother.

"A teaspoon and a file would be nice."

Phillip gripped the bars of his cell. "There's a few things that you can get me, honey."

I spun around and faced the drunk for the first time. "Like what?"

"India," Mains said, as he stepped between us. "Let's—"

"Mr. Rosengard?" I squeaked.

The drunk blinked. "How—"

"You were my third-grade teacher at Eleanor Elementary."

Phillip blanched.

Once upstairs, Mains insisted on walking me to my car. "Go back inside," I said. "This isn't exactly the 'hood."

"Not a chance. If anything happens to you between here and your car, your parents will have my head on a platter."

My car rusted under a lamppost, quietly forlorn. I unlocked the door. "See? Perfectly safe."

"I'm sorry about Phillip's behavior in there," Mains said.

"It's not your fault, but I'm in serious need of a shower. My entire perspective of third grade has changed."

Mains laughed that awful laugh again, but it didn't seem as

awful as before. Like a Byzantine bas relief, half of his face hid in the shadows, the other half was overexposed in the garish yellow light. I wished I had paper and charcoal pencils to capture it.

I was reluctant to leave and oddly torn. Mains wasn't playing for my team; he was on the other side.

"I remember you, you know," he said when I was about to say goodnight.

"What?"

"From the time Carmen and I dated in high school. You must have been twelve or thirteen then. And I came over to your house to see Carmen. You were sitting in the front yard, plopped right in the middle of the lawn, scratching away in a sketchbook. You wore a peace T-shirt and your glasses were about to fall off your nose. I had to repeat your name five times before I finally got your attention. And when you did look up, you said, 'Carmen's not here,' and went right back to sketching." He paused. "Do you remember that?"

"No," I answered.

But I did remember.

CHAPTER THIRTY-TWO

The next morning, I was back at the library. "I could never be a librarian; it's too much like work," Nasia complained.

I wondered if Lasha would be sad to hear that her daughter would not be following in her footsteps. Probably not.

Andy, a lanky student worker at the library, raised one eyebrow at her. "What would you like to be?"

The fourteen-year-old thought for a minute. "A professional snorkeler."

"A professional snorkeler," Andy teased. "There's no such job."

"Yes, there is," Nasia countered with heat. "Like when people snorkel, they need someone to show them how. That's what I'm going to do."

"Where are you going to snorkel? Lake Erie? The Cuyahoga River? You know the river caught on fire once."

"Obviously," Nasia said, with a look that indicated she was talking to the mentally deficient. "I'd have to move to Tahiti."

Erin interrupted their banter. "Why am I the only one working?" She held a pile of reference books that began at her belt buckle and ended at the tip of her eyebrows. I followed Erin with an equally large stack.

Andy, who had an irrepressible crush on Erin, quickly took the stack from her and placed it on the carpet. Nasia and the two student workers were helping me shift the reference collection. Books can become overcrowded on the shelves with new purchases, and shifting is a method to make more room on tight shelves. Unfortunately, it causes almost every book in the collection to move, creating quite a job, which is why I put it off until the last minute. After one full bookshelf, Nasia had demoted herself from active participant to head cheerleader.

I hoped the physical activity of shifting five hundred heavy reference books would keep my mind off the fast-approaching afternoon and Olivia's funeral. It wasn't working.

Our progress was slow, and a third of the way in, the recruits were already waving their white flags.

Nasia picked up a microbiology tome that weighed more than she did. "Who cares about this stuff?"

"Maybe a microbiology major," Andy said.

"Hey," Erin said. "Don't get those out of order. I organized that entire stack."

"Chill," Nasia replied.

"Okay, guys," I relented. "Let's take a break."

Andy slumped onto the floor, limbs flung out. "Thank God."

When I reached my post at the reference desk, Nasia had fled the scene and Erin and Andy had planted themselves behind the checkout desk. Andy tried to strike up a conversation with Erin, leaning his elbows and back against the counter. She grunted in reply. I laughed to myself and didn't notice Bobby and Bree enter the library until they stood directly in front of me. I suppose they were wearing what could be classified as funeral chic: dark colors, sedate, well cut, and understated.

Clever as ever, I said, "Oh, hi." I really needed to sharpen my greetings; my speech continually regresses to that of a fifteen-year-old—and not an especially bright one.

"Hello, India," Bree spoke mournfully.

Bobby nodded; we hadn't spoken since I had accosted Bree in the parking lot on Monday afternoon.

"India, I'm so sorry. I promised to tell you when Olivia's

funeral service would be. When I didn't see you at the visitation hours yesterday, I remembered I hadn't told you," Bree said.

"No need to apologize, Bree," I said.

Bree licked her glossed lips. "I'm so sorry about the position you're in. We all know that you're not responsible for your brother's actions."

I bit the inside of my cheek. Unable to speak, I forced a snarl into a sad smile.

"We'll look for you at the funeral," Bree promised.

"India, can I have a word?" Bobby asked.

"Why not?" I said, but my tone was sharp.

Bobby grimaced. "Bree, I'll meet you in the car."

If Bobby's dismissal surprised her, she didn't show it.

"Shoot," I said after she disappeared.

"Not here." Bobby motioned to the stacks.

I sat at the reference desk longer than necessary to make my point and then followed him. Bobby led me to the farthest corner of the library's main floor by the microfilm machines. To see an undergraduate this deep into the recesses of the library would be like seeing snow fall in Miami.

I brushed dust off the end of the microfilm reader, leaned against it, and crossed my arms. "You couldn't speak to me at the reference desk because . . ."

"Please, India, don't be a brat," Bobby said.

"A brat? You heard what she said. She thinks Mark did it."

"Bree doesn't know Mark, okay? She's making a decision that she can understand from the information she has, and from what the Blockens have told her."

"Have you told her otherwise?"

Bobby played with the collar of his hundred-percent-cotton dress shirt. I had my answer.

"We don't really talk about it," he conceded.

"What do you talk about?"

"Other things. Give her a break. Her mother's ill."

"What's wrong with her mother?" My tone was more civil.

"Multiple sclerosis."

"Oh," I said, subdued.

"Yeah. Her mom's only fifty-eight. She's in a nursing home somewhere in Virginia, and not a very good one either. Bree's having a tough time, being away from her."

"I'm sorry to hear that," I said, mollified.

Bobby patted me on the shoulder, accepting the weak apology. "Don't worry about it."

"Is Bree still staying at the Cookery Inn?" I asked as we trekked back through the labyrinth of shelving to the reference desk.

"For now." He gave me a sidelong glance.

"Oh," I replied, wondering what *for now* meant. I promised myself to study the thesaurus during my late shift. I recovered. "You know, she's a perfect heroine for one of your stories."

Bobby laughed. "I think so, too."

"I'm not copyediting that one," I said.

"We'll see you at the funeral?" Bobby asked.

I nodded, although the thought of going to the funeral and seeing Mrs. Blocken again made my stomach clench. I slid into my seat behind the desk.

He winked and walked over to Bree who was sitting on one of the couches by the new bookshelf. She looked very prim with her legs crossed and her hands folded on her lap. She was a much better bridesmaid candidate than I ever would be. Not that either of us were bridesmaids anymore.

Chapter Thirty-Three

I waited until the last possible minute to leave for the funeral. If I timed things correctly, I would be able to slip into the sanctuary before the service, but avoid greeting anyone.

On the square, I parked in the Presbyterian lot and hurried across the square to the opposing side.

The Lutheran church's whitewashed siding and narrow steeple juxtaposed against the Presbyterian's red brick and leaded stained glass. Minivans, SUVs, and family cars crowded the parking lots around the square. Even more vehicles blocked the tiny Lutheran lot. The hearse and caravan were primed and ready to drive to the gravesite.

The church's open doors allowed the summer breeze to tease the mourners in the unair-conditioned building. Ushers in sedate Sunday suits flanked the sanctuary's tight entry.

"Running late, Miss?" one whispered. He led me to my seat, thankfully in the back.

I smiled weakly at him. I found myself seated next to a Martin professor I recognized, but couldn't name. She nodded at me and glanced at her watch.

A pipe organ droned from overhead in the balcony. No matter how well the non-denominationals have marketed a praise band, you would never find a drum set or a synthesizer in these Lutherans' midst, only a stately pipe organ, and when they felt frisky, an upright piano.

The ceiling peaked at eighty feet high; wooden buttresses

supported its weight. The room held approximately twenty rows of pews split down the middle by a three-usher-wide aisle. The Blocken family and Kirk sat in the first two rows left of the aisle along with some members of the Blockens' extended family who looked vaguely familiar. O.M.'s blue hair glowed in the muted sunlight that shone through the narrow windows. My seat was one row up from the last on the right.

The coffin, which dominated the center of the aisle, stood closed with a blanket of yellow lilies and pink roses draped across its length. I exhaled an unwittingly held breath at the sealed casket. I'd been given the gift of remembering Olivia in life alone.

The professor gave me a look of reproach. Perhaps she taught etiquette to the plethora of home ec majors on campus.

Bobby and Bree sat in the row behind the Blockens, shoulders touching. Bobby glanced over his right shoulder every few seconds, scanning the crowd. I slunk low in my seat.

The minister rose from his seat behind the pulpit. Rev. William Myer had been the senior pastor at St. Jude Lutheran Church since before I was born. For the last year he had been on the verge of retirement but had yet to make any formal announcement. He would be sorely missed by his congregation when he did decide to trade in his prayer book for a garden trowel. Many of the Lutherans feared their synod would send a fresh-faced seminarian to their majestic grounds to promote church growth and attract young people. Rev. Myer hadn't bothered with either of those pursuits in decades.

My mother and Rev. Myer traded wedding or funeral gigs when one or the other was out of town, which usually consisted of my mother on an idealistic crusade or Myer fishing in Canada.

The funeral bulletin contained a short biography of Olivia and a copy of her obituary, which I hadn't read. I didn't read it then either. The service would be short with a brief sermon from Rev. Myer and a few hymns. No eulogies or Bible readings from family or friends. The simplicity of Olivia's funeral stood in stark contrast to the extravagance of her wedding.

Rev. Myer motioned for the assembly to rise. The organist caressed the chords of *In the Garden.*

When the final note of the hymn ceased, Rev. Myer spoke in his somber baritone. "We are not here to mourn, but to celebrate the vibrant life of Olivia Blocken. When the young are taken from us, the pain is that much greater. But we have hope in the resurrection of our Lord Jesus Christ."

The more I strained to listen, the less I heard. Only snippets of phrases broke through my barrier: "loving," "excellent student," "community involvement," "Olivia." I bit the inside of my lip, shoulders tense with barely managed emotion. For the last few days, my brain had known Olivia died, but my heart hadn't accepted that fact. I was an expert at diversion, and I distracted my heart with work, my parents, the Blockens, and Mark. But now, my heart slammed into a sharp learning curve.

A kernel of fear crept into my mind like the haunting note of a hymn. If I had never befriended Olivia, if I had never allowed Mark to run around with us, maybe Olivia would never have been on Martin's campus that day. She'd still be alive with a different bridesmaid number three, one that's more attentive, one that's more caring, one like Bree. I shivered.

The ushers *cum* pallbearers marched up the aisle two-by-two. Rev. Myer turned his back to the assembly and placed his hand on the sealed casket in silent prayer, smothering a lily. The Blocken family, including Kirk and Bree, rose and shuffled out of the sanctuary to the melancholy chorus of the pipe organ. Rev. Myer followed them in his black robe. The procession ended with the coffin and pallbearers.

Another pair of ushers dismissed the mourners row-by-row. From my row, I noted who attended the service and who did not. The mayor and his wife were among the first to leave, followed by some Martin dignitaries, including Lepcheck and the president. Cowardly, I pretended to read Olivia's bio when Lepcheck passed my shoulder. Even after I knew he was gone, I continued to stare at Olivia's bio. Three brief paragraphs. Again, I couldn't read it.

Someone pinched my arm. Bobby smiled down at me. I smiled back. The reception line had stalled. The Martin professor leaned over me. "Bobby, it's so good to see you. Are you a friend of the family?"

Bobby glanced past me. "Good afternoon, Adele. A friend of a friend."

"Oh, it's so nice that you would sacrifice your afternoon for a friend of a friend."

Bobby grimaced. I looked away, afraid that I would laugh.

"I know this isn't the best time, Bobby, but I was wondering how the library plans to increase its materials budget for the philosophy department. If Martin wants to add such a prestigious major, they need to have the right resources for those students," Adele droned.

"You're absolutely right, Adele."

She beamed at him.

"The line's moving." He gave my arm another pat and moved on.

Adele settled back into her seat in a huff. An academic scorned. I kept my mouth shut about the materials budget for the philosophy department. Lasha had mocked the proposal when it had crossed her desk.

A pimply faced usher fidgeted next to my seat. I led my row into the reception line.

The narrow narthex and doors of the church made it impossible for me to escape the line. I rubbed my sweaty palms on my skirt as I shuffled closer to the Blocken contingent.

Bree shook my hand first. "So good of you to come."

I nodded. I tilted away from the Blockens, who were greeting the stream of mourners.

Bree, clinging to my hand, yanked me toward her. I stumbled. "I see an opening after the woman in that god-awful bird hat. You can sneak through the door," she whispered in my ear.

I glanced at the woman in the hat, which was truly hideous, a wide black mesh number with a small starling clinging to the brim. A small opening revealing summer sunlight twinkled behind her, enough for a small man or an aggressive woman to slip through. I whispered a thank-you to Bree.

Safely on the sidewalk, I rotated my tense shoulders under my thin suit jacket. The square was congested with mourners, hearse, and caravan. A Stripling police officer stepped out of his cruiser to direct the gridlock. I wove through a tangle of autos to the relative safety of the square's center green, a tiny park with ancient sycamores, park benches, and a gazebo for weddings. I hurried through it and another tangle of vehicles to the Presbyterian lot.

The steering wheel burnt my hands. As I rolled down both windows and leaned back on the scorching vinyl headrest, I clenched my eyelids.

A loud metallic pop like an exploding aluminum soda can startled me. A featureless face leaned into the car. I screamed, giving any B movie heroine a run for her money.

CHAPTER THIRTY-FOUR

"Relax," a voice broke through my hysteria. "India?"

I gulped down the last cry on my lips. Psycho killers don't usually know your name. Unless they're stalkers, my brain added. I took a breath to scream again.

"It's Rick."

Rick? Rick who? Mains. Oh. Does he want me to call him Rick? I'm not calling him Rick, I thought.

I peered through the open window. Mains's face loomed white as Santa's beard. Served him right.

I braced my hands on my chest and thrust my heart back behind my sternum. He backed up from the car door.

"You nearly gave me a heart attack. I could sue the city for this. Terrorizing law-abiding citizens," I said.

"Whoa there," he said as if I were a testy gelding. "I didn't mean to scare you, but you overreacted."

"Overreacted? Overreacted." I struggled out of my car and the heavy door pinched my left calf on the way out. After freeing myself from the metal beast, I slammed the door shut. "Maybe you haven't noticed, but I'm a little on edge."

Mains threw his hands up like one of his perps. "I said I was sorry."

"Yeah, well." I couldn't think of anything to end the sentence. I leaned on the hood of the car to mask my confusion.

I noticed how the sunshine reflected off Mains's dark hair. Carmen had been right: he did have great hair. No, no, no, no. I will not do this. He's not cute, I told myself. I can't think that. I tried to focus on Mark freezing to death in the Justice Center jail cell. Leave, my brain begged. Leave now.

Mains interrupted my inner debate. "Who was that guy you were chatting up at the funeral?"

"You were at the funeral? I never saw you."

"I sat directly behind you. You never looked back."

He must mean Bobby, I thought. I took a breath. "Why do you care who that guy was? Is he wanted for something?"

He scowled and wiped his damp forehead with a gray handkerchief that matched his tie. "We need to talk."

The metal hood burned the back of my thighs, but I didn't move. The temperature camped in the high eighties and the humidity was as stubborn. I removed my jacket and tossed it through the open window onto the seat. "Why, Detective?"

"Your brother was arraigned this morning. To my surprise, Lewis Clive stated that bond would not be posted on Mark's behalf."

I ignored the implied questions. "How much?"

"A hundred thousand."

"A hundred thousand dollars," I whispered. "Why?"

"The judge believes Mark is a flight risk."

I had a sinking feeling. "Who was the judge?"

"The Honorable Martha Luckas."

As I feared. Back when the Honorable Martha Luckas was only a public defender, she was my family's next-door neighbor on Kilbourne Street. Many times, my daydreamy brother would ride his mountain bike through her impeccable front lawn and flower beds in his haste to return home to his beloved calculus problems.

"Of course, it would be her." I laughed mirthlessly. "A flight risk? Mark doesn't know a soul outside of Stripling." I pressed the heels of my hands into my eyes and willed myself to breathe normally.

"By the way the judge was staring down your brother, Mark's lucky she set bond at all."

I removed my hands. "Is Stripling really this corrupt?"

"Not corrupt," Mains said, nonplused. "Small." He folded his arms across his chest. "Why isn't your family posting bail?"

Before I could answer or avoid an answer, heavy footsteps approached from behind. Unwilling to be caught unaware again, I spun around. Kirk jogged across the parking lot. He waved a hand over his head. "Detective!"

Mains stepped away from me and approached Kirk.

Despite the humidity, Kirk wasn't winded from his jaunt across the square, a fringe benefit of his peak physical condition. Another benefit would be the ability to crack Brazil nuts with his biceps.

Mains greeted Kirk in muted tones, but Kirk spoke normally. "How's the case going? Are you going to get him? I would've been at the courthouse today, if it hadn't been . . ."

Mains made uninformative and generic statements about the case against my brother, obviously aware of my proximity.

"I can testify," Kirk declared. "Anything to put that bastard away."

My best recourse was to slip into my car and drive away. The ancient door hinges wailed under the simple movement. With the speed of a greyhound, Kirk was beside me. He smacked the hood of the car. I wondered if the automobile would require body work after all its post-funeral love taps. Not that the pounding could make it look much worse.

"What the hell are you doing here?" he demanded. "You shouldn't have been at her funeral. You weren't invited." His face was the color of an overripe raspberry.

"Last time I checked, Kirk, funerals didn't require RSVPs.

Furthermore, I've known Olivia my entire life and have every right to attend her funeral."

Kirk stood inches from me, pressing me back into the car. I straightened to my full height and looked down at him. "You and that brother of yours orchestrated Olivia's death," he growled.

"What kind of crock conspiracy theory is that? And is *orchestrated* your word for the day?"

"India," Mains warned, edging closer.

"Mark had nothing to do with Olivia's death, and neither did I."

Kirk pressed against my body and lifted his hand as if to strike. Mains was there in an instant.

He grabbed Kirk's wrist in a viselike grip. "If you hit her, Mr. Row, you will spend the rest of the day in jail, no matter who Regina Blocken calls." He released Kirk's wrist.

Kirk lowered his hand. "Tell that brother of yours it's prison or the funeral home."

Mains yanked Kirk away from me. Kirk stalked off across the parking lot.

Mains watched him cross the street, then turned to me. "Are you all right?" His expression was one of true concern.

"Fine," I whispered.

Maybe Mark was better off in jail. Even with that in mind, I would do my best to get him out.

CHAPTER THIRTY-FIVE

I had resituated myself behind the reference counter at Ryan when Erin approached the desk with a handful of yellow while-you-were-out slips. She fanned them on the counter. "I didn't go to college to be a secretary, you know."

I thanked her, and she looked at me strangely, probably because she expected a smart retort; I disappointed her.

"Four messages from your mother, each more hysterical than the last, and another two from some dude named Lewis Clive."

The first message from my mother read, "India, call me immediately." Followed by "India, call the second you get in." Then, "India, turn on your cell phone and call me." Finally, "India, this is your mother. I'm expecting a call."

Erin leaned on the counter. "She had me read them back to her to make sure that I got the emphasis just right."

"Fantastic."

"India, what's going on? Rumors on campus say that your brother's in jail for murdering that woman in the fountain. Everybody already knows that he's been fired."

I took a deep breath. "Suspended," I corrected.

"Whatever," she said, as if the distinction meant nothing.

"Erin, I really can't talk about this with—"

"Anyway, I told them they were full of it. Professor Hayes would never hurt anyone." Before I could respond, she turned and retreated to her post at the checkout desk.

During my break, I went to the student union to return Lew's phone call. A lone graduate student slept in a dimly lit booth. Piles of books, notebooks, and printouts hid the table's dark surface and his face.

I slipped into an empty booth and turned on my cell phone. The tiny digital screen announced that my mailbox was full. I bet I knew who most of those messages were from. I dialed Lew's number.

"It's about time you called," Lew rasped.

I made no apology. "Isn't a hundred thousand dollars a little steep for bail?"

"Oh, you heard. Your mother called, I suspect."

I didn't correct him.

I heard Lew take a long drag. I feared my eardrum would be inhaled through the phone. "A hundred thousand is not unusual for a murder rap, but I agree that it is high in Mark's case. I asked the judge to release him on his own recognizance, just as a formality, but I knew she'd never buy it. With Mark's ties to the community, etcetera, I can't understand the exorbitant amount, especially since the DA is only charging him with manslaughter. I objected heartily, but no go."

Oh, only manslaughter. Well that makes things so much better, I thought.

"The judge and Mark have a history," I said and told him about the trampled flower gardens.

"Oh. God, I hate this small-town crap."

I agreed and longed for the anonymity of Chicago. Maybe I should have stayed there after art school.

"That explains that. The judge took one look at your brother and set her jaw. It didn't help that your parents were kicked out of the courtroom for disturbing the proceedings. Do you know they had T-shirts made up? But I don't have to tell you about your folks, do I?"

"No, you don't. Were the Blockens there?"

"Just the doc as far as I could see, and pretty unemotional. Olivia's funeral was today."

"I know; I was there."

"Ah." He inhaled.

"How did Mark react?"

"He sniffled a little. Thank God, he didn't cry." Lew coughed and took another mouthful of nicotine.

"I mean, to my parents not posting bond."

"I haven't had a chance to tell him yet. The courtroom was in such an uproar after Luckas's decision that he was taken from the room before we could speak. I'm on my way to the jail right now."

I ended the call and walked back to the library.

By late afternoon, I was more than ready to go home. The week had robbed me of what little librarian fervor I'd had, and my eyes drifted shut, then jerked open at a tapping on the reference counter. I opened them to Lepcheck's scowl. His perpetual grimace matched his understated, but pricey funeral suit nicely. Lasha stood behind him with her arms crossed over her expansive chest in a gleaming kelly green pants suit. Ina would've approved of the ensemble.

"Do you have a reference question, Dr. Lepcheck?" I asked in my best helpful librarian voice.

He tugged on the tip of his goatee, a perturbing habit. "Ms. Hayes, Dr. Lint and I would like to speak to you in her office."

"Who will watch the reference desk?" I asked, instantly regretting it.

He scowled. "Now."

I followed their ridged backs, one black, one kelly green, toward Lasha's cramped office. We passed Andy and Erin. Erin glanced up from a novel and Andy from a gamer Web site. The looks on their faces were those of witnesses watching a friend enter a Texas gas chamber. Dead librarian walking.

Lasha hadn't tidied her office for the occasion. The innumerable stacks of library books in varied stages of acquiring or discarding covered every flat surface including the four chairs. Lasha pushed the piles off three.

Lepcheck looked around, but refrained from comment. His thin-lipped expression spoke volumes, though. He walked around Lasha's desk and sat on her desk chair. Lasha's expression spoke volumes, too. She sat on one of the three armchairs facing the desk. I chose the chair closest to the door, but before I could sit down, I tripped over a stack of library catalogs, falling into Lasha's desk and knocking a pile of magazines to the floor. Clumsily, I restacked the magazines. I bit my lip to stop myself from speaking. Furtively, I glanced at Lepcheck.

Lasha sighed, and I let out an exhale of relief when Lepcheck didn't say anything.

Lepcheck tugged his academic goatee twice more and steepled his fingers, which were slender and long, his nails buffed to a shine. Lasha crossed her legs and her arms as if to shield herself from the arctic draft wafting off of Lepcheck's person.

"Ms. Hayes," he said. "You've startled the college this week with your behavior."

During any moment in academic life that the college was subjected to personification, it's time to duck and cover. Lasha winced, making me feel more at ease. She wasn't on his side.

Lepcheck studied me over his manicured hands. "I fear that the unfortunate situation with your brother has skewed your focus."

"Skewed my focus?" My tone was ironical.

"Martin College is an institution of great esteem and respect in this community."

Esteem and respect. I hadn't known.

"With that position, a level of prestige and honorability must be retained. In the last week, Martin College has fallen short of its expected level of . . ." he paused, ". . . respectability. Olivia Blocken's misfortune was a sad circumstance for her family and for the town of Stripling. But, Ms. Hayes, it was also an unfortunate circumstance for Martin College, due primarily not to the location of the act, which is disheartening to say the least, but to the involvement of a Martin faculty member. The college has received innumerable phone calls and emails from parents concerned about their children. Martin College has fostered a reputation as a safe environment, but with the latest turn of events, that reputation is beginning to wane."

I gripped the arms of my chair. I was going to be fired. I could feel it in my bones. Fired for failing to curtsey when Lepcheck entered the library, fired for being the offspring of crazies, fired for being the sister of Stripling's most wanted. It would obviously be a wrongful dismissal. Lew would certainly litigate on my behalf, and my parents' like-minded friends would take up arms, but would I be able to survive a long court case? And if I won, would I be able to return to Martin?

Lepcheck spoke a few more sentences that I missed. I tuned in when he was in mid-tirade. "However, the college understands that you are not responsible for your brother's actions."

"Alleged actions," I said. They don't think I'm responsible. Maybe I won't be fired. Or at least not today, I thought.

Lepcheck affected a weak smile. "Nevertheless, we are concerned about your involvement on your brother's behalf. Please understand that as long as Mark Hayes is a suspect in Olivia Blocken's death, the college cannot in good faith reinstate him as a member of the faculty. The prime objective for Martin College is student safety."

Followed closely by tuition revenue, I mentally added.

Lasha frowned. "Sam, is there a point to all of this?"

Lepcheck winced most likely at Lasha's casual use of his

moniker. He adjusted his position in her desk chair, maybe to remind her where he was. "The point of all this, Ms. Hayes, Dr. Lint, is simple. Martin College can no longer tolerate disturbance to the education and betterment of the young people on this campus. This goes for any planned or impromptu rallies established by your parents and/or friends on your brother's behalf. If these disturbances continue, the college will be forced to take action."

"What type of action?" Lasha asked.

"That will be determined when or if the time comes." He tugged on his goatee one more time. The lord and master had spoken. I knew that he was expecting a bow or at the very least a brief round of applause, but Lasha and I are not obliging in these types of situations.

Lepcheck looked at his watch, nodded as if in satisfaction, and rose. Evisceration in less than twenty minutes—a new personal record.

After he'd run off to ruin someone else's day, Lasha spoke, "Martin doesn't have a leg to stand on if they fire you. You know that. Lepcheck's a weak man with weaker threats. He's threatened me half a dozen times, and I'm still here."

"True," I agreed, cheered a tad.

Lasha looked thoughtful. "The sooner this mess with your brother is cleared up, the better for your brother, for the town, and for you."

"I know." I shifted in my seat.

"Are you still taking the weekend off?" she asked.

"The weekend?"

Lasha walked behind her desk to the staff calendar. "You requested it off months ago for Olivia's wedding. Take it off, and figure out who killed your friend while you're at it."

As if it were that easy, I thought.

CHAPTER THIRTY-SIX

I thought about going home and changing first, but I knew myself well enough and what a great big coward I was. If I didn't go directly after work, I would never go at all. Instead of turning the prehistoric automobile toward my duplex, I drove in the opposite direction toward the town square.

The Cookery Inn came into view as I turned off the square onto Blossom Avenue, which snaked behind my mother's church. The Cookery was an old Tudor-style mansion that had been revitalized into an inn in the late nineties under the threat of demolition. I remembered the event well, as my parents had chained themselves to the front door in order to block the city's wrecking ball. By some miracle, they had found an investor who had the imagination and the means to transform the languishing building into the town pearl it is today.

The estate itself had once been very large, but was sold piecemeal to those businesses that couldn't afford property directly on the square, leaving the inn on a postage stamp–sized property. All that was left of the grand estate was a large circular driveway and a garden in the back.

I parked in the circular drive behind a red compact car. A half dozen or so honeybees buzzed amidst the pink cosmos that flanked the door. The bees made me sad, because I knew how much they would have charmed Olivia.

I pushed open the heavy wooden door, which led directly into the reception hall. Dark wood chair rail ran the length of the room. Below the chair rail, the wainscoting was polished to a high sheen, and above the rail a floral wallpaper seemed to burst from the walls. The blossoms were so real they looked as if I could pluck them. On the right side of the room, a woman sat behind a desk reading a magazine. She looked up with a smile. When I approached her, her smile widened into a grin as we both recognized each other.

"Well, India Hayes, what are you doing here?" Maggie Riffle asked in her unmistakable raspy voice. During high school the sound of her approaching voice had made underclassmen throw themselves into their lockers just to avoid her. Shaped liked the little, squared-off robot that my brother played with as a child, Maggie had been my prime tormentor from kindergarten through the twelfth grade. Although I wasn't her only victim, her favorite prey had always been artsy nerds, such as myself.

I swallowed hard and greeted her. "Wow, Maggie Riffle. How are you?"

"Not Riffle anymore. I got married. Last name's Blankenship now." She held out her hand to display an enormous diamond.

"That's wonderful," I said with as much enthusiasm as I could muster. The stone was at least an inch across and two inches high. It was a wonder she didn't stab herself with it on a regular basis. "I thought you moved away after high school."

"I did," she said. "I lived out west for a few years. My husband and I moved back to buy this place. I had always loved it and when it came on the market, I just had to have it."

"That's great," I said, surprised. Maggie had never struck me as a historic building buff, but, then again, we did not share our opinions about architecture when she was tripping me in the cafeteria lunch line. "Where'd you live out west?"

"Dayton."

I mentally rolled my eyes. A three-hour drive west of Stripling to Dayton, Ohio, wasn't exactly the Rocky Mountains.

"Coo-coo." A pause. "Coo-coo."

"What was that?" I asked, looking around.

"It's those damn doves."

Quickly, I stepped away from her, hoping to avoid any bolts of lightning that came shooting from the sky to strike Maggie dead. I was pretty sure it was a cardinal sin to use a curse word when referring to a dove. Instead of the bolt of lightning as expected, I locked eyes with a large white dove that was perched at the top of the crystal chandelier hanging from the hall's ornately carved ceiling. The dove was as large as a hen. More coos echoed through the room, and I followed the sound around the high ceiling with my eyes. Two more doves roosted together in an unlit candle sconce near the French doors that led into the Cookery's impressive English-style garden. A fourth dove watched me from the black walnut railing that led up to the second floor.

"Why . . ." I trailed off.

"You mean *who*. I have Regina Blocken to thank for those buzzards. They were supposed to take part in Olivia's reception in our ballroom Saturday. That's not going to happen now. I suppose you know why." Maggie's eyes narrowed and even though I hadn't seen her in several years, I recognized her killer instinct look. I imagine that it was the same expression that a hungry cheetah wore when spotting his four-legged dinner. "I suspect you know all about that. I read about your brother in the paper. I'm surprised the little weakling had it in him. He was such a wimp in high school."

I gave her a wan smile. "Well, Maggie, that's why I'm here. I'm looking for her fiancé, Kirk Row. I was told he was staying here."

"He is, but he won't be much longer if he doesn't make good on his bill. He better not pull a fast one like the Blockens are trying to pull."

"A fast one?" I asked, confused.

"The caterer, the cake decorator, the dove trainer, or whatever that guy is, and us are all getting stiffed. The Blockens claim since the wedding was canceled, they shouldn't have to pay their bills. Luckily, I have a non-refundable deposit to fall back on for the reception hall. I guess the dove guy wasn't so lucky. Not that I won't be taking a major loss. I had three other people who wanted to rent the ballroom for this week, and I had to turn them all down because of the Blocken wedding. I called them earlier today to see if any of them were still interested, but they'd made other arrangements months ago."

"Wow, that's too bad," I said, barely containing my anger at her callousness. Had I not needed her to tell me where I could find Kirk, I would have hit her; I've wanted to hit her for years.

"You're telling me." She leaned on the reception desk, resting her arms on the guest book.

The doves cooed in tandem from above.

"If there won't be a reception, why are the doves still here?"

Maggie grimaced and shot a nasty look at the bird clinging to the chandelier. If I were a dove, I would be up in a chandelier out of Maggie's reach, too. She looked like she wanted to serve the bird up for dinner. "The trainer said he was leaving the doves here until he was paid. I told him it would be a cold night in hell before he gets his money out of Regina Blocken. If he doesn't pick them up by the end of the day today, I'm calling animal control. If he wanted to make a statement to the Blockens about the birds, he should have left them on the Blockens' doorstep, not on mine."

I felt bad for the doves, but knew that I couldn't add four large doves to the mix of warring felines back at my apartment. "I'm sure he'll come. They must be very valuable to him."

The doves cooed agreement.

"Why are you looking for Kirk, anyway?" Her dark brown

eyes were trained on me.

"I wanted to see how he was doing. I'm worried about him." This was technically true. I was worried about Kirk—worried about what he would do to Mark if he ever got his hands on him.

She shrugged. "I'm not supposed to do this, but since I'm going to kick him to the curb if he doesn't pay up, why not?"

"Gee, thanks," I said.

Either Maggie missed the sarcasm or didn't care, because she said, "He's in room twelve on the second floor." She pointed to the staircase. "Just take that staircase up there."

"Is he here?"

Maggie shrugged again. "I haven't seen him, but I can call up to his room to check and let him know that you are here."

"No," I said quickly. "Don't bother. I'll just run up there and see for myself."

Maggie's eyes narrowed. "He has a temper on him, so don't get him riled up. I don't want any damage done to my Cookery. If there is any trouble, I will have to finish that swirly that we started in high school, understand?" The seriousness of her threat was carried all the way to her eyes.

I swallowed and headed up the stairs without a word. The doves watched me warily. Upstairs, a corridor lined with wallpaper patterned after peacock feathers led to my right. An Oriental floor runner lined the passageway. The corridor was dark. The overhead light was off, and I had only the natural light from the large rosette window that loomed over the staircase to guide me. At the end of the hallway, I was grateful to see another small window. I hadn't noticed it so much on the first floor, but the Cookery Inn had that particular smell that is common to many older buildings, a mixture of must, old wood, and something else I could never quite identify. Brass plate numbers marked each door. Number twelve was the very last room.

No light escaped through from under the door. I knocked lightly. There was no answer. Of course, I had knocked so gently that it wouldn't have disturbed one of my mother's church mice. I stood up straighter and gave the door a brisk rat-a-tat-tat. Still, no answer.

The door to number ten opened instead, and a slim figure stepped out. In the dimness, I couldn't make out a face.

"India?" Bree asked. "What are you doing here?"

"I . . ." She'd caught me off guard, but even though it felt strangely like I was doing something wrong, I saw no reason to lie. "I want to talk to Kirk."

She stepped closer. "He's not here."

"Do you know where he went?"

She shook her head. "I was just about to go across the street to the café to grab some dinner, why don't you join me? We haven't had much opportunity to get to know each other."

I hesitated. I was still wary of her. If I was completely honest with myself, it was because she was the thinner, prettier best friend who had replaced me when Olivia and I went our separate ways after high school. Now, I feared that she would be taking Bobby, who was decidedly smitten with her, away from me too. But I wasn't in high school anymore and should stop acting like I was. "I'd like that," I said.

Bree and I walked downstairs to the coo of the dove. Maggie looked up from her computer screen. "You find him?"

"He wasn't in his room," I said.

"Do you want to leave a note for him?"

"No, no, that's all right. I'm sure I will catch up with him sooner or later." The last thing I wanted Kirk to know was that I was looking for him.

Maggie turned her beady stare on Bree. "I'll need payment

for your room tonight, Miss Butler."

Bree's beautiful face crumbled. "But the Blockens were going to pay for my room."

Maggie's face was hard. "Not anymore, they aren't. You and Mr. Row will be paying. I have your bill right here." Maggie slid a printout across the desk to Bree, who instantly paled when she saw the number. "But I don't have that kind of money. That's more than one of my paychecks."

"If you can't pay, I suggest that you start packing."

Bree looked as if she was about to cry.

I patted her arm. "Come on, Bree, let's go eat and sort it out."

Bree folded the piece of paper and placed it in the large leather handbag looped over her arm. She followed me out the front door

Before the door completely shut behind us, Maggie called out, "And I don't take out-of-state checks."

CHAPTER THIRTY-SEVEN

Bree and I walked to Pioneer Roast, a small coffeehouse on the square, which also served soup and sandwiches. We sat at one of the metal tables outside of the shop underneath a gauzy yellow umbrella that barely shielded us from the sun. All the other sidewalk tables were empty as most of the customers had chosen to dine in the air conditioning.

The thin waiter who I recognized as a Martin student took our order. A veggie wrap, an old standby, for me. Bree selected a chef salad.

"I don't know what to do. Olivia promised me when I agreed to help her with the wedding that her family would pay for everything."

"Well, this turn of events was unexpected." I felt the need to defend my childhood friend. "She couldn't have known what her parents would do if the wedding was canceled."

"You don't know everything I did. I addressed all the invitations. I made all the decorations for the church and the centerpieces for the reception. I spent countless hours on this wedding, and for what?" Bree's voice was high-pitched.

I frowned.

She gave me a sad smile. "I'm sorry; this has all been so horrible. I can't believe this is even happening."

"Maybe you can talk to her mother."

But Bree wasn't listening. "I don't know where to stay. My flight doesn't leave for two days." She folded her paper napkin in a series of tiny triangles, unfolded it, and started again.

"Maybe you can stay with the Blockens," I said, knowing full well that if I had been a nicer person, I would have invited her to stay with me. But truth be told, I wasn't completely comfortable with Bree, and I already had an extra cat to deal with.

She shook her head, then looked at me. "Maybe Bobby will let me stay with him. He mentioned that he had a three-bedroom house."

"Bobby?"

"He's been so nice since I arrived. Don't you think he'd want me to stay there? You're his friend; you know him better than I do. What do you think he would say?"

Knowing Bobby, and how attractive he found Bree, I knew he'd say, yippee, but I wasn't going to tell her that. "You'll have to ask him yourself," I said, hoping that she wouldn't.

The food arrived, and I dove into the wrap. I hadn't realized how hungry I was. Bree picked at her food. Not one bite reached her mouth.

I used the food's arrival as an opportunity to change the subject. "Dr. Blocken said that they are missing an engagement photo of Olivia and Kirk. Have you seen it?"

Bree shook her head. "No, but it'll show up. Everything has just been turned upside-down this week."

That was the understatement of the century.

"I hope it does," I said. I bit into my wrap and chewed thoughtfully, barely tasting it despite my hunger. "I keep wondering how Olivia got to Martin that morning."

"Oh?" Bree said, pushing a tomato to the side of the plate with her fork.

"Dr. Blocken told me Olivia didn't have car, and, according to campus security, there were no strange cars on campus that day. The only logical answer is someone drove her there and left campus before security noticed."

Bree looked up from her salad, eyes level with mine. "Your brother could have picked her up."

"He didn't," I said, putting down my wrap. The sun pounded on my back. I started to sweat. We should have eaten inside with the sane customers.

"Have you asked him?"

"Not in so many words," I admitted. "But I know that he didn't. He was on campus long before Olivia got there."

"How do you know that he didn't leave and come back later with her?"

"I checked with security. His car never left."

Bree's cell phone rang from deep in her purse. The bag was enormous, and she placed it on the table's edge in order to root through it. At the same time I reached for my water glass, knocking against it and sending it tumbling. Her possessions flew every which way, scattering on the cement walk.

"I'm so sorry." I jumped up to gather her things.

Bree instantly dropped down beside me. "It's all right. I'll get it."

I picked up her cell phone, which was now silent. Surreptitiously, I checked the caller ID and recognized Bobby's cell phone number. Then, I reached for her bag, noticing a glint of metal. Curious, I righted it, peered inside, and found myself staring down the barrel of a gun.

"Here, give that to me." She grabbed the bag, haphazardly threw her possessions in, then sat back down, her bag clutched to her chest as though she thought I'd steal it from her.

From the look on my face, she must have realized that I had seen the gun. "I need it for protection. I live alone," she said defensively.

"I live alone too," I said, "and I don't pack heat."

Was suburban Virginia so different from suburban Ohio that she really needs a gun to protect herself? I wondered.

"Is it legal?" I pushed what remained of my wrap to the far side of my plate. The sight of the gun had made me lose my appetite.

"Perfectly legal," she said. "I have a license from Virginia to carry a concealed weapon."

"But you're in Ohio. Does that type of license cross state lines?" I honestly didn't know.

"I don't have to take this lecture from you." She threw her napkin down on her uneaten salad.

I watched her go. My, some people were touchy. It wasn't until she disappeared around the corner that I realized that she'd left without paying her half of the meal. I suddenly felt touchy, too.

I walked back to the Cookery to retrieve my car with a considerably lighter wallet, my mind on Bree and her gun. But when I saw my car, thoughts of Bree fled.

Someone had keyed the hood of my car. KILLER'S SISTER was spelled out in letters a foot high. A chill ran through me, followed by fury so powerful that it made my teeth ache. Sure, it was an ugly car, and, sure, the keying didn't depreciate its financial value, especially since I would probably have to pay a dealer to take it off my hands anyway. But this was a personal attack on me, and on my brother, which was worse than the vandalism. I knew of only one person who could have done something like this.

I stomped into the Cookery. I threw open the door so violently its leaded glass shook and threatened to break.

Maggie, writing in her ledger, looked up in shock. "What's gotten into you?"

"Is he here? Is Kirk Row here?"

The doves were silent as if they feared their cooing would attract my wrath. Maggie silently pointed up the stairs. Her mouth opened, and she did not remind me to leave her beloved

Cookery unharmed.

I took the stairs two at a time. At Kirk's door, I pounded on it with all my might. He opened it almost at once.

"What are you do—" He stopped short when he saw the look on my face.

I forced my way into the room. "Did you key my car?"

Kirk folded his arms across his chest, his muscles bulged, and for the first time, I paused to consider the stupidity of my actions. Kirk may be a few inches shorter than I was, but he was at least forty pounds heavier and every ounce of that extra weight was pure muscle.

I moved back toward the door, but he was faster and blocked my way. Now, I'd done it. I'd trapped myself in a room with a man who could be—probably was—a murderer. My only salvation was my old high school bully downstairs, who, I had no doubt, would love to see me pounded into jelly. I had my cell phone in my shoulder bag, but I was afraid that any sudden movements would spur Kirk into action.

I noted the half-packed suitcase on the bed. I wondered if Maggie had given him the same ultimatum that she had given Bree.

"So what if I did. It's the truth. Your sorry excuse for a brother killed my wife," he spat.

"She wasn't your wife yet."

Kirk's face fell as though I'd slapped him across the mouth. Slowly, he slumped onto the bed, holding his head in both of his hands. Loud, heart-wrenching sobs wracked his body.

I stood over him, like a judge. "Did you plant that scarf in my brother's apartment?" I didn't mention the engagement picture since it wasn't discovered by Mains or his officers.

"No, I didn't." He wiped the tears from his eyes and stared at me, eyes glinting with anger. "He did it; he killed her. That's the proof."

He said it with such ferocity that I knew that he truly believed that Mark was guilty.

I squatted beside him, taking care not to touch him. I softened my voice. "Kirk, do you know how Olivia got to Martin that morning? Did you drive her?"

"No. I don't have a car; her parents picked us up at the airport." His voice became a hoarse whisper. "I didn't even see her that day. The last time I saw her alive was when I left her at her parents' house after the picnic. They insisted that she stay with them before the wedding instead of here at the inn with me. Olivia said it was easier to go along, rather than making a big deal out of it. I wished that I had insisted. Then she wouldn't have gone to meet your brother. She would be my wife."

He looked up again, directly into my eyes. His eyes were bloodshot. His tan cheeks were pale and drawn, giving him a startling cadaverous look. "I will hate the Fourth of July for the rest of my life."

Looking into his haunted face, I believed him.

A few minutes later, I walked through the Cookery Inn's entry once again. Maggie was still at her post behind the reception desk.

Something cold and wet suddenly splashed my bare shoulder. Instinctively, I put my hand up and came away with fingers dripping dove doo. I glared at the large dove on the chandelier. He looked back, and I could have sworn he had just a hint of a smile on his beak. All my sympathy for the abandoned doves evaporated. "Gross!"

Maggie grabbed a roll of paper towels from under her desk and hurried to my side. She thrust them at me. "Here. Hurry up and clean that up before it gets on the floor."

As if the floor was my biggest concern. I cleaned myself up the best that I could. Through the window, I saw Bree climb into the driver's side of the red compact parked in the circular drive.

"Bree has a car," I said.

Maggie blinked, holding a paper towel in mid-air. Maggie followed my gaze and watched as Bree drove away.

Maggie shrugged. "She listed it as a rental at check-in. I always ask so that I know what vehicles should and should not be on my property."

I thanked her and headed out the door.

CHAPTER THIRTY-EIGHT

Twenty minutes after I left The Cookery, I threw my keys and shoulder bag in my apartment's entryway and bid them to sit. Templeton slept in the middle of my sheet-covered sofa, opening one eye before uttering a contented sigh and curling back up. Genius that I am, I deduced that Theodore was not on the premises. Undoubtedly, Ina shielded him from devilish Templeton by hand-feeding him boneless chicken breast.

The answering machine on my snub-nosed kitchen counter blinked incessantly and declared ten missed calls, a personal record. I assumed that at least seven of those messages were from my mother. I was not disappointed.

The first nine messages were either from Carmen or my mother. I skipped those. The tenth message was from Lew, who'd called only ten minutes before I walked in the door.

Curious, I dialed his number, which I'd now memorized.

"Thanks for calling back. I just got back from the jail. I told Mark about your parents' decision about the bond." Lew let that pronouncement hang in the air.

I sat in the rocking chair. "How did he take it?"

"As well as could be expected. Shocked mostly."

"God," I murmured in a half curse, half plea.

"I just spoke with your parents. They're not budging."

I clenched my jaw. "So much for all their talk about equal rights and the common man."

"Your parents are wrong in this case. You know it, and so do

I, but they've done a lot of good in this town for a lot of people. Heck, without them, all the Martin yuppies would have total control."

"Yes, everyone should have equal opportunity to rot in jail."

Lew inhaled a mouthful of smoke. "Are you still interested in posting Mark's bond?"

Student loans be damned. "Yes."

"I called in that favor to hold Mark at the Stripling PD longer than normal, but the best I was promised was Saturday morning. If you don't want Mark to go to the county prison to await his trial, you'll have to bail him out before then." He repeated the names and numbers of three bond agencies. "You've got collateral, right?"

"Sure," I said, even though my only collateral was my car, which was suspect at best even before Kirk took a key to the hood.

Lew sighed as if he knew the true answer to the question. He probably did.

"Lew, how are you working this case? Are you looking for other suspects?"

Lew took another drag on his before-dinner cigarette. "I'm just a one-man show, and Mark's isn't my only case."

"Did Mark tell you that he heard someone with Olivia at the fountain?"

"He did. Cell phone." He echoed my own thoughts.

I thought of the engagement picture, which weighed heavily on my conscience. "That's not all."

"I'm listening."

Pounding shook my front door, followed by the mechanical click of the lock giving way. Ina barreled into the room, Theodore slung over her thin shoulder like an obese newborn. "India! Fella's sick." She rushed toward me. Theodore did look a little green. Templeton, who slept the slumber of the victorious, arched his back and hissed.

"Are you under attack?" Lew's voice came over the line. He didn't seem that concerned.

Before I could respond, my parents walked and wheeled through the open door in matching Free Mark Hayes T-shirts. My brother's likeness behind roughly drawn, black bars was preserved in blue cotton.

I cut Lew off in the middle of another raspy question as to whether I was witnessing Armageddon. "My parents are here. I'll talk to you later. Tomorrow." I hung up the phone.

My mother and Ina lobbied for my attention.

"India, where have you been all day? Why haven't you returned any of my calls?" my mother demanded.

"I think he's fainting," Ina cried and shoved Theodore's fuzzy mug into my face. "See, isn't his coloring bad? I killed him!"

Templeton was long gone by this point, in my bedroom, no doubt shredding my slippers.

My father interjected his own admonishments.

Despite my mother's powerful pulpit voice, for which the elderly removed their hearing aids, Ina won the shouting match by sheer hysteria. "He's going to die. Call the vet. Call the vet!"

"Okay," I yelled over the racket. I took Theodore from Ina's shoulder and felt his nose. It was cool and damp, although his eyes were slightly glazed. I ignored my parents, who continued to yell in my left ear. "What happened?" I asked Ina.

"Nothing, nothing," Ina protested. "I treated him like a king."

"What did you feed him?"

"Not much. Cat food," she said defensively. "And a can of tuna. A little frozen shrimp. Some cheese cubes. Oatmeal. A sauerkraut ball."

"A sauerkraut ball?" Theodore seconded the motion as I felt his stomach rumble in my arms. Oh no. I ran through the open door and threw the cat into the yard. He landed with a solid thump and threw up sauerkraut ball and God-knew-what-else on Ina's sailor-outfitted leprechaun.

My parents and Ina stood behind me dumbfounded.

"You could have killed him," Ina said. Then she saw the unfortunate leprechaun. "Oh, Fella, not on Ralphie!"

My dad wheeled over. "India, that is no way to treat an animal."

My mother heartily agreed.

Theodore stumbled and slumped onto the grass and, after a moment, began to eat it. I ignored the yelps and proclamations in my ears as I marched around the house, unraveled the garden hose, and dragged it to the front yard. I cleansed Ralphie and returned the hose to its place beside the driveway. My movements were deceptively smooth.

I stepped in front of them. Ina wrung her hands over her head; my mother shook her entire right hand at me, one finger apparently not expressive enough; and my father snapped his fingers in my face.

"Stop it," I said.

They froze like puppets with tangled strings.

Across the street, an open-mouthed neighbor, who pretended to prune her double petunias, gave up the charade and watched the spectacle, as did the man three houses down on his riding lawnmower.

"Stop it, all of you!" I became painfully aware that I was yelling at the top of my voice, but was unable to reduce my volume.

"India, you're making a scene," Mom said.

"Making a scene? What do you think you're doing? Or what you're always doing, huh?"

My father opened his mouth to speak.

I held up one hand to stop him. "No. I'm sorry that I didn't call you back. I had to work. I went to a funeral—" I stopped mid-sentence, choking on the word. The finality of it, the finality of Olivia's life was too much. For better or worse, Olivia had been my best friend for the vast majority of my life. She was a friend who listened to me whine for countless hours about my parents, a friend who came to all my art exhibitions even though it was most definitely not her crowd, and a friend who saved me from the evil clutches of Maggie Riffle and her coven of bullies-in-training. Seeing Maggie again had reminded me that it was Olivia who had saved me from that near swirly. That had to count for something. That loss was worth the inattention to my parents. Apparently, they did not agree, and I knew never would.

I shook my head, trying to sort out my thoughts, trying to think of something that I could say to them that could make them understand. In my silence, my parents and Ina began shouting again. The words I needed did not come to me because they did not exist. I turned away from them, stepped into my apartment, and shut the door. I secured the lock, deadbolt, and chain. After unplugging my landline and turning off my cell, I went to bed.

A half hour later, the knocking at my front door finally stopped.

CHAPTER THIRTY-NINE

The next morning, I woke up in my funeral outfit with Templeton kneading my head with his forepaws. I reached up to pet him and felt the dried dove poop on my sleeveless blouse. I shuddered. I blinked my eyes, fatigued from staring at the ceiling most of the night, and stumbled into the shower fully clothed.

An hour later, dressed in shorts, T-shirt, and running shoes, I felt twenty percent human and eighty percent idiot. The guilt from my outburst haunted me. Ina was right—I would make an excellent Catholic.

I plugged in the phone and grabbed a new box of raspberry toaster pastries, Ina's favorite. I hopped over the iron railing that divided our porches. It was seven-fifteen; Ina would be on her third mug of Irish Cream coffee.

There was no answer when I knocked. I knocked again, and Ina threw open the door.

My hand caught suspended in the air. I waved. "Good morning," I said brightly.

Ina scowled. Her ensemble that morning was lemon yellow pedal pushers and a lime green tank top.

I held out my peace offering like a Girl Scout making her pitch. Giving the inside of my cheek a good chomp before I spoke, I apologized. "Sorry I blew up at you yesterday. I was angry at my parents, not you."

Ina took the box of pastries from my outstretched hand.

Taking this as a sign of goodwill, I pressed my luck. "I know that you were just worried about Theodore. You're a terrific cat sitter. Mark's really grateful." Or, he would be if he knew.

Ina examined the box. "Raspberry?"

I nodded.

Ina's withered face broke into a glorious grin. "Come on in, Sweetie. Let's have breakfast."

If things were that easy with my parents, I'd write a personal letter of thanksgiving to the cereal company.

The layout of Ina's apartment was the mirror image of my own, but that's where the similarities ceased. Ina's apartment had all the novelty and, well, greenness of an Irish specialty shop skirting Boston Common. The carpet was green; the curtains were green; and the walls were green. Shamrocks decorated the lampshades and doilies, and clay pots of house-plants were painted to resemble pots of gold. A large icon of St. Patrick held center stage on the wall directly across from the couch. However, the apartment held remnants of Ina's former life—the life before the senator's letter—in the heavy mahogany furniture and silver frames of deceased relatives.

Ina dropped the pastries in the toaster. "Fella's doing much better. He's in the bedroom, sleeping it off."

"Ina, I'm sure that he only had a stomachache from all he ate yesterday. You should only feed him cat food, at least for a while," I told her as gently as possible.

"I gave Archie table scraps all the time. He always turned up his nose when he was full, but Fella never turned up his nose. He kept eating. Made me wonder if that brother of yours ever fed him."

I sat on the bar stool by the abbreviated counter. "Theodore is well fed. Any scale will tell you that. He doesn't understand the concept of full, or, for that matter, self-restraint."

The toaster popped, and Ina tossed two extra crispy treats

onto a saucer for me. The edges smoked. I bit off a corner and burned the roof of my mouth. Penance. I ineffectively waved my hands in front of my mouth,

"Yes, some don't understand self-restraint," she remarked.

After Ina's pastries were charbroiled, and mine had cooled to a temperature akin to the shady-side of the equator, I took three steps, Ina took six, and together, we sat on the green plush sofa.

Ina spoke. "What's got you spooked, honey?"

After burning my mouth twice more, I fanned my mouth again. "Spooked? I'm not spooked."

She wiped a few stray crumbs from her tank top to the floor. Theodore would eat them after his nap. "I've never seen you so uptight."

I scooted away from her for a clearer view. "I'm not uptight."

Ina shook her head slowly.

"It's been an unusual week, and under the circumstances, I've held together very well."

Ina shook her head again. "You're three tantrums away from the psych ward. You'll never survive if your brother goes to trial."

Frequently, Ina rambled on in incomprehensible psychobabble, but I wasn't in the mood to indulge. "What on earth are you talking about?"

Ina placed her saucer on the low coffee table. Sprinkle crumbs were all that remained of her breakfast. She licked her right index finger and picked up the crumbs, putting them in her mouth. I was ready to throttle her when she finally spoke. "A tiny part of you thinks that Mark could be guilty."

I jumped from the sofa, tipping my own saucer and half-eaten pastry to the floor. "I do not."

"He had motive, means, and opportunity." She ticked the three points off with her hands.

I lowered my volume to a roar. "You are not Hercule Poirot,

for goodness sakes. You just can't check off these elements and have the answer."

"My dear, I know this is hard for you, and I truly believe that Mark is innocent, but the only way you are going to find out who is really responsible for Olivia's death is to assume that Mark is guilty and prove that he's not."

"You've got the legal system backward, Ina." I slid back onto the sofa and picked up the pastry and saucer.

"You do want to know what happened, don't you?"

"Of course I do."

She shrugged. Case closed.

"I'm trying to help Mark as much as I can. I've talked to people about it. I'm going to bail him out, at least try to bail him out. What more can I do?"

"We know the police aren't going to figure it out with that bloody Englishman in charge."

I laughed in spite of myself.

"So, let's hash it out. You can be the brilliant detective; I'll be the wise sidekick. The sidekick is usually the fat one, but he's the one that gets to write everything down." Ina pulled a notepad and a pen out of the small drawer in the coffee table.

"Ina, I'm not a private eye, and neither are you." I rose and took my plate to the counter. "Thanks for the offer, but I'll pass. Now, if you'll excuse me, I have to go try to bail my brother out of jail."

"Can I come?"

"No."

Her face fell.

Theodore lumbered into the room and begged Ina for a bite. "I'm all out little Fella, but India still has some of hers."

I threw my uneaten pastry in the trash. "Ina, he cannot have people food."

She nodded solemnly. Theodore licked crumbs from the carpet.

CHAPTER FORTY

"Ms. Hayes, is it?" the burly man across the metal desk asked me. His arm was twice the circumference of my thigh. A blue plastic nameplate sat on his desk: Norman North, Bond Officer.

"Yes," I said, wearing a gray summer suit reserved for job interviews and meetings with bond agents. My right foot tapped on the gray linoleum floor.

"You have no collateral. You don't own any property. Your car is way past its expiration date, and you're up to your ears in student loans."

"I have excellent—"

"Frankly, North and South Bond Offices can't afford such high-cost or high-profile cases. We specialize in juvenile violations, petty theft, auto theft, minor stuff. I wouldn't touch your brother's bail with a forty-foot pole." He shrugged. "Sorry."

The sweaty vinyl tugged the hem of my skirt as I leaned forward in my seat. "I understand your concerns. But I have a stable job and . . ."

"I'm sorry and wish you luck, but no." He rose from the desk. He towered over me and the ugly chair. "I'll show you out."

We walked through the brief reception area and passed the clerk, who was sharpening her nails to a vicious point with a rainbow-colored emery board.

North opened the dingy glass door. "You ever have a friend

arrested for carjacking, send him my way."

"Uh, sure. Who's South?"

"Huh?"

"North and South Bond Offices." I pointed to the sign by the reception area.

He grunted. "It sounded good."

I stepped out into the late-afternoon sunlight filtered by city haze. On the west side of Akron, North and South Bond nestled between an exotic dance studio and a suspect-looking video rental store with iron bars on the windows.

I marched to my car, left undisturbed on the street. Even in this neighborhood, my car was a clunker. Inside the car, I locked the doors and rooted in my shoulder bag for the list of names and numbers of bond officers that Lew had given me. I scratched off North and South Bond Offices, the last name on the list. I was out of bondsmen and out of luck. I couldn't buy Mark any more time—not with my measly resources and lack of collateral.

I sat there for a few minutes collecting my thoughts. Both of the car windows were rolled all the way down, but no breeze cooled its interior. A local denizen spat tobacco juice in a beer can and crossed the street when we locked eyes. He looked away and ambled on. I wondered if his parents wouldn't bail him out of jail, and that's how he ended up where he was. There had to be a way I could help Mark. I thought about talking to my parents again, but knew it was a lost cause. When they were taking a stand, they wore blinders.

Suddenly, I had the heart-stopping fear that the engagement picture was no longer in my trunk. Sure, the trunk was locked, but the car was old and the lock could be jimmied with a screwdriver. I'd even used that method to get into the truck a few times when I couldn't find my key.

I jumped out of the car and popped open the trunk. In this

neighborhood, I wasn't afraid of anyone recognizing me. I pushed back the carpet and exposed the tire well. There it was, wrapped safely in my T-shirt. I didn't realize until I unwrapped the engagement picture to study it that I had used a Martin College T-shirt to protect the frame. I was sure there was some significance in that fact, but I was too drained to dwell on it. Carefully, almost lovingly, I rewrapped the framed photograph back in the T-shirt and pulled my cell phone from my jacket pocket. I hit the speed dial for Lew's cell.

"How did it go with the bond officers?" Lew asked, clearly expecting my call.

"Three strikes, you're out," I said.

A man with a long, ratty ponytail walked out of the exotic dance studio.

"I'm not surprised," Lew said.

"Not surprised. Well, that's encouraging." I kept an eye on the man so that I could kick him where it counted, if need be.

He lit a cigarette and leaned against the studio's door.

In my ear, I heard Lew light a cigarette. "It never hurts to try."

"It hurts me," I muttered. "What's our next step? Give me some more names."

"That's all I got. Those were the only names I thought would have even a remote interest in bailing out Mark."

"But . . ."

"I'm sorry, India, but unless your parents take the initiative to post bond, he's going to prison."

I scratched my head angrily. "Will you speak to them?"

"I'll do my best," he promised.

I paused.

"What?" Lew rasped. Lew was a good attorney and knew when someone was holding something back.

"I found something," I said, still unsure if I wanted to make a confession.

To my relief the pony-tailed man finished his cigarette. Throwing the stub back on the sidewalk, he reentered the studio.

"India," Lew said impatiently. "What did you find?"

"A picture."

"Am I going to have to guess of what?" He took a drag of his cigarette.

I took a breath and told him about my clandestine adventure and the engagement photograph.

Lew was not pleased. "Do you know how much trouble you could get into for this? Even if I can prove that your brother is innocent, you can still be charged with tampering with evidence."

My chest constricted. I knew he was right. "It seemed like a good idea at the time."

Lew snorted into the phone so loudly, I jumped.

"Don't you see? This proves that Mark was framed."

"It would have, if you hadn't removed the evidence," he complained.

"Listen, Lew, I'm giving you a heads-up. I'm turning the photo over to the police."

"I don't know if that's . . ."

"My mind's made up. I can't keep driving around with it in my car. It's making me crazy. Maybe, I can use it to show them that Mark really was framed. I found the picture before the scarf was found, didn't I? This shows that whoever planted the scarf in his apartment, first tried the picture. I foiled the first plot when I found it before the police did."

"That, my girl, is called conjecture." Lew took another drag of his cigarette. "You can keep Mark company in county prison."

On that note, I said good-bye and disconnected.

I reached through the open window for my shoulder bag.

After sifting through it for a few seconds, I dumped its contents on the hood and over the ugly message that Kirk had keyed there the day before. Compact, wallet, spare change, a small army of pens and pencils, sketch pad, used tissues, and gum wrappers clattered onto the metal surface. I rummaged through the mess and located the card, crumpled and covered with charcoal pencil.

Standing outside North and South Bond Offices, I examined it. Medium-weight paper with simple black lettering and the department's seal in the upper left-hand corner. I gathered my things back into the bag.

With shaky fingers, I punched the number into my cell. Mains's line at the police station rang four times before his voicemail picked up. "This is Detective Richmond Mains of the Stripling Police Department. I'm sorry to have missed your call. If this is an emergency, press one. If you'd . . ." The recording stopped abruptly. "Mains speaking."

I held the phone away from my ear, dumbstruck. I was hoping to just leave a message that said something like, "Oh hi, Detective Mains, I happen to pick up Olivia Blocken's engagement picture, and I wanted to turn it over to you. Oh, and by-the-way, I found it in my brother's office just a day or so after she was attacked. Thanks. Bye."

"Hello?" Mains asked.

I found my voice. "Rick?"

"Yes." He was impatient.

"This is India, uh, India Hayes." I mentally slapped myself on the forehead; how many other Indias could he know?

"What's up?" I heard a smile in his voice. I could've imagined it, or worse wished it. Focus, India, I told myself.

"I think we should meet about my brother's case." I couldn't bring myself to tell him what I had done over the phone. It was better to get the confession over with and turn over the picture all at the same time. Or, so I thought.

Mains agreed to meet me in Ryan Memorial Library's parking lot in thirty minutes.

I climbed into my car, made an illegal U-turn in the middle of the deserted street, and headed back to Stripling.

CHAPTER FORTY-ONE

Summer students lounged on the quad as I drove through campus. Two coeds of indeterminable gender played catch on the edge of the library's lot. Mains waited outside of his cop sedan. His arms were folded across his chest.

When I got out of my car, I pulled at the hem of my shorts. "How's Mark?"

Mains took a pair of sunglasses out of the breast pocket of his shirt and shielded his eyes from the afternoon sun. "He asked for paper and pencil so that he could work on calc problems in his cell. I gave him a box of tissue too. He's been crying off and on. He hasn't really said much."

"That sounds like Mark." I pushed the worry for my brother to the back of my mind.

"You could have asked me that over the phone."

"You're right." I looked at the ground.

"Is there something else you wanted to tell me?"

I looked at the trees, the sky, the library, the sexless catch couple, everywhere but his face. When I had decided, I looked him directly in the eye. "Someone is framing Mark."

He uncrossed and crossed his arms. I saw my reflection in his sunglasses—I looked small, misshapened, frightened. I straightened my shoulders, reset my jaw, and walked toward the back of the car.

Mains followed but then stopped short. He removed his sunglasses and stared at my car's hood. "What the . . ."

"It's nothing," I said.

"Nothing? It's a threat." Mains clenched his jaw. "Who did this?" He leaned over to examine the angry letters more closely.

"It doesn't matter. The car's a piece of junk anyway. Bobby's been begging me to buy a new one for years. Now, I have the proper incentive."

Through clenched teeth, "Who did this?"

I turned to face him. "I didn't ask you to meet me here to show you that." I gestured at the hood as if I didn't care, as if every time I saw it, it didn't hurt me.

"Well, I'm seeing it, and I can't ignore it. No one could. You need to file a report."

"No," I said resolutely.

"You could be in danger," he protested. "Whoever did this is obviously not stable."

I placed my hand on the warm hood and let my fingers trace the *r* in *killer*, such an ugly word. "I'm not in any danger." I was certain that Kirk wouldn't harm me. If he had wanted to, he would have taken his opportunity when we were in his hotel room.

Mains's voice was gentler. He put his hand on my wrist, encircling it with his fingers like a bracelet or a handcuff. "At least tell me who did this. Something tells me that you already know, which is why you are reluctant to file a report."

"Do you promise not to do anything about it? You have no crime if I refuse to file a complaint."

He grimaced. "Fine. I promise that I won't do anything without your permission."

I nodded in acceptance. "It was Kirk."

He let go of my wrist. "That son of—" he stopped in mid-curse and slammed his fist on the hood of my car. The couple playing catch glanced over.

"Don't you think my car has had enough abuse already?"

Mains's eyes blazed. "I'll have a little talk with him."

"No, you won't," I said, using my sternest voice, the one I use to tell rowdy undergrads to pipe down in the library. "You promised. Besides I already talked to him about it."

"You talked to him? Alone?"

I nodded.

Mains's jaw twitched. "There was something you wanted to show me."

I walked around to the back of the car and unlocked the trunk. Mains peered inside it. I waved him away, threw back the tire well cover, picked up the T-shirt-wrapped frame, and handed it to him.

"Where'd you get this? Why do you have it?"

"Let me explain," I pleaded.

Mains examined the frame and the photograph. Angrily, he said, "I'm waiting."

"I found them in Mark's office."

He wrapped the frame back up but didn't return it to me. Not that I expected to ever see it again. "When?" he asked.

"Monday." I didn't clarify that it had been just before he'd arrived with a search warrant for Mark's office on Monday. We both knew the exact time.

Mains took a quick breath.

"Someone planted it," I said. "Just like they planted the scarf."

Mains opened his mouth to protest.

"Hear me out. You arrested Mark because you found a scarf in his apartment that matched the dress Olivia was wearing the day she was attacked. How could Mark have such a scarf? He hasn't seen Olivia in years, and I doubt she was wearing the same dress at the time. There was no time for him to take the scarf those few minutes he was at the Blocken picnic."

Mains tried to speak.

"Wait, let me finish. If there was no time for Mark to take the scarf, there was certainly no time for him to swipe this engagement picture. Someone wants you to believe that Mark stole both."

Mains peered down at the package in his hands. "The Blockens haven't reported anything missing to the police."

"With the funeral and everything, something like this would be easy to forget. I saw Dr. Blocken two days ago, and he mentioned that Mrs. Blocken was missing the picture, so they do know that it is gone. Dr. Blocken told me that his wife was talking about reporting it missing to you. Maybe she changed her mind because she thought it was misplaced in the confusion and not actually stolen." I took a breath. "Or, maybe she doesn't want you to know."

"I know what you are implying, India, and I know that you don't have the best relationship with the Blocken family."

It was my turn to protest.

"I'll be sure to ask the Blockens about this picture; you can bet on that. But that doesn't change the facts about the scarf. You've neglected to consider that Mark could have taken that scarf from Olivia just before or after he pushed her into the fountain." Mains walked back to his sedan, opened his trunk, pulled out a huge plastic bag, and placed picture, T-shirt, and all inside. He zipped that bag closed, dropped it back into the trunk, and slammed the lid. "I don't want you talking to anyone about this case anymore."

"What?"

"Contrary to what you might think, the police can do the job. Those stupid cop shows will be the death of me," he mumbled under his breath. "I won't arrest you for the time being, but taking and hiding evidence is a serious offense."

Gee thanks, I thought.

"I didn't know that it was evidence when I took it," I said.

Mains gave me a look. We knew this was merely a technicality.

"You'll need to stop by the station to make a statement. I have to speak to my superiors about the mess you've created, but I'll expect you within the hour." Mains opened the sedan's door.

"Won't you at least consider the possibility of Mark's innocence?" I asked.

"This is my first murder case; I won't screw it up." He looked at me, and an emotion I couldn't name crossed his face. "If your brother is innocent, I'll do whatever I can to keep him out of prison. However, I would do much better if I didn't have your bumbling help."

I imagined that comment was more of a boost to his confidence than it was to mine.

He squeezed my wrist again, so quickly that I couldn't be sure that it even happened. Then, he jumped in his car and drove away with his lights flashing.

CHAPTER FORTY-TWO

My cell rang as I was driving through town. The feeling of Mains's fingers encircling my wrist lingered as much as I wanted to ignore it.

I plucked the phone off the passenger seat and checked the caller ID. A picture of Bobby's face rolled its eyes at me on the tiny screen. I smiled as I remembered that I took that picture during a particularly boring faculty meeting the year before.

Bobby's voice was apprehensive. "I need to tell you something, but you have to promise not to freak out."

"That's an encouraging opening," I said.

"Promise?"

"Okay, I promise, but if this has something to do with Martin Campers' Week, all bets are off."

"Must all our conversations revolve around the library?" he asked.

I stopped at a red light. "Nope. Spill it."

"Bree's been turned out of her hotel and needed a place to stay." He took a deep breath. "So she is crashing with me."

A pause. The light had turned green, but I didn't take my foot off the brake. The guy in the car behind me honked and saluted me with his middle finger. I rolled the car forward.

"India?" Bobby asked. "Bree told me that the two of you had a misunderstanding over dinner last night."

A misunderstanding. The woman was carrying a gun. I bit my lip and wondered if I should tell Bobby about the gun.

Would it make any difference? Would it change his mind about her?

"Why are you telling me this? You're your own man; you can spend time with whoever you want."

"I know that, but things have been weird between us this week and I just thought . . ." He trailed off.

I made another turn onto a commercial road lined with fast-food restaurants, grocery stores, and discount supercenters. "You just thought what?"

"I just thought you should know."

"Consider it noted," I said and snapped the phone shut.

My cell rang again, almost immediately, and Bobby rolled his eyes at me again from the screen, but I ignored him. I knew that I would regret hanging up on him later and would have to do some serious groveling to get in his good graces again. However, I'd reached my limit. My first priority had to be Mark.

I turned the car into the parking lot for Topaz Bridal. In the store window stood the exact replica of the wedding dress Olivia had described to me in excruciating detail so many months ago. The antique-white gown was full-length and strapless with thousands of delicate silver stars and a gold sunburst embroidered on the bodice. The waist was so narrow that it crushed the headless mannequin's Styrofoam innards. The bodice exploded into a full multilayer skirt heavy on taffeta; silver and gold threads wove in and out of the cloud of fabric. In that dress Olivia would be—would have been—breathtaking. I almost walked away.

A bell chimed at my entry. A voice called from the back, "Be with you in a minute."

I walked around the store. Being so surrounded by wedding gowns and their trappings, my stomach clenched. I glanced at a few price tags and whistled. Each one had the Topaz trademark and a lofty declaration that each gown was one of kind. I glanced at the mannequin in the window. One of a kind, I thought.

If I ignored what the dresses signified—commitment, a lifetime of compromise, companionship in old age—and considered the gowns with a purely artistic eye, Topaz was an amazing designer. I wondered, and not for the first time, why she lived in Stripling. She was obviously talented. Wouldn't she be more successful in New York, L.A., or Atlanta?

A teenage boy emerged from the back room. He walked with a pronounced slouch and had an unfortunate case of acne.

Topaz followed behind him. "I'll see you in two weeks for your final fitting."

The boy grunted and fled the store.

"He's buying a wedding dress?" I asked dubiously.

Topaz chortled. "No, I do alterations and tailoring on the side. I'm glad you're here. It's all ready."

Ready? I must have looked confused because Topaz said, "You're here to pick up your bridesmaid dress, aren't you?"

"Well, I thought—"

"Don't tell me you're not going to pay me. I feel horrible about Olivia, but I have to run a business. I've spent hundreds of hours on the gowns for the Blocken wedding and that doesn't include the time I spent on the bride's gown. And no one wants to pay."

"No one?"

"Didn't you see Olivia's dress in the window? It's for sale. Apparently, the Blockens are no longer interested."

"That's Olivia's dress?" I asked, hoping that my assumption about the dress had been wrong.

"Of course it is. Every Topaz wedding gown is one of a kind." Topaz paced around the room adjusting and readjusting gowns every few steps.

"How much?"

She beamed. "Perfect. Follow me." Topaz led me to the back

of the shop and through a heavy curtain that obscured the back room. The room held thick pallets of fabric organized by an expert's hand shelved along the right wall. White, white, and more white. Each shade of white was one wash darker than the last. I peered through the small doorway into an adjacent room that housed Topaz's many sewing machines. Several works in progress were pinned to much-abused dress dummies. To my left a long metal rack held dress after dress, all wrapped in plastic. I suspected that my gown was among them.

Topaz sat behind an antique writing desk, pulled a leather ledger from one of its impractical drawers, and quoted a figure. My eyes boggled. My hands shook when I tore the check out of my checkbook. The price was more than two months' rent for my apartment. Templeton would be living on generic cat food while I would be dining on saltine crackers for the remainder of the summer.

Topaz thanked me, confirmed the amount, folded the check, and slipped it into her jeans pocket. She handwrote a receipt.

"You can change behind that screen there." She pointed to a paisley-patterned screen in a small corner of the room.

"Excuse me?"

Topaz glanced at her watch. "I have time for your final fitting."

"Fitting?" I was slow to catch on.

"Of course I can't let you buy the dress without trying it on first." She pulled a plastic-wrapped gown from the rack and handed it to me. *Déjà vu.*

I held the garment bag at arms' length. "Really, Topaz, I trust your expertise. I'm sure it's a perfect fit. I know you're very busy. Summer is the height of wedding season, right? I don't think—"

She pointed, and I ducked behind the screen with the garment bag. Remembering my temporary blindness, I didn't look directly at the dress while I put it on. This time it zipped up without a hitch. I walked out from behind the screen. The hem of the skirt brushed hardwood floor.

Topaz placed a stout pedestal in front of the unforgiving three-way mirror. Moors during the Spanish Inquisition never faced such a horror.

"Arms out," Topaz directed.

Three sharp pins glistened in the right corner of her mouth. I unlocked my knees and shifted my feet on the small pedestal, intended for someone with a shoe size smaller than ten.

The gown's painful golden color against my pale skin, my genetic destiny passed down by Celt and Fin bloodlines, remained hideous, but it did fit, or at least I thought it did until I saw my reflection in Topaz's torture chamber. The three-way mirror was merciless and considered my figure from the worse possible angle. I closed my eyes.

"Were you surprised when Mrs. Blocken asked you to bring the bridesmaids gowns to her house on the Fourth?" I asked.

Topaz snorted.

"She can be demanding."

"You could say that." Topaz circled me like a lioness contemplating a baby zebra.

I shifted my clown feet and nearly fell off the tiny pedestal.

"Stop moving."

"Sorry. Did you notice anything strange at the picnic?"

"The only strange thing I saw was your brother crash the place. This is about your brother, isn't it?"

"Yes," I admitted. "But after we left, what happened? Anything that you can tell me might help. I know Mark's innocent."

"You're a nice girl, but I can't discuss my clients if I want to pay the rent." She stepped back. "You can get down now. The dress is a perfect fit."

Not according to the three-way mirror, I thought. "You mean your former clients. You said Mrs. Blocken refused to pay for Olivia's dress." I stepped off the pedestal. My feet sang the Hallelujah Chorus.

"Go ahead. I know that you're dying to change."

I leapt behind the Chinese screen. "Mrs. Blocken hates Mark and me—that has to give us some credibility."

I tugged at the zipper and sighed with relief when it gave way. I put on my own clothes as quickly as possible. Why anyone would wear a bridesmaid's dress when there are T-shirts and jeans in this world, I would never know.

When I emerged, Topaz was sitting behind the desk. "I wish I could help you, I really do, but nothing happened after you left. The group was shocked, but that's no surprise. Lady Blocken put a stop to that fast. I took O.M. upstairs for her fitting, and that was the end of that. While I was in the upstairs hallway, I heard some debate as to whether you"—she gave me an apologetic smile—"should still be a bridesmaid. Olivia was determined that you would be. She didn't seem to be overly concerned about seeing your brother. I remember Kirk was pretty fired up about it, but Olivia said not to worry."

"What about Dr. Blocken or Bree?"

Topaz thought for a minute. "Olivia's father didn't really react. He sat off away from the group with some book that made *Moby Dick* look like a thriller. Bree's behavior didn't change at all. She ran around the room being annoyingly helpful. I finally had to make up something for her to do so that she'd leave me alone during O.M.'s fitting."

"Did Olivia order the dresses from you?"

"The Fourth was the first day I ever saw Olivia, although I spoke to her on the phone a few times, for measurements and things. All of the business went through her mother. From now on, I'm getting the money up front. I had a commission contract with Regina to design that dress. I suppose that I could sue her for breach of contract. But I know she'd bury me with some high-priced lawyer."

I made sympathetic noises. Topaz zipped my bridesmaid's gown into its dress bag and handed it to me. "Know any good lawyers, cheap?"

I gave her Lew's name.

She wrote his name in her ledger. The bell chimed. I peered through the sheer curtain.

"She never tried it on, you know," Topaz spoke, barely above a whisper.

"What?" I asked, thinking I misheard her.

"Olivia never tried on her wedding dress."

Topaz put on her customer service face and stepped through the curtain into the showroom. I followed with the garment bag draped over my arm

A girl in her early twenties and a dour-looking woman stood by the mannequin wearing Olivia's dress. "Oh, look at the bodice. It's perfect. You know I love suns and moons," the girl gushed.

The older woman teared up. "This is the one. Oh, honey, you'll be breathtaking."

Topaz smiled brightly at the pair. She turned to me. "India, thanks for coming in. You might want to buy some form-shaping lingerie for that dress."

From my car, I watched Topaz remove the mannequin from the display window. The girl jumped up and down excitedly and the older woman sobbed.

I wiped the moisture from my cheeks and backed out of my parking space.

CHAPTER FORTY-THREE

Back at the duplex, I found a note from Mains taped to my front door telling me rather gruffly to come down to the Justice Center for questioning. I wondered why he hadn't called my cell phone, until I realized much to my relief that he didn't have the number. My stalling over my statement about the purloined picture wasn't going to help me in any way, but I had decided to go to Topaz's shop first, since it closed at six. Now that it was well after that time, I knew I should drag myself to the Justice Center.

Ina, who sat on her resin lawn chair, said, "Don't worry, honey, I held down the fort." She waved the garden hose's nozzle. "I got rid of him real quick." Theodore snored in her lap.

I thanked her and unlocked my door. Inside my apartment, my answering machine displayed six messages. I suspected a good number of them were from Mains with a healthy selection from my mother. Instead of listening to the machine, I called Carmen.

"Nicholas! Don't put that into your mouth!" my sister shouted into my ear.

"Are you listening to me?" I asked.

A frustrated sigh. "Yes, India, I'm listening to you." A pause. "Nick, find your father. Dinner will be on the table soon."

I spoke over her cries to her son. "Carmen, you have to talk to Mom and Dad about Mark. We can't let him go to prison."

"We've been over this before. Do you honestly think our parents will let that happen?"

I didn't respond.

She sighed again, louder this time. "Lew bought Mark a couple extra days at the Stripling jail, right?"

"Well, yes, but time's up tonight . . ."

"Mom and Dad are waiting till the last possible minute. They're making another elaborate point. You know that."

"But it takes time to speak to bond agents. I went to several this morning; they all turned me down."

"Mom and Dad shouldn't have a problem. They probably have a favorite agent who's gotten them out a time or two, and they're more reputable than some twenty-something kid who still has thousands in student loans."

Not exactly thousands. I ground my teeth. "You won't speak to them."

"No, I won't. You're not the only one this is happening to, India. I want you to remember that."

"You're right. It's happening to Mark. Let me ask you this, Carmen. What if it was Nicholas?" I hung up.

I grabbed a pad of paper and pen off the end table and half-sat, half-crouched at the end of the sofa. I wrote a list of all the people that had reason to frame or could have possibly framed Mark. I included everyone that was at the Fourth of July picnic at the Blockens: Dr. Blocken, Mrs. Blocken, O.M., Bree, Kirk, Bobby, and Topaz. Mrs. Blocken was my number one suspect, but my theory stalled. I couldn't think of any reason why Mrs. Blocken, who worshipped her daughter and, maybe even more so, the upcoming nuptials, would hurt Olivia. Maybe it was an accident. That was it. She could have pushed Olivia into the fountain accidentally.

Number two on the list: Kirk. He'd proven to have an outrageous temper, and he was certainly strong enough to push Olivia into the fountain. However, there was no denying that he was devastated by Olivia's death. Could he be so upset because he knew he was the one responsible?

Dr. Blocken was a suspect for the same reason Mrs. Blocken was, but I still couldn't fathom a reason why either one would hurt their daughter.

Bree was also a suspect merely because she was present at the picnic, but again, she had no motive. And the thought of fifteen-year-old O.M. killing her sister was more than I'd let myself fathom. I knew some teenagers were violent, and O.M. definitely had an attitude problem, but . . .

Topaz had made it plain that she didn't know Olivia, and Olivia's death had cost her a lot financially. If it had been Mrs. Blocken who was found in the fountain, Topaz would be a much more likely suspect. After Topaz, I considered Bobby. He'd just met Olivia the day before she was attacked, hours really. Furthermore, the thought of Bobby up that early on his Saturday morning off from the library was ludicrous.

I added a final name to the list, the most likely suspect, the one person who had indisputable means, motive, and opportunity: Mark. Ina said to solve the crime I must assume that Mark is guilty. He had motive. He still loved Olivia, and she was marrying another man in his hometown. He had means and opportunity. He could have easily pushed Olivia into the fountain and returned to his office at Dexler without any problem. During the summer, the campus was deserted early in the morning. No one would see him. In fact, no one did see how Olivia ended up in the fountain, even with the ill-placed surveillance cameras and Mutt's rent-a-cops roving the grounds.

My front door opened. Ina ambled in with a mug of steaming liquid.

I hid my list underneath a throw pillow. "Ina, I need to get ready to go to the Justice Center. I have to give Detective Mains a statement. I should get it over with before he throws me in the cell next to Mark."

She set the mug on the coffee table in front of me. "Now, honey, I know that you're upset about Mark, but everything will work out just fine, you'll see. Why don't you drink this cup of tea I made for you?"

"It's too hot for tea."

Ina sat on my rocker stubbornly. "I'm not leaving until you drink every last drop." She scooted to the front of the chair and planted her feet firmly on the floor. "I've heard you rambling around here in the middle of the night. When is the last time you were able to get any real rest?"

I picked up the mug and took a sip. It tasted awful. I gagged.

"It's good for you."

I'll bet it is, I thought.

"I wanted to bring Fella over to sit with you, but I was afraid of what your wild cat would've done. I don't trust that cat as far as I can throw him."

I took a big gulp and swallowed the last of the tea. I opened my mouth to show her. "See, it's all gone."

Ina started telling me a long, detailed account of her and Juliet's cruise plans for August. "It's the perfect time of year to see Alaska, don't you think?"

"Sure," I said. "I really . . ."

"Juliet is such a hussy. You should have seen the dress she bought yesterday."

"That's nice." I paused, "Oh!"

"What is it?"

"I feel a little woozy." I sat farther back on the couch, shaking my head.

"You do?"

I started to nod, but the action took too much effort. I stretched my legs onto the couch, and Ina covered me with the orange cotton sheet.

I was in my dorm room in art school. The phone rang, and I answered it. Sobs sounded on the other end. "Mark? Mark? Is that you?" More sobs answered me. "Is everything okay? What happened?"

"I miss her. Why'd she leave?"

"Olivia?" I couldn't help but ask.

He cried, and I couldn't get another word out of him.

Suddenly, I was on the telephone with Olivia. "How's Mark?" she asked.

"Like you care," I said.

"India, that's not fair."

"He's crushed," I said.

"He'll get over it."

I remained silent.

"Don't let this thing with Mark come between us," she said.

The scene changed, and I was just a child. Olivia pushed me on the swing in our neighborhood playground.

"Higher!" I called. "Higher!"

She threw all of her weight against my back, and I soared into the air over the treetops and into the clouds.

Frightened, I screamed. "Stop it! That's too high! Livie, that's too high!"

I jerked awake, grasping my thundering chest. Ina was knitting an emerald green scarf on the rocking chair. The light in the living room was dim. The VCR clock read ten after nine. I'd slept for nearly three hours. Templeton perched on the back of the couch, his back arched.

"What happened?" My head throbbed.

"Oh, you're awake. Did you have a nice rest?"

"How could I have slept that long?" I held the side of my head.

"A little sleeping draft I whipped up. It was my mother's recipe."

"What?" I asked. Templeton jumped off the couch.

She kept on knitting. "It's all natural, all herbal. You have nothing to worry about. I've taken it many times myself."

"You drugged me?"

"There were no drugs involved, and you needed the rest." She gave me her elfin smile.

I jumped off the couch. I grabbed the arm as I started to topple over. "I can't believe you did this."

"It was for your own good. I was helping," she said, as if that was a completely reasonable explanation for lacing my drink.

I clenched my jaw and mentally counted to ten. I blew out a long breath. "Mains is going to kill me, I was supposed to be at the Justice Center four hours ago."

"Oh, dear." Ina hopped out of the rocking chair.

After a minute, the dizziness passed. I grabbed a dark, paint-splattered hooded sweatshirt from my closet and slipped my wallet and cell phone in the pockets of my shorts. "I have to go."

"Isn't it too late," Ina said.

"It's better that I go now than wait until tomorrow."

I left Ina in my living room, knowing that she would lock up my apartment for me before she left.

CHAPTER FORTY-FOUR

After nine at night, even during the summer, the people of Stripling roll up the sidewalks. Despite the fact that Stripling is a college town, it is not a party town. If the students of Martin are looking for any night life, they drive the fifteen miles to go to bars in Kent.

The Justice Center parking lot was just as deserted as it had been several nights ago when I visited my brother. I walked up the steep steps, both dreading and hoping that Mains would be there. Instead of Mains, I was greeted by Officer Knute, who was again behind the desk. He scowled when I walked in.

"I'm here to see Detective Mains," I said.

Knute gave me a bored look. "Name?"

"For crying out loud, you know who I am."

Knute's face was impassive. "Name?"

Through gritted teeth. "India Hayes."

"Ahh, yes," he said. "Detective Mains said I was to take your statement if you bothered to show up tonight."

I kept my mouth shut. I was in enough trouble as it was. I didn't think that Officer Knute would think twice before throwing me in a cell.

As the reception area was empty, he asked me to write my statement right there. Thirty minutes later, I signed it and handed it to Officer Knute.

With my conscience cleared, I left the station. I didn't bother to say good-bye.

In the parking lot, I stood under the same lamppost where Mains had asked me if I remembered him, and where I'd lied and told him that I didn't. I was reluctant to go home. Mark would be moved to a prison most likely the next day if I didn't do something. I knew there was one person I still hadn't talked to, who I needed to talk to. I looked up into the lamppost light. Two huge moths knocked themselves silly against the glass. Why did I feel like I'd be doing the same if I spoke to Regina Blocken?

I got in my car and headed to Kilbourne Street.

I knocked on the Blockens' door with a firm hand. Lights flickered on. The door opened. Mrs. Blocken wore royal blue satin pajamas and matching robe, but her face was still in full makeup.

"I need to talk to you." As it was a wide doorway, I slipped past her into the parlor.

Fury replaced her shock. "It's after eleven. How dare you invade my home like this?"

I paced the room. "I need to talk to you about Mark."

"Whatever you have to say can wait until morning." She tightened her robe around her waist.

"No, it can't wait because in my mind it keeps coming back to you. You were the one who was in control of the wedding. You were the one who noticed the engagement picture missing."

Mrs. Blocken paled, and I knew I had been correct.

"You know, the engagement picture that someone conveniently placed in Mark's office right before the police got an anonymous tip to search it."

"I don't know what you're talking about."

"I think you do. You had access to the engagement picture and to the scarf you planted later in Mark's apartment when the first try didn't work. I found the engagement picture before the police, by the way."

"That's tampering," she accused.

"Don't worry. The police already know about it." I paced the room. I didn't hear any movement from upstairs, and I wondered where Dr. Blocken was.

A cruel smile played on the corner of Mrs. Blocken's face. "You can't prove anything."

"You're right," I admitted. "But you and I both know it was you. You've been waiting to blame something on Mark for years. He was never good enough for your Olivia."

"Oh, please, you knew that it wouldn't last."

I shrugged. "So I did, but my brother didn't. He really loved her. He still loves her."

"So, you are here to tell me that your brother is innocent, and that I framed an innocent man."

"Yes. I can assure you that the last thing Mark wanted in the world was to hurt Olivia."

She glowered at me. "I suppose you also think I killed my daughter."

"No," I said honestly, because as much as I disliked Mrs. Blocken, that was the one thing I could not picture her doing.

Mrs. Blocken was silenced by my unexpected answer. She fell into the armchair in tears. "Then who did?"

It was a rhetorical question, so I didn't answer. Her pain filled the room like an unexpected storm that comes on a summer night with violence and speed.

I looked out onto the darkened patio and remembered Olivia that day at the picnic. When I remembered her another person came to mind. Bree. Bree who was bustling around the party following Olivia's every command, taking the maid of honor responsibilities to the extreme. But why? Why had she behaved that way? A prick of unease crawled up my spine.

"What do you know about Bree?" My voice was low.

She looked up. Her perfect makeup was ruined. "Bree?"

I sat across from her. "Yes, it's important. What do you know about her?"

She blinked and rubbed her cheek, smearing mascara into her hairline. "She's a sweet girl."

She looked pointedly at me, silently saying that I was not. The fire was back in her eyes. I was relieved. I found a sad Mrs. Blocken made me more uneasy than an angry one.

"She was always helping Olivia with this and that. I don't know how many times I called Olivia, and she said that Bree was there helping her with this project or that project. Also, Bree was always volunteering at Kirk's gym."

"Why?" I asked.

"Why what?"

"Why was Bree so helpful?"

"Why wouldn't she be? Olivia was her friend." Again, she looked pointedly at me.

"That's true to a point, but all that helping out sounds like it was more than friendship."

Mrs. Blocken's eyes narrowed. She pulled tissue from her robe pocket and dabbed at her eyes. "What would you know about what it means to be a friend?"

I let that comment pass. "Why would Bree volunteer at the gym? Kirk's business was making plenty of money. He mentioned at the picnic that he just opened a new fitness center. He can afford to pay someone."

"I know that Olivia was giving her money." She was on the stairs. Neither Mrs. Blocken nor I had noticed her. I wondered how long she'd been standing there. How much had she heard? She came down the stairs in a rock band nightshirt.

Mrs. Blocken looked up, shocked. "What are you talking about? Olivia wouldn't do that."

O.M. shrugged. "I overheard them talking before the picnic. Bree asked Olivia for a check, and Olivia said that they would talk about it later."

I felt very cold as my brain put the pieces into place. "O.M., this is important. Did you see Bree the morning that Olivia was attacked?"

O.M. bit her lip. "No, I was asleep." Her eyes darted away.

She was lying, and we both knew it. Her eyes flicked over to her mother.

"Whatever it is, I promise you won't get in trouble," I said.

"You can't make any such promise," Mrs. Blocken said.

I shot her a look so fierce that it silenced her immediately. That was the first time in the history of the world that anyone had silenced Mrs. Blocken with a mere look.

O.M. swallowed. "It was about seven in the morning. I was just getting home."

"You stayed out all night?" Mrs. Blocken roared.

O.M. shrank away from her. "My band had a gig, Mom." Her voice was small like a child's. "I knew you would never let me go."

"Of course, I wouldn't let you go. You're only fifteen."

"Mrs. Blocken, please," I said. I turned to O.M. "What happened?"

"When I got home, I was just going to slip upstairs. I knew Dad would have already left for the office, and that both Mom and Olivia sleep late. But when I got there, I saw Olivia in the kitchen window, already up, so I had to hide out by the garage. I didn't know how I was going to get inside without her seeing or hearing me, and I knew she would tell Mom if she caught me. Finally, around seven thirty, just when I thought that I couldn't stand it any longer and was going to go inside and face my sister and Mom, Bree pulled up in this tiny red car. She didn't get out. Olivia must have been looking for her, because she ran out and jumped right in." O.M. looked down. "I remember thinking at the time how lucky I was that Bree came and got her."

Mrs. Blocken stared at her youngest daughter as if she didn't even know her. Maybe, she didn't.

"O.M., call the police," I ordered.

"What? Why?" She looked scared and more like the fifteen-year-old that she was than I had ever seen her.

"Because Bree Butler killed your sister, and now she is alone with my friend." I told her Bobby's address.

Mrs. Blocken gaped.

I ran out of the house and jumped in my car. I threw the car in reverse, running over a rose bush in the process.

CHAPTER FORTY-FIVE

A weak yellow glare backlit Bobby's mini blinds. I shifted on the balls of my feet and rapped the brass knocker.

Bobby blinked at me. "India? What's wrong?"

"Bobby, thank God," I exclaimed. I tugged on the sleeve to his red flannel robe. Embarrassed, I looked down. "Is Bree here?"

Bobby belted his robe more tightly over his blue boxer shorts and white T-shirt. "Yes," he said cautiously.

"Where is she?"

"She's sleeping. Not that it's any of your business." He smoothed his tangled hair.

I pushed through the threshold. "Let her sleep."

"What's—"

"There's an emergency at the library. We have to go." I scanned the room, seeing Bree under every table and behind every chair. Bobby's laptop and trashy romance notes sat on the dining room table. A mug of coffee topped a short stack of romance novels.

"Wait." He waved his hands in my face. "What happened? Sit down. I can't understand you if you jump around the room like a deranged kangaroo."

"Didn't you hear me? It's an emergency. There's no time to sit down."

"No way. Not until you tell me what happened." He sat on an armchair. "You look horrible. Did you remember to brush your hair today?"

"Someone broke into the library. We have to get down there."

"If you think I'm going to run into the library to stop someone from stealing the *Oxford English Dictionary* or the change in the fine drawer, you're crazy."

"The robber's gone. Lasha wants us down there to inventory what's stolen." I became more agitated, wringing my hands and pacing. I tired to keep my voice low. I didn't want to wake Bree up.

"The robber?" Bobby asked in disbelief. "Is it time to circle the wagons?"

"The thief, burglar, perp, whatever you want to call him."

"Why do you automatically assume the robber's a man? I think I'll have to write women's liberation about you." Bobby tsked.

"We have to take inventory right away so the police can find the stuff before it goes on the black market." My story sounded ridiculous to my own ears, but I would wait to tell Bobby the truth after I got him out of the house, after he was safe.

Bobby chortled. "Forget women's lib. Watch out thriller authors, we have a new espionage writer in town."

"Come on," I pleaded, pacing the room.

Bobby mellowed at my sincerity. "If it's that important . . ."

"It is. It is."

"Just let me go to the bedroom and change." He rose from the couch.

"No!"

"India," he warned.

"I mean, no, you look fine. It's in the middle of the night and everything, I bet half the people there will be in their pjs."

"You're not."

"Yes, I am," I lied. "I always sleep in this outfit. It's very comfortable."

Bobby became suspicious. "If Lasha wanted me so badly at the library, why didn't she call me?"

"She thought it would be easier coming from me."

Bobby wasn't buying. "Let me call her." Bobby pulled his tiny cell phone out of his robe pocket.

"No."

He glared at me. "What the hell is going on?"

I stepped closer to him and he backed away. "Okay, I lied. The library's fine." I seized his arm. "But we have to leave your house. Just trust me, please."

He jerked his arm away from me. "Why?"

"It's Bree, Bobby."

"What about her?"

"She's not who you think she is."

Bobby glared at me. "You've had it in for her since day one."

"I haven't. Bobby, she—"

"She's having such a horrible time here, and you're like everybody else, tearing her down."

"Who tore her down, Bobby?" I whispered.

He threw up his hands. "Everyone. All she tries to do is help her mother and everyone else. She did everything for Olivia's wedding."

"You don't understand."

He ignored me. "At least I'm able to help her."

"Help her how?"

"A loan. It's the least I can do so she can afford a better nursing home for her mother. Can't you leave Bree alone? She's leaving tomorrow to move her mom."

"Bobby, listen to me. Bree killed Olivia."

"What? How can you say that?" He shoved me. I collided with the sofa and sat down hard.

"Please, just step outside with me and I'll tell you everything. Trust—"

"Bobby?" Bree stood in the hallway, outlined by the bathroom's dim nightlight. She wore one of Bobby's tweed blazers over her nightgown. She buried her hands deep into the jacket pockets.

Bobby rushed to her side. "India claims you had something to do with Olivia's death."

Bree's right hand flashed out of her pocket. In the low light I saw the unmistakable glimmer of metal.

"Bobby!" I screamed, jumping up from the sofa.

Bree whacked Bobby on the back of the head, and he crumpled onto the carpeted floor. Then she turned the gun on me. It was the same gun that she'd claimed she needed for protection. It was small and fit snugly in her hand, but I didn't doubt that the danger it presented was real, no matter the size.

Why hadn't I warned Bobby about the gun? I thought frantically. Why had I made up that crazy story about the robbery at the library? Maybe if I had told the truth right away, Bobby and I would be outside now; we would be safe. But I knew as infatuated as Bobby was with Bree, had I told the truth from the beginning, he wouldn't have believed me.

I flopped back onto the couch. Bree stepped over Bobby.

I squeezed my eyes shut and prayed, Please, don't let him be dead. Please, don't let him be dead.

I opened my eyes and saw Bree pointing the tiny gun at my chest. "Can I check on Bobby, please? If you cared about him at all, you'd at least make sure he's breathing."

Bree glanced at Bobby. Her right arm shook, which was little comfort. "Stay there!" Bree stepped over to Bobby and felt his wrist. "He's fine. He'll be fine." Her eyes watered.

I silently agreed. Bobby's head was made of granite.

Bree stepped in front of me again, her entire body quivering.

I couldn't help myself. "Were you going to take Bobby's money and run?"

"No. Bobby gave me a loan. I'll pay every cent back. I need the money. My mother . . ." She began to cry, but the gun's aim did not falter.

"What happened?" I asked. I hoped my voice sounded gentle, that it didn't betray the terror that I felt.

"You'd understand, wouldn't you?" she whispered to herself. More loudly, "Olivia has . . . had . . . everything. Great looks, great job, great fiancé, great life."

"Bree, I've known Olivia my entire life. I understand," I soothed. Please, don't let her shoot me. Please, don't let her shoot. I'll be more respectful to my parents. Okay, I'll *try* to be more respectful to my parents, but they're cracked, I thought.

Bree broke into my thoughts. "By the time I started college and met Olivia, my mother had had MS for ten years." She began to relax as she told the story. "And in my freshman year of college, Mom moved to a nursing home, the best one we could afford with a small inheritance from my grandparents. Olivia was there for me the entire time. She was so supportive." Tears slipped down her flawless cheeks. "She told me that if I ever needed help, she'd be there." The gun began to droop in her hand. I watched it fall millimeter by millimeter. Bree noticed the oversight and retrained the gun on my chest.

"After college, Olivia got a job at Kirk's gym as a physical therapist. Kirk was planning to franchise it when he and Olivia started dating." She gave a short, bitter laugh. "My mom was worse, and we were running out of money. Mom was awarded disability insurance, but she had worked odd jobs all her life, cleaning, waitressing, serving people like Olivia's family. She has no pension, no retirement. With my teaching salary, I couldn't keep her in the nursing home. They were threatening to kick her out. The only place I could barely afford was . . . was . . . not acceptable."

"You asked Olivia for help," I whispered.

"Yes. Wouldn't you? I was desperate. And Olivia said she would. She said that after she and Kirk were married, we'd work out a loan." Bree paced back and forth on Bobby's Navajo rug, trampling the pipes and players.

"She backed out of the promise."

"Of course, she backed out. I'd been her lapdog for weeks, afraid that at any moment she'd change her mind." Bree mimicked Olivia's voice, " 'Bree, could you be a dear and call the florist for me?' 'Bree, honey, could you wait for the delivery man to drop off our washer and dryer on Thursday. He'll be there between eight and five?' And 'Could you spend the week in Ohio with me to prepare for the wedding? I really need your help.' I did everything she asked me. I even drove her to see your brother. She begged me to go with her. She wasn't afraid of Mark, but she said that it would be easier for her if I was along. So of course, I went."

I bit the inside of my lip and tasted blood.

"We were walking across campus when I asked her about the loan. I didn't want to pressure her, and I'd already asked her the day before. She'd planned to talk it over with Kirk, as soon as she could." Bree's tears were gone, replaced by cold anger. "That's when she said that she didn't think it was going to work out." She spoke more quickly. "I asked what she meant, and she said that she'd talked it over with Kirk, and they'd decided that it wasn't a good idea when they're starting out. I asked her how she could do this to me. To my mother. I reminded her of everything I'd done for her, for the wedding. And she thanked me. She thanked me, but said no."

I held my breath.

Bree ran her left hand through her tangled curls. "I was so angry, I pushed her into the ugly fountain. She wasn't expecting it and lost her balance. She fell and hit her head. She didn't move; I thought she'd died right there." Bree stopped pacing

273

and began to cry, her bare feet firmly planted on the Navajo rug.

As she spoke, I slowly bent down.

"I didn't know she was still alive," Bree continued to speak but her words were unintelligible through her sobs.

I grabbed the end of the rug and yanked. Bree flew into the air and landed flat on her back. Her skull hit Bobby's tiled entryway with a dull crack.

The gun went off.

Oh God! I've been shot, I thought. But, I didn't feel anything. I looked behind me and saw Bobby's shattered coffee mug.

The sound of sirens penetrated the walls. Bree moaned. I sprang from the couch. I found the gun under an end table. The sirens became louder, just outside. I leapt over Bree and out the door. Police cruisers crowded the street. One by one they trained their spotlights on me. I was blinded.

"Drop your weapon," the voice of God commanded.

Weapon? What weapon?

"Drop your weapon!"

I realized the gun was in my right hand and threw it onto the lawn. Two police officers materialized out of the bushes and rushed me. They threw me onto the grass and handcuffed me behind my back. The grounds smelled like earthworms and fertilizer. A sharp pebble dug into my right cheek.

"Let her go," someone ordered.

I felt male hands remove the cuffs from my wrists and the weight off my back. A hand grabbed my shoulder and pulled me up. I felt dirt in my teeth, and grass stains covered my sweatshirt, shorts, and legs.

"Are you all right?" Mains asked.

"Fine, I think." I spat a piece of grass out of my mouth. Officer Knute stood behind Mains, his uniform conspicuously grass stained. Figured. Then, I remembered, "Ohmigod, Bobby's still in there. She hit him. Bree's the—"

"I know. O.M. called me."

A pair of paramedics hurried into the house. "Knute," Mains said. "Call the station and tell the desk sergeant to stop Lana and Alden Hayes from posting bond to free their son. He'll be out on his own accord very shortly."

I picked a stray blade of grass from my front teeth and beamed at Mains.

EPILOGUE

The steaming humidity of July had translated into the weighty air and heavy clouds of August that settled into the hovels and creases of Stripling and the surrounding Cuyahoga Valley. The summer term ended, and the library closed for a few blessed days to recuperate and prepare for the fall semester.

I sat on the vinyl glider on my half of the duplex's front porch. With one foot folded under me, the other kicked a soft rhythm on the damp cement with bare toe tips. My sketchbook lay in my lap, but the etchings were frail. I idly doodled, accomplishing nothing of worth.

That morning, I had visited the Blocken home one last time. When I arrived, there was a moving van in the driveway, and O.M. sat on the curb. I set the package I brought with me on the devil strip—a truly Akron term that described the area of grass between the street and the sidewalk. Without a word, I sat beside her.

"My dad's moving out," O.M. whispered.

"I'm sorry, O.M." I couldn't think of anything else to say.

"It's okay. They haven't really gotten along since Olivia went to college."

For lack of anything better, I nodded.

"What's that?" she asked, gesturing toward the package.

"It's for you."

I handed it to her, and she ripped off the brown paper. It was Olivia's portrait inside a simple black frame. I had been able to mend the tear in the canvas as if it had never happened.

"Did you paint this?"

"Yes."

"It's good," she said, and I knew she meant it.

Her comment was one of the most cherished critiques I ever received.

"Thank you. You know, she looked a lot like you," I told her.

She cocked her head, looking at the painting, looking for herself inside of it. "I hope so," she whispered.

A crack from the street jolted me off the glider and out of the memory. A massive off-white and faux wood paneled camper backfired. It rumbled to a jerky stop in front of the duplex. I stood on the porch waiting for someone to exit the vehicle, believing it was one of Ina's eccentric cronies. Maybe Juliet—I could imagine her behind the wheel of a camper. To my astonishment, Mark, with Theodore on a leash, exited the side door. I walked across the lawn and around the perpetually cheerful leprechauns to meet him.

Mark walked toward me. He wore baggy carpenter pants, much like our father's, and an outrageous Hawaiian shirt. Theodore sat docilely on the unruly grass and began to eat it.

"What do you think?" Mark asked happily and gestured to the camper.

"Yours?" I asked in disbelief.

"Yup. I bought it at a nice price too."

"Because?"

"I saw the ad in the Akron paper. Couldn't pass it up."

Not really the answer I was looking for. "Why did you buy the camper, Mark? Are you going camping?"

"In a manner of speaking," he remarked.

He stuck his free hand in his back jeans pocket and pulled out a folded sheet of white office paper. He handed it to me; it was a photocopy of a letter. Dated the day before and addressed to Samuel Lepcheck, the provost of Martin College, the letter began, "Dear Dr. Lepcheck: I respectfully resign from my position . . ."

"You quit your job? After everything that has happened. After everything we did to get it back?"

Mark shook his head sadly, as if he expected, but pitied, such a reaction. "We didn't fight to get my job back, India. You did. And Mom and Dad, and maybe Lew. I had nothing to do with it."

Before I could protest, he continued, "Do you know what my first thought was when you told me I was suspended from Martin, even with everything else that was happening? Thank God. That was my first thought, thank God. Because the next day I knew that I wouldn't have to go back to the hole in the basement of Dexler or pound equations into apathetic freshman heads or create some useless theorem so I could publish my dissertation. For one brief second, those cares were gone."

"If you didn't want to fight the suspension, why did you let us fight it for you?"

Mark laughed. "And deny Mom and Dad a worthwhile crusade?"

"I don't understand. I thought you liked Martin; you even went to undergrad there."

"It's all I've ever known," Mark said quietly.

"Your PhD?"

"What about it?"

"But all you have to do is finish your dissertation, and you're done. You're so close."

"I've dabbled on that dissertation for years and never even completed the research stage."

"But you're so good at math."

"Just because you're good at something doesn't mean it will make you happy," he said sagely.

I was at a loss.

"I have a favor to ask you."

Dumbfounded, I nodded.

"I've always loved the travel logs and journals of adventurers and pioneers. I've always wished I could leave everything and hit the open road and discover America, discover the world like they did. While in jail, I promised myself I would do just that. Olivia isn't around to wait for anymore." He paused as if to let those words sink in. "I finished the summer term at Martin, sold my car, and bought this camper. I'm doing it, India. I'm leaving Stripling."

"Where will you go?"

"Anywhere, everywhere."

He handed me Theodore's leash, and I took it. "But I worry about taking Theodore on such a venture. Will you take care of him while I'm gone?"

"How long will you be gone?"

"I don't know. A month. A year. Please, India, it's the only thing I ask."

Tears welled in my eyes, and I glanced down at Theodore to hide them.

"You understand why I have to leave, don't you, India?"

I did. "Because you never have," I whispered.

Mark knelt down and hugged Theodore, kissing the cat's furry head. Then he hurried to the camper and brought out a large blue duffel bag that had THEODORE embroidered on the side in bright orange letters.

Mark patted the cat again on the head. "I'd better be off."

"You're leaving *now?*" I exclaimed.

He nodded.

"What about Mom and Dad? And Carmen?"

"Could you tell them for me?" He laughed again. "I guess that's two more things I need you to do for me." He turned and strode to the camper.

"Mark! Wait!" I yelled as he reached for the camper's door. I dropped the duffel and scooped up the protesting cat. I smashed us into a three-way hug that Theodore did not appreciate.

"Bye." I let go.

Mark waved as he stepped into the camper. It backfired as he pulled away from the curb and then disappeared around the curve.

An empty tear rolled off my cheek and onto Theodore's ruff. I dumped him onto the lawn, where he discovered a peace-loving cicada and promptly ate it. Wiping my eyes with the hem of my T-shirt, I told Theodore, "You'd better pray Ina has the room."

ABOUT THE AUTHOR

Amanda Flower is an academic librarian for a small college in Ohio's Western Reserve. When she is not at the library or writing her next mystery, she is an avid traveler, aspiring to visit as much of the globe as she can. Recent trips have taken her to Slovakia, Ireland, and Israel. She lives and writes near Akron.